I0618650

The Dragonbutt Itch

The Adventures of Trumper Gallant and Bingo Malloy

BOOK TWO

JP Gunby

MAOS
Publications

For Fox and Flynn

Contents

Dragonbutt, the village where Trumper Gallant and Bingo Malloy lived with their aunty and uncle was really not just one village but two. In point of fact, it encompassed Greater Dragonbutt and the neighbouring yet smaller village of Lesser Dragonbutt. However, because so many houses had been built over the centuries, you can no longer see where Lesser Dragonbutt ends, and Greater Dragonbutt starts. So these days everyone just calls the two villages, Dragonbutt...

One

Shug Monkeys

"Finished!" exclaimed Trumper, at a decibel level that was unnecessarily high considering Bingo was sitting barely two feet away from him on the brown leather sofa.

"Dragonsbutts!" shrieked Bingo, as he leapt to his feet in such a hurry the old journal he was quietly reading fell onto the hard concrete floor of MAOS (*pronounced 'mouse'*) headquarters. This stood for MONSTERS ARE OUR SPECIALTY, which was the name given by Bingo to the red-brick shed situated behind the little old house at Twenty-Two Counting House Lane, where the two boys lived with their aunty and uncle. "You gave me such a fright, Trumper. I was just reading about the outbreak of shug monkeys in Dragonbutt and thought that a bunch of them were attacking me."

"Don't be silly, Bingo," replied Trumper, who, during the two hours since the boys' hefty lunch of toad in the hole and burnt custard with fresh boysenberries, had been busy typing the last few pages of something very important on his laptop. "It's taken me a whole

1

week of the Christmas holiday, but I've finally finished writing my first journal. 'The Little Vampire of Counting House Lane' is at last ready to be printed so that it can join the rest of the Entwhistle journals. All I need to do is email the manuscript to Uncle P, and he can print and bind the journal in the print shop at the Dragonbutt Smoker."

"Good timing," grinned Bingo, while picking up the journal he had dropped before strolling over to the heavy oak shelves that stored the entire collection of Entwhistle journals. Once there, he carefully placed it in the section marked with the letter 'S', between 'Screeching Sybil of Creaky Hollow' and three rather large volumes of 'Everything you need to know about snoswanglers but was afraid to ask' that were wisely labelled 'NOT FOR THE FAINT OF HEART' in blood-red ink. "My tummy is rumbling, so it must be time for hot chocolate and a snack. Let's go back to the house and hopefully Aunty J can rustle up something yummy for us to eat while she's making the hot chocolate."

"Alright, just give me a minute," agreed Trumper, who had just sent his manuscript to Uncle P and was now powering down his laptop before sliding it into a DPS embossed protective case. "And what was that you were saying about shug monkeys? I don't believe I have read that journal yet. What did you learn about them? Anything interesting?"

"Did I ever. They were dreadful creatures," uttered Bingo, as he reached into the large chest of drawers which was nestled against the wall facing the brown leather sofa. Smiling, he retrieved Little MO, the two-headed battleaxe that had been forged during the dark days and had the letters M and O carved into its short yet solid wooden handle. Their uncle had told them that the letters stood for Monster Obliterator, and already the fearsome weapon had helped Trumper and Bingo capture a bloodsucking vampire. Little MO, the younger boy believed, would be invaluable in their fight against all sorts of grisly monsters that according to the Dragonbutt prophecy, would one day return to the village.

As Bingo paced up and down in front of Trumper, who was still sitting on the brown leather sofa, he excitedly swung Little MO to-and-fro, which was his habit when talking about monsters and other types of beastly things. It was therefore not a surprise to the older boy to see that Bingo was eager to tell everything he had learnt about shug monkeys. The journal, he announced in a rather animated fashion, had the ominous title 'The Great Shug Monkey Incursion', and this he went on to explain had taken place at the height of Dragonbutt's dark days.

The shug monkeys that caused such a nuisance in Dragonbutt were not one of the regular types which were big and clumsy and usually quite docile. Those ones liked to live in the more isolated and mountainous parts of the country where few people were ever unwise enough to tread. No, these shug monkeys were much worse and came from a neighbouring district, some twenty-five or so miles north of the village.

They were not large; as a matter of fact, they were quite small, with the body of the now-extinct Acheronian Hound. This meant they were longish with very short legs, just like a Basset Hound but in place of patches of brown and white, they were as black and menacing as a starless sky at night. It was not their body though that made shug monkeys look so scary, it was really their monkey faces, and their large oval eyes the colour of crimson which looked like they were always staring at you.

And it wasn't just the terrible mistake of cross-breeding the Acheronian Hound with a monkey that led to the creation of this particularly monstrous type of shug monkey and the subsequent demise of Dragonbutt's neighbouring and once populous village. Instead, it was the reprehensible meddling of a dark witch who cast a despicable spell that allowed an extremely unpleasant demon spirit to enter the very soul of the shug monkey.

This would not have been such a calamity for the residents of the village if they only had to deal with one shug monkey. Unfortunately, akin to commonplace monkeys, shug monkeys had an insatiable drive to reproduce. And being neither male nor female but something in-between, they found it extraordinarily easy to multiply from one to two, then four and eight, until there were literally too many shug monkeys to count. In fact, so numerous were the devilish creatures, they formed themselves into hunting packs numbering around half a dozen in what was known as a bevy.

In many ways, shug monkeys were no different from everyday monkeys, who are well-known for doing all sorts of naughty things. Although, most would say they were probably ten times worse. This, along with their unquenchable appetite for all the food they could eat, literally drove every resident of the village hopping mad and downright crazy. Within a matter of weeks since the creation of the first shug monkey, the residents had vacated their village and all but abandoned the surrounding district, leaving the shug monkeys to eat as much food as they could find and do all sorts of mischievous things.

For a time, the shug monkeys flourished in the village, but once they had eaten their way through all the food, they realised that a rumbling tummy was no fun at all and no amount of naughtiness could make up for it. Besides, without food, the shug monkeys found they could no longer reproduce. This in itself was a devastating blow for the shug monkeys who prided themselves on their ability to multiply. Worst still was the fact they never lived longer than a month, which meant they absolutely had to produce more shug monkeys to replenish the ones that had already departed and those about to go, and fast. Or, as they quickly realised, there would be no shug monkeys left at all.

To begin with, the shug monkeys scoured the surrounding district for food, and at first, they were more than happy with what they found.

But once they had eaten every scrap of food for miles around, the shug monkeys had to search further afield. A bevy was sent north but never returned, and so two more were sent out, one to the east and another to the west. However, like the first bevy, these too were never heard of again.

In desperation, the shug monkeys headed south. Not just one bevy this time, instead, all the remaining bevies left the village in the hope of finding food, and of course to get up to as much mischief as they possibly could. Luckily they did not have to travel far before they came across another district, one that was fertile and had an abundance of tasty fare. This new district, they would soon find out, was called Dragonbutt. Though unluckily for the naughty shug monkeys, one of its residents would prove to be too much of a challenge for even the most resourceful of them, leading to their eventual demise.

It could not have been more than a week or so before the shug monkeys ate their way across the district of Dragonbutt leaving the lush green fields barren of crops, and once flourishing apple orchards wilting and fruitless. The people fled as the misbehaving shug monkeys wrecked their homes by smashing the windows, using the beds they found as trampolines, and even doing all sorts of impolite and scurrilous things on the floor. The only things left unharmed were the animals because even shug monkeys have a limit to what they will and will not do. And being an animal themselves, eating other animals was definitely one of those things they would never ever do.

During this time there were two unconnected villages in the district of Dragonbutt, Greater Dragonbutt and the neighbouring yet smaller village of Lesser Dragonbutt. The shug monkeys would probably have swept through both of these villages to wreak havoc on their residents, but as luck would have it, they reached Lesser Dragonbutt first. Even though it was by no means as imposing as Greater Dragonbutt, it was renowned in the district for one thing, and that was its exceedingly potent cider, Butts Batch. This was brewed by the Braithwaite family at the Dragonbutt Cider Mill and was located in the very heart of the village.

As bevy after bevy of shug monkeys stormed into Lesser Dragonbutt, the residents ran as fast as they could to their larger neighbour for help. Expecting the shug monkeys would soon follow, the villagers believed that all was lost and they would certainly have to flee Greater Dragonbutt as well. To their surprise, the shug monkeys halted their advance when one bevy came across the Dragonbutt Cider Mill and the thousands of bottles of Butts Batch that were stored there.

Being full of devilment and unaccustomed to strong brews, the bevy of shug monkeys greedily started drinking the Butts Batch. Not only did this make them eager for more naughtiness, but they also found it necessary to sing chorus after chorus of foul-mouthed songs as well. This, of course, attracted the attention of the other shug monkeys who had been busy eating and causing all sorts of devastation in the once tidy village of Lesser Dragonbutt.

By the time the rest of the shug monkeys had joined the first bevy to drink their way through bottle after bottle of Butts Batch, it quickly became obvious to the villagers that shug monkeys simply could not handle their cider. And so the shug monkeys partied at the Dragonbutt Cider Mill like there was no tomorrow, almost forgetting about their hunt for food and constant craving to cause untold carnage in their pursuit of mischief.

Due to the sudden and completely unforeseen onslaught of shug monkeys into the district, the residents of Greater and Lesser Dragonbutt were not only ill-prepared; they simply had no idea how to defend themselves. Let alone drive the horrendous creatures from the two villages, and as the old saying goes, send them back from whence they had come.

Shocked and panic-stricken, the residents of both villages could clearly hear the shug monkeys singing their dreadful and utterly detestable songs. Certain the supply of Butts Batch would soon run out, the villagers were forced to use their time wisely to plan the defence of Greater Dragonbutt. Knowing that if they failed then both their beloved villages would be devastated, and due to the diabolical nature of the shug monkey, they would more than likely be left ruined and beyond repair.

In all the excitement, no one remembers who came up with the idea of using butt sticks, the name given to what looks like a modern-day tennis racquet. Although back then they were most commonly used in the village for the shooing of pigs from the Hogswood Piggery to Baverstock's the Butcher's, along what in those days was called Pigs Alley. However, as it turned out, butt sticks were also perfectly suited for whacking the butts of the always badly behaved shug monkeys, which became a necessary part of Dragonbutt's now-famous shug monkey expulsion.

As it turned out, it was a young girl who not only saved Greater Dragonbutt and its smaller neighbour from the awful shug monkeys, but also the prosperous surrounding district. Fannie Entwhistle, the eldest daughter of Brinley and Maida Entwhistle, while only twelve years old, had already taken the Entwhistle Oath to always protect the residents of Dragonbutt. She was an extraordinarily gifted girl, uncommonly well-read for those times and blessed with a remarkable ability to always know the right course of action to take in times of crisis.

Fannie, because of her fondness for reading, knew quite a lot about many things, and one of those things happened to be monkeys. The one thing that monkeys hated, Fannie had learnt, was simply being clean. And shug monkeys, being quite like regular monkeys, but obviously much worse, would more than likely be terrified of anything that would wash away their filth and offensive odour, forcing the noxious creatures to be fragrant smelling and for once in their short lives just about clean. For that reason, it was Fannie Entwhistle who was responsible for coming up with the ingenious plan to rid the district of Dragonbutt of shug monkeys.

Without much ado, Tomkin Blewitt and his small band of carpenters started the monumental undertaking of making enough butt sticks to arm every resident who was capable of giving a shug monkey a good firm whack on the butt. Tomkin and his team worked tirelessly for three long days and nights, fortuitously managing to complete their task before any of the partying shug monkeys quit Lesser Dragonbutt.

Meanwhile, Fannie implored the Dragonbutt soap maker, Hedwig Gribble, to make as much soap as she possibly could with the help of the other ladies in the village. But not just any soap would do because if her plan was to work it had to be made using Butts Batch, and she stressed to Hedwig, the stronger the scent, the better.

During this time the whole village could hear the shug monkeys raucous and thoroughly objectionable singing all through the day and most of the night. And every resident knew that once the Butts Batch was all gone, the singing would cease and the shug monkeys would resume their destructive rampage right into the centre of Greater Dragonbutt.

While Tomkin and Hedwig, along with their helpers, were busy toiling away, the remaining men and children in the village were given the job of collecting as much food as they could readily find. Being careful, of course, to avoid anything that contained meat and then to cart it down to Dragonbutt pond. Once there, the food was then ferried over to a small island at its centre by Arley Dingle. He was the closest the village had to a sailor, having once rowed all the way to Merman Island, a voyage of a little over five hundred yards. Or at least it is when the high tide covers the cobblestone causeway that connects the island to the mainland.

By the time the small island had been piled high with a tempting assortment of all kinds of yummy food that would have delighted even the most pernickety of shug monkeys, both Tomkin and Hedwig had finished making enough butt sticks and soap that Fannie Entwhistle's plan just might work. With every resident armed with a stout butt stick, Fannie had already instructed the hulking Hogswood boys; Hodden, Hadley and Halbert, to build a good strong blockade at the entrance to Dragonbutt High Street. This was to ensure that when the bevies of shug monkeys eventually rolled into Greater Dragonbutt, they would be forced to take a course that was not of their choosing, but one Fannie had carefully planned out.

After the shug monkeys had emptied the last bottle of Butts Batch, it was not long before their tumultuous and by now rather tuneless singing finally died down. Fewer in number than when they had arrived, like a fearsome tornado, the remaining bevies burst into Greater Dragonbutt. Though due to the Hogswood blockade, and as Fannie had intended, it was clear to each of them that they had no alternative but to enter Pigs Alley.

It was called Pigs Alley and not Pigs Willow Alley as it is officially known today (or Pigswill Alley to the locals) because during Dragonbutt's dark days there was not a single willow tree growing on any part of the muddy passageway. Instead of the willow trees that were planted several centuries later, the Hogswood family had built a sturdy fence on either side of the alley to ensure their pigs could never escape. This was one of the reasons why Fannie had chosen Pigs Alley as a necessary component of her plan. The other being that part of the way along the alley, there was a large gate built into a section of the fence. And when this was open, it not only blocked the entire width of Pigs Alley, it also meant that the only way forward was towards Dragonbutt pond.

With the villagers safely crouched behind the two fences on either side of Pigs Alley, they were able to completely surprise the unsuspecting shug monkeys. As they clamoured their way down the alley, dozens of butt sticks could be heard whacking the butts of the wailing creatures to the cheers of everyone present. And to make certain there was no chance of the shug monkeys retreating to Lesser Dragonbutt, the Hogswood boys chased them with their own oversize butt sticks held high in the air.

By now the howling shug monkeys were not only extremely annoyed because of their painfully sore butts, but they were also ravenously hungry. So without slowing down, they ran through the open gate that led to Dragonbutt pond and at once saw the mountain of scrumptious food on the small island. As if presented with an endless buffet, the shug monkeys unfortunately and to their everlasting regret did not hesitate even for one second. Consequently, they dived right into what their noses told them was a vat of their newly discovered favourite tipple, Butts Batch.

All anyone could hear were the terrible screams of the shug monkeys, who after coming into contact with the water, had very quickly realised they had been out-and-out tricked. Dragonbutt pond, they found to their horror, was not full of their prized Butts Batch after all, but rather hundreds of bars of the sickeningly clean and refreshing soap they loathed and feared so much.

As the Hogswood boys whacked the butts of the few remaining stragglers sending them shrieking and tumbling into the pond, the other villagers did the same with any shug monkey who tried to escape their Butts Batch infused soap bath. It took a good hour of whacking and the shug monkeys desperate splashing before Fannie was satisfied that the odious creatures were passably clean. Now that their frightful ordeal had come to an end, one by one, they dragged themselves out of the soapy water. And although each of them was visibly cleaner with a new-found and rather pleasing smell, they were also less mischievous looking and decidedly more placid as well.

Guarded by the now victorious residents of Greater and Lesser Dragonbutt, the shug monkeys were marched in single file back along Pigs Alley. With an occasional whack on a wayward butt, they passed by the Hogswood blockade on Dragonbutt High Street and made their way into the near ruined Lesser Dragonbutt. What the villagers saw was row after row of wrecked houses and the remains of the Dragonbutt Cider Mill. This, not surprisingly, was now littered with a vast number of empty bottles of Butts Batch, many of which had been unceremoniously smashed by the partying shug monkeys.

When they reached the northernmost limit of Lesser Dragonbutt, the shug monkeys just kept walking. Not daring to look back as they would most likely receive another whack on the butt if they did. As the villagers came to a halt and cheered once more, the incorrigible creatures were last seen heading in the direction they had originally come. Only the three strapping Hogswood boys, with their butt sticks to the ready, followed the shug monkeys until they had left the district of Dragonbutt. And by all accounts, thankfully, they were never heard of again.

"Dragonsbutts! It was lucky Fannie Entwhistle was there during that time to save the residents of Dragonbutt," exclaimed Trumper, who by now was sitting at the far end of the brown leather sofa, which happened to be the safest place to sit when the younger boy was holding Little MO. "You see, Bingo, Fannie used her brains to defeat the shug monkeys, and that is what I intend to do when we encounter our next monster."

"Well if I had been around during the great shug monkey incursion those shug monkeys certainly wouldn't have gotten away with just a bath and a whack on the butt. I would have given them an extra close shave with Little MO," laughed Bingo, as he lifted his trusty battleaxe into the air once more, before placing it back into the large chest of drawers. "Come on, Trumper, my tummy is rumbling even more now, so let's head back to the house for some hot chocolate and a snack."

Before Trumper had a chance to reply, Bingo had already grabbed his DPS woolly hat and warm woollen gloves, pulled on his coat, and had run out of MAOS headquarters. This left the more responsible Trumper to turn the heater and lights off and lock the door. And then with his treasured laptop under one arm, he followed Bingo up the long garden path to the little old house where he hoped his hot chocolate and snack would be waiting.

Two

Mumford

"Don't forget to take off your wellingtons before you enter the house, Trumper," shouted Aunty J, who had been busy making the boys their hot chocolate when she heard the loud thud of the back door being flung open for the second time in as many minutes. "It's still quite muddy outside, and I don't want you bringing all that dirt into the house and ruining my nice new carpet."

Without a word of complaint, Trumper promptly removed his boots while standing on the doorstep, which as his aunty had suspected were more than a little muddy. Seeing Bingo's even muddier boots sitting on a copy of the local newspaper, the Dragonbutt Smoker, he neatly placed his beside them. And finally, after taking off his outdoor clothes and hanging the sky blue coloured coat he liked so much on one of the hooks by the front door, he eagerly made his way into the pleasantly warm kitchen that smelled of chocolate and freshly baked cake.

Just as Trumper entered the kitchen, his aunty placed two steaming mugs of hot chocolate onto the table, both of them topped with a huge dollop of fresh whipped cream and a large marshmallow. At its centre was one of his favourite cakes, the somewhat regally appointed Victoria sandwich, which was named after a long-departed queen of the same name. It came as no surprise to Trumper that Bingo, who always seemed to be hungry at all times of the day and night, was already halfway through eating an enormous slice of the mouthwatering cake.

"You know what I don't like about starting a new year," declared Bingo, while swallowing another mouthful of the delectable cake. "It means I won't be able to eat any more mince pies until next Christmas. Although if I could eat a Victoria sandwich every day, then I probably wouldn't miss them too much at all."

Victoria sandwiches were not one of those difficult types of cakes to bake and were certainly not what you would call fancy. It was all too important though if one was to create the perfect Victoria sandwich, to use only the finest ingredients. Which is why Aunty J always used the best flour, eggs, caster sugar and butter that Dragonbutt had to offer, and of course all of them were purchased from Gribble's the Grocer's. And when it came to the filling, she always preferred the traditional approach, using only the choicest of jams and would never consent to use cream.

"Wash your hands at the kitchen sink, Trumper, while I get you a slice of cake," urged Aunty J, who without waiting for an answer, cut another slice from the Victoria sandwich that was just as large as the one Bingo was rapidly polishing off. "We have Old Mrs Dingle to thank for the jam. It's her homemade raspberry jam that she brought over the other day as an apology for all the trouble Baxter caused before Christmas. She said he's much better now and back to his old self again, and so I told her you would both go to visit him tomorrow before you start the new school term on Monday."

"Alright, Aunty J," replied Trumper, as he hungrily gorged himself on the heavenly cake. At first thinking, the rich sponge was as good as he remembered, but once he tasted Old Mrs Dingle's raspberry jam, he decided that it was even better. "I've been so busy writing my journal that I haven't had a moment for anything else. The last time I saw Baxter was in a cell at Dragonbutt Police Station."

"I'll bring Little MO with me. Just in case he turns into a bloodthirsty vampire again," added Bingo, who by now had finished eating his slice of cake and was spooning the gooey marshmallow out of his hot chocolate before popping it into the gaping hole of his open mouth.

"Oh no, you won't!" snapped Aunty J, as she sat down at the kitchen table clutching her own mug of hot chocolate. "I've already told you, I don't want to hear you have been waving that dangerous weapon around again. And for the umpteenth time, vampires don't exist!"

Bingo made no attempt to challenge his aunty, knowing he would never be able to convince anyone who was not Dragonbutt born, that not only did vampires exist during Dragonbutt's dark days, but he had actually been responsible for catching the little vampire who had terrorised the village just two weeks earlier. Instead, he gave Trumper a sly wink, while the two boys quietly drank their mugs of hot chocolate and thought about what exciting adventures would be in store for them next.

"Has the Dragonbutt Smoker arrived yet?" asked Trumper, while draining the last drop of hot chocolate from his mug.

"Yes, it came when you were in the red-brick shed, and so I placed it on the coffee table in the living room for you to read on your return," answered Aunty J, who could not resist the smell of the Victoria sandwich and was now cutting herself a small slice to eat with her hot chocolate.

"It's no longer called the red-brick shed, insisted Bingo, rather stubbornly and using a tone that his aunty was unlikely to appreciate. "I told you before, it's now called MAOS headquarters."

"Yes, you did, Bingo. But considering I don't believe in monsters, to me it will always be called the red-brick shed," responded Aunty J, quite firmly as she gave him one of her 'don't push your luck young man' type of glares.

The boys knew this was probably a good time to excuse themselves, and so they thanked their aunty for the cake and hot chocolate and then strolled into the living room to read the latest edition of the Dragonbutt Smoker. After Bingo had tossed a couple of logs onto the glowing fire, they sat down on the sofa where Trumper began to read the front-page headlines, which were written in big bold black letters. This, he presumed, was to let everyone know the article contained something of the utmost importance to the residents of Dragonbutt.

"'Mooner Mayhem Comes To Dragonbutt!'" read Trumper aloud, and then he explained to Bingo the article was written by their fellow vampire hunter and the Dragonbutt Smoker's best reporter, Barry Beasley.

At around nine-thirty on Wednesday evening, the participants of the Reverend Pinkerton's bingo night were disturbed by a loud banging noise on the front door of Dragonbutt Victory Hall, followed by the ear-piercing din of what sounded like an air-horn. At first, the Reverend continued calling out the all-important numbers, knowing it would take a braver man than him to interrupt the final game of the evening. After several minutes of listening to the dreadful racket, Emilia Baggot, the oldest resident of the village at ninety-seven and two numbers shy of calling bingo, pulled herself up from her seat and with the aid of a walker angrily made her way to the entrance of the hall, with everyone else only a few steps behind. Flinging the door open, she was about to give the unwelcome intruders an earful of her notoriously colourful language when in the distance she saw a truly shocking sight. MOONERS was all anyone could hear her shriek, as she pointed towards Pigswill Alley before promptly fainting, leaving everyone present to witness three bare butts bent over in unison that were recklessly facing their direction. And then seconds later they simply disappeared into the darkness.

"Dragonsbutts! Do you think they're monsters?" screeched Bingo, while trying to imagine what type of loathsome beasts they could be.

"I don't think so, but we should do a little investigating tomorrow to find out," stated Trumper, and then he continued to read the rest of the story.

Old Mrs Dingle, a regular at bingo night, administered first aid to the unconscious Emilia Baggot. A good firm shake and a generous swig of Dragonsbreath, Boosey Dooley's infamous and extremely alcoholic homemade potato and acorn vodka, was all it took before the grizzled old woman was back on her feet. In the interval, the Reverend Pinkerton had sensibly called Dragonbutt police who arrived with Staff Nurse Bone Cruncher Trudy Fanshaw to examine the elderly lady. By this time she had all but drained Old Mrs Dingle's hip flask and was merrily singing a song about a sailor she once knew named Shanghai Joe. Detective Huntress, therefore, interviewed the other eyewitnesses to the incident, who confirmed that it was indeed three shameful and utterly indecent mooners they all saw. Although regrettably, no one could remember seeing any notable features that could identify the three butts in question. In a statement issued by Dragonbutt police, Detective Huntress said, 'It has been twenty-five years since the last outbreak of mooning in Dragonbutt. Unfortunately, this wretched problem has once again reared its ugly head. However, I would like to assure every resident in the village that Dragonbutt police will not stop until we get to the bottom of this outrageous spectacle and find those responsible'.

"We should talk to Old Mrs Dingle about the mooners when we go to visit Baxter," suggested Bingo, who was already thinking that a good sideways whack from Little MO would put an end to all this abominable mooning. "And don't forget we still have plenty of questions to ask her regarding the DWI."

"Yes, of course, Bingo," nodded Trumper, rather thoughtfully. "I've been thinking about the DWI since the day Old Mrs Dingle revealed their existence, and so it's about time we started our investigation. Which means tomorrow we will not only ask her what she saw during the mooning last Wednesday evening, we will also question her about this mysterious organisation she belongs too – the Dragonbutt Witch's Institute."

"Alright, but I can't really be expected to think that far ahead on an empty stomach. First things first, Trumper," stressed Bingo, who had just jumped up from the sofa and was walking to the living room door. "What I want to know right now is what are we going to eat for dinner tonight?"

Wisely, Trumper did not disagree with the younger boy. And so without a word passing his lips, he followed Bingo into the kitchen to see that Aunty J was still sitting at the kitchen table. Although now, she was no longer drinking a mug of hot chocolate and eating a slice of Victoria sandwich, instead, their aunty was thoroughly engrossed in her favourite dental magazine, the fittingly named, 'Cavity'.

"What's for dinner?" demanded Bingo, whose tummy was not rumbling just yet, but from years of experience, he knew it soon would be.

"Well it's Saturday, and your uncle will be eating at the Dragonbutt Arms, as usual, so I thought it would be nice to treat ourselves to a takeaway this evening," answered Aunty J, as she placed her magazine on the kitchen table and smiled at the two boys.

"Goodie," thundered Bingo, who was always happy to eat a takeaway, no matter what type of food it happened to be. "Are we ordering from Butt Hut or Chilli Dilli?"

"How about we try the new fish and chip shop that is opening today on Dragonbutt High Street. I believe it's called 'Oh My Cod!'," proposed

Aunty J, knowing the boys would certainly agree. "It doesn't have a delivery service, but it won't take you any time at all to ride there and back on your nice new bikes."

"Wow, Dragonbutt is becoming a real culinary mecca," rejoiced Bingo, in a fit of excitement as he jumped up and down. "We've got kebabs, pizza, Indian food, pies, and now we have fish and chips."

Besides several smaller presents and of course a stocking full of forty-two Choco Bombs, which was Bingo's reward for capturing the little vampire, each of the boys had received a brand new shiny bicycle from Father Christmas. Trumper's was unquestionably larger and came in a striking shade of cobalt blue. Whereas Bingo's impressive-looking bicycle could only be described as candy apple red.

"Aunty J, what time is Oh My Cod! going to open?" inquired Trumper, who at that moment was checking the time on the kitchen wall clock.

"Five o'clock sharp according to the advertisement in the Dragonbutt Smoker," she replied, while noticing the time was already a quarter to five. "You better leave soon to avoid the queue. It's Dragonbutt's first fish and chip shop, and so in all likelihood, opening night will be very busy. And boys, don't forget to turn your lights on as it's dark outside and make sure both of you wear your helmets."

"Do I have to?" appealed Bingo, who claimed the extra weight of his helmet would slow him down. And because his tummy was just now starting to rumble, he wanted to get to Oh My Cod! as quickly as possible.

"Yes, you do if you want to do well in school," asserted Aunty J, while giving Bingo another one of her stern glares.

"But what if I don't want to do well in school?" retorted Bingo, looking decidedly stubborn once again.

"Bingo, just wear your helmet, or none of us will be eating fish and chips tonight," barked Aunty J, which sounded like the subject was not going to be up for further discussion.

"Come on, Bingo, why don't you go and get your Dr Who backpack to carry the fish and chips, and I'll take our bikes out of the garage and bring them around to the front of the house," interjected Trumper, as the younger boy's protests regarding his helmet were just wasting time and getting them absolutely nowhere. "So I guess it's cod and chips three times, Aunty J?"

"Yes, thank you, Trumper, and don't forget that I like plenty of salt and vinegar on my fish and chips. Just give me a minute while I find the money in my purse," said Aunty J, relieved that one of her boys was wise enough not to argue. "And hurry back because the weather forecast indicated it will probably snow tonight."

No more than five minutes later, the two boys were standing outside the front door dressed in their winter coats and warm woollen gloves. Trumper was already wearing his helmet, and Bingo, with his Dr Who backpack slung over both shoulders, was grudgingly fastening the strap attached to his helmet securely under his chin.

"Alright, Bingo, turn your headlamp on and then I'll race you to Dragonbutt High Street," uttered Trumper, who was impatient to be on his way as it was already quite nippy outside. "And I don't want to get our new bikes muddy just yet so let's ride along Hunnickle Drive. But make sure you stay on the pavement."

It was not necessary to tell Bingo twice. And because he always liked to win any type of race, he enthusiastically jumped onto his bicycle and sped down Counting House Lane. It took Trumper a good five minutes before he caught up with the younger boy, who had already ridden over the old Dragonbutt Bridge and was now turning the corner into Lower Dragonbutt High Street. Seeing that Trumper was close on his heels, he put his powerful legs into overdrive and peddled with all his might until he could see the flashing red neon sign of Oh My Cod!. This, quite conveniently, was located just a few doors down but on the opposite side of the street from the Dragonbutt Arms.

"Winner!" shouted Bingo, triumphantly waving his arms in the air as Trumper's bicycle came to a halt next to his. "It looks like Oh My Cod! is already open, and we're the first ones here."

Trumper and Bingo immediately pulled off their helmets and hung them from the handlebars of their bicycles before walking over to Dragonbutt's new gastronomical sensation. Underneath the ingeniously overstated and intentionally in-your-face neon sign was written 'Proprietor: Morweena Ogglejay'. The pungent and always addictive smell of deep-fried fish and chips was too much to resist. And so the boys marched right through the open doorway, only to see a remarkably pretty young lady in her mid-twenties standing behind the counter ready to greet them.

"Ah, customers," she announced, rather obviously, but with a great deal of enthusiasm as she clapped her hands together after seeing the boys enter. "Hello, I'm Mor-w-w-weena Ogglejay, and I w-w-would like to w-w-welcome you to Oh My Cod!."

Morweena was a poor choice of name for her because ever since childhood, try as she might, she always had tremendous difficulty in pronouncing the letter 'W' due to an unfortunate hereditary lisp. Notwithstanding, she was extraordinarily slim for someone in the fried food profession and quite small. In fact, she was no more than five feet in height with long raven coloured hair that reached to nearly her waist. And this was neatly tied back in three thick braids that seemed to somehow complement her unusually large and rather cat-like looking green eyes. Her smile though was by far her most notable feature, full of life that matched her youth with just a hint of mystique thrown in.

"I'm Bingo," gushed the younger boy, seemingly full of confidence in an obvious effort to impress the young lady.

"Not, Bingo Malloy, the brave man who captured Dragonbutt's little vampire?" inquired Morweena, as she looked in disbelief at Bingo who was already starting to blush. "Then that means you must be Trumper Gallant," while turning to look at the older boy who was closing the door.

"That's right," nodded Trumper, secretly quite pleased that he and Bingo were getting quite a reputation in the village, and a good one at that. "Are you new to Dragonbutt?"

"Oh no, I'm Dragonbutt born. Though my family moved away a long time ago, and I have only recently returned," explained Morweena, as she smiled at the boys while carefully studying the two of them with her strangely penetrating eyes. "Now w-w-what can I get for you?"

"Cod and chips three times please," requested Bingo, who had all but forgotten that his tummy was still rumbling. "And lots of salt and vinegar please, Morweena."

"Yes, of course," nodded the young lady, and then she suddenly clapped her hands together and loudly called out someone's name. "Mumford!"

In no time at all, a slow thud-thud-thud sound could be heard coming from the kitchen at the back of the fish and chip shop, and then the boys saw him. If Mumford had been a tree, he would undoubtedly have been a hundred-year-old willow tree, or so their uncle would have said. Be that as it may, Mumford did not only look like he had been around for a hundred or more years, he must have been at least seven feet tall. And so if he was Dragonbutt born, Trumper thought, it had to be a long-long time ago indeed, and someone must have kept him well hidden.

"Dragonsbutts!" yelped Bingo, as the two boys stared at the enormous figure standing before them. "It's Frankenstein's monster."

"There's no need to be afraid of Mumford," giggled Morweena, while lifting her hand to pat him on the shoulder. Although due to her diminutive stature, she only managed to reach his elbow. "Mumford is my trusted and profoundly mute manservant, and he's been in my family since before anyone can remember."

Mumford was not only a colossal size and downright intimidating looking at that, but he also had a peculiar and rather dense look about him. And this definitely made his hard to read features appear as if he possessed little to nothing up-top. As he looked down at his mistress, he slowly lowered himself onto one knee, while she bellowed Bingo's order into what the boys noticed was his one and only and quite badly mangled cauliflower ear.

Before Trumper and Bingo had time to really contemplate what they were looking at, Mumford dutifully started frying up three portions of cod and chips and two sausages in batter. At that moment, the door of Oh My Cod! abruptly opened, giving the boys quite a start. And then Morweena clapped her hands together once again and said, "Ah, another customer."

"Dragonsbutts! I thought I'd be the first one here," groaned the boy who had just entered. "I should have known that when it comes to food; Bingo Malloy will always be at the front of the queue."

The new customer was no stranger to Trumper and Bingo as he was in the younger boy's class at Dragonbutt Primary School. Chugher Harris was his name, and he was the best friend of another of Bingo's classmates, Chomper Baverstock Junior. He was about Bingo's size and had what one would call nondescript medium brown wavy hair and unremarkable matching brown eyes. That was probably all anyone could say about Chugher, except for the fact he had a very annoying and easily recognisable high-pitched laugh which sounded very much like a guffawing hyena.

"I understand that you two were busy over the Christmas holiday," squawked Chugher, who just like the rest of the village, had heard all about the boys capturing the little vampire. "And what's this new organisation you have formed to deal with Dragonbutt's monster problem? Can Chomper Junior and I join?"

"It's called MONSTERS ARE OUR SPECIALTY or MAOS for short, and it's not open to new members, not yet anyway," pointed out Trumper, thinking that if they were ever going to open MAOS to others, Chugher Harris and Chomper Baverstock Junior would hardly be at the top of the list.

In return, Chugher was about to say something he considered exceedingly funny when all of a sudden, he noticed the gargantuan figure of Mumford behind the fish fryer. "Dragonsbutts! It's Frankenstein's monster," jabbered the DPS student, and then he quickly retreated to the door.

"I said the very same thing barely five minutes ago," sighed Bingo, while pulling the Dr Who backpack from his shoulders. "His name is Mumford, and he works here."

Just then, Morweena stepped out of Mumford's huge shadow and introduced herself, lisp and all. Chugher, who had a rather extensive list, read off his order to the young lady and she then repeated it to Mumford. This, of course, was done somewhat loudly and directly into his solitary mangled ear. By the time she had finished, the boys' order had been wrapped in plenty of sheets of the previous week's edition of the Dragonbutt Smoker and was ready to go.

Bingo placed the three portions of fish and chips into his Dr Who backpack while Trumper paid Morweena. With a pleasing smile, she handed them the two sausages in batter that Mumford had just finished frying and said, "These are on the house for the two heroes of Dragonbutt." And although they were very much appreciated by the boys, Trumper thought he detected a slight air of sarcasm in her outwardly kind words.

"Thank you, Morweena and Mr Mumford," echoed the two boys, as they walked past Chugher Harris and made their way to the door.

"It's just, Mumford," corrected Morweena, waving emphatically. "I hope you come back soon."

"No need to worry about that, Morweena," added Bingo, who had already taken a large bite out of his sausage in batter and was happily savouring the taste of the fried pork and greasy batter treat. "I'm pretty sure we are going to be your best customers because I am putting Oh My Cod! at the top of my takeaway list."

"Is she your girlfriend or something?" muttered a sniggering Chugher to Bingo, as Trumper opened the door and the two boys stepped out into the cold night air once again. "I hope that Morweena gives me a free sausage in batter as well. Anyway, it's supposed to snow tonight and if we get enough then let's meet at ten in the morning and have a snowball fight at Dragonbutt pond. You bring Bertie and Flitcher, and I'll bring Chomper Junior along with a couple of others, so we'll have four on each team."

"Good idea," replied Bingo, who was pleased they would have a snowball fight the next day so that he could get his own back on the annoying Chugher Harris.

As the boys walked over to where they had parked their bicycles, they devoured the sausages in batter with ravenous glee. Bingo, as usual, was the first to finish. And now that they were out of earshot of the fish and chip shop's occupants, he announced, "I never dreamt I would meet anyone bigger than Angus Hogswood in Dragonbutt. Mumford is ginormous, and did you notice he never said a word and only stares and nods his head."

"Yes, I did," acknowledged Trumper, who had also finished eating his sausage in batter and was now sitting on his bicycle. "They make quite an odd pair that Mumford and Morweena Ogglejay."

"Oh no, Morweena is first-rate. Anyone who gives me a free sausage in batter is more than alright by me," objected Bingo, as he pulled on his helmet and climbed onto his own bicycle. "It was Mumford who was the strange one, not Morweena."

"Perhaps, Bingo, but let's talk about this another time," implored Trumper, while peddling as hard as he could to stay ahead of the younger boy. "I can feel snow in the air, and you know that Aunty J is waiting for these fish and chips, so let's ride back to Counting House Lane as fast as we can."

Three

The Snowball Fight

"It's five-thirty, Aunty J, and it looks like it snowed a bucketful during the night," shrieked an excited Bingo, as he ran into his aunty and uncle's bedroom. "We're burning daylight hours, so I'll wake Trumper while you cook breakfast. And I think you should make it a big one because I get the feeling I'm going to need plenty of energy today."

Even though Aunty J was now wide awake, in no way did she agree with the young boy that daylight had actually arrived. And by the look of the dark sky full of twinkling stars, doubted it would be materialising anytime soon. Nevertheless, this did not stop her from crawling out of her warm and extremely cosy bed, pulling on her dressing gown and slippers, and trudging down the stairs and into the kitchen. The boys believed this selfless act was solely for their benefit, but it was really because of her husband's thunderous snoring, which meant more sleep would be nigh on impossible.

By the time Trumper and Bingo had descended the stairs and entered the kitchen, their aunty had already made them both a mug of steaming hot chocolate with a large dollop of fresh whipped cream and a gooey marshmallow to boot. And to the boys' delight, she was now mixing the batter for their customary Sunday breakfast, which comprised a mountain of fluffy pancakes smothered in oodles of their favourite honey and lots of melted butter.

"I'm not sure where you put all this food you keep eating, Bingo," laughed Aunty J, who was now placing her first batch of pancakes on the kitchen table next to a large pot of honey from Botters of Chelmsford and a slab of creamy Dragonbutt butter. "Last night you not only ate a huge portion of fish and chips and a sausage in batter but also half of my chips and the remainder of the Victoria sandwich as well. And then there were the three bottles of Braithwaite's you drank to wash it all down."

"What can I tell you, I'm a growing boy," chortled Bingo, while jabbing his fork into the last of the pancakes and placing it onto his own plate before Trumper had a chance to object. "Any more pancakes, Aunty J? I've only eaten five and will need at least five more if I'm to win the snowball fight this morning."

"You mean, we win. Don't forget that it will be a team effort with you and me, and hopefully Bertie Bovington and Flitcher Jenkins. It's going to take the four of us working together if we are to beat Chugher Harris and Chomper Baverstock Junior, and whoever else they bring along," stressed Trumper, who often had to remind Bingo of the merits of team play, since he was all too prone to go it alone as the older boy had witnessed on many an occasion. "I could eat a couple more of your delicious pancakes as well, Aunty J, if it's not too much trouble."

"Yes, of course, Trumper, I've made plenty of pancakes for both of you," answered Aunty J, as she placed another large stack on the kitchen table, only to see Bingo greedily place two of them on the older boy's plate and the rest onto his own. "But don't forget to visit Old Mrs

Dingle and Baxter before you leave for this snowball fight. And to celebrate the start of your new school term, your uncle has reserved a table for twelve-thirty at the Dragonbutt Arms. So please don't be late."

"Goodie!" exclaimed an ecstatic Bingo, who by now was struggling a little with his tenth and thankfully last remaining pancake. "I hear it's going to be an all-you-can-eat buffet, so I'm going to wear my running bottoms with the elasticated waist. They're perfect for buffets because they give my tummy plenty of room to expand."

Once the boys had finished their more than ample breakfast, they both thanked their aunty and quickly scurried upstairs. Taking turns in the bathroom, they washed, brushed their teeth, and slipped into some warm winter clothing in preparation for their much-anticipated snowball fight at ten. This allowed Aunty J a few moments for a little break and some well-deserved peace and quiet. And of course, just enough time to eat a couple of pancakes herself and drink a nice hot cup of freshly brewed English breakfast tea.

Standing before their aunty in the kitchen once again, it was still only seven-thirty. Although this was somewhat of an early hour on a Sunday morning to be calling on one of their neighbours, it was already getting bright outside with the first rays of sun glistening on the newly fallen snow that had blanketed the village during the night. Besides, the boys knew all too well that Old Mrs Dingle was not one of those types of people who like to lay in bed on a Sunday. Rather, she always rose by sunrise to prepare a hearty breakfast for herself and Baxter. And then, dressed in her Sunday best could always be relied upon to attend the morning service at Dragonbutt Village Church between the hours of ten-thirty and twelve.

Before they left the house, Trumper quickly jotted down a few words onto a piece of paper, and then he folded it and wrote Bertie Bovington's name on one side before handing it to Bingo. "What's it say,

Trumper?" inquired Bingo, though before the older boy could answer, he read the note out loud, "'Bertie – snowball fight at Dragonbutt pond around ten. It's going to be me and Bingo along with you and Flitcher against Chugher Harris and Chomper Baverstock Junior, and they will bring a couple of others with them. We'll meet you at your place sometime after nine-thirty and make sure you invite Flitcher – Trumper'. Good idea, Trumper. We can push it through the Bovingtons' letterbox on the way to Old Mrs Dingle's house."

"You know the drill, boys," proclaimed Aunty J, just as they were walking out of the kitchen and into the hallway. "I want to see you wear your coats, woolly hats and warm woollen gloves before you step out of this house. And make sure you are home by twelve."

"Yes, Aunty J, we promise," replied the boys, who had guessed she was going to say something like that and were already anticipating her next remark. So they were both standing on the mat by the front door and pulling on their wellingtons to ensure they did not get mud on her new and still spotlessly clean hallway carpet.

Clutching the note addressed to Bertie, Bingo was the first out of the front door, although Trumper was only a few steps behind. Kicking the heavy snow as they ran, the boys raced over to the large Bovington house at number eleven Counting House Lane. Regrettably, though, Bingo lifted up the hefty cast-iron knocker that had been forged in the shape of a horizontal letter B. And before Trumper could stop him, he slammed it against the chocolate brown coloured front door three ear piercingly loud times.

"Dragonsbutts! If that is Flitcher Jenkins again I'm going to strangle him!" screeched the unmistakable voice of Bunty Bovington, whose bedroom was unfortunately located directly above the front door.

"Come on, Bingo, shove the note into the letterbox and run!" beseeched Trumper, who was already backing away from the front door because Bunty's bedroom light had been turned on. And now the heavy thud of someone furiously storming down the stairs could be clearly heard. "Trust me; you really don't want to mess with Bunty when she's angry, especially at this hour in the morning."

"But, Trumper, Bunty is always angry," argued Bingo, rather unwisely, as he pushed the note through the letterbox in the front door just as the older boy began to run. He then thought Trumper might just be right, and so he hastily ran after him so as not to end up being the brunt of Bunty Bovington's early morning wrath.

The boys did not risk looking back, dare they make eye contact and provoke Bertie Bovington's enraged older sister any further. And they did not stop running until they came to Old Mrs Dingle's somewhat dilapidated house with the faded blue front door at the entrance to Counting House Lane.

With a short pause between each knock, Trumper firmly knocked on the door three times so that the old lady knew it was a social call and not an emergency. Though it was not Old Mrs Dingle who reached the front door first, instead, it was her funny-looking dog, Baxter. Hearing the older boy's loud rapping, he had hurriedly scampered down the hallway to greet them, and naturally, the old lady had followed him, albeit at a far slower pace.

"Hello, boys, I haven't seen the two of you since before Christmas," called out Old Mrs Dingle, as she opened the front door a little too much. Whereby Baxter leapt out and jumped on a surprised Bingo, who immediately fell backwards and landed in the soft snow.

"Ah, vampire!" yelled Bingo, now regretting he had listened to Aunty J and had left Little MO in the large chest of drawers at MAOS headquarters. "Get him off of me."

"Oh, don't worry about Baxter, he's no longer a bloodthirsty vampire, and besides, Azalia Blenkinsop defanged him on Christmas Eve. So the worst he can do now is nip you with his front teeth," explained Old Mrs Dingle, as she and Trumper watched her little black Bedlington terrier, that looked more like a sheep than a dog, drool over the young boy. "Come along, Baxter, it's time to go back inside for breakfast, and you boys should join us."

Hearing the word 'breakfast', the funny-looking dog pricked up his ears and happily trotted back into the house, though not before giving Trumper a big sloppy lick on the way. Almost immediately, Bingo picked himself up from the ground and brushed the snow from his clothing before entering Old Mrs Dingle's house. And smiling, he thought it would not be such a bad idea if he and Trumper were to accept the old lady's invitation.

Once inside, they quickly slipped out of their wellingtons and slung their outdoor clothes over an old chair in the hallway. During this time, the boys could smell the tantalising and always mouthwatering aroma of Hogswood thick-cut smoky bacon, which had been smoked using applewood supplied by Typsy Braithwaite. And although Trumper and Bingo had already eaten a rather large quantity of pancakes earlier that morning, both of them would never dream of turning down the opportunity to eat a plate or two of their favourite breakfast treat.

As the boys followed Old Mrs Dingle into the kitchen, they found Baxter was already eyeing the mountain of bacon that was sitting on the table. And next to the bacon was a large slab of creamy Dragonbutt butter along with a rack containing half a dozen slices of lightly browned wholemeal toast. This was not too soft or too crisp, which was just the way the old lady liked it, and coincidentally, so did Trumper and Bingo.

"I hope you like bacon sandwiches, boys," said Old Mrs Dingle, while placing two more slices of bread into the toaster. Because with two guests for breakfast, she knew they would certainly need more toast, especially when one of them was Bingo. "Please take a seat, and I will bring each of you a plate and a bottle of Braithwaite's."

"Wow, there must be two pounds of bacon here," uttered a thrilled

Bingo, his mouth already salivating at the sight of the enormous mound of Hogswood bacon.

"Actually, it's three pounds. Baxter and I always like to treat ourselves to a hearty breakfast before we attend church," replied Old Mrs Dingle, happy that the boys had finally plucked up the courage to visit. "Now, here are your plates and two bottles of Braithwaite's, so please dig in while I give Baxter his bacon in a doggy bowl. He just likes the bacon you know, no toast and butter for him."

"Thanks, that's perfect," beamed Bingo, who had already helped himself to half a dozen rashers of bacon and was now layering them between two slices of toast that had been coated with lashings of creamy butter. "Old Mrs Dingle, you must like church a lot because you go there every week."

"To tell you the truth, I'm not really religious," giggled the old lady, as she handed the funny-looking dog his bowl that was now piled high with crispy bacon. "I only go because the Reverend Pinkerton has such a small congregation these days and so I would hate to disappoint him. Furthermore, he even allows pets into the service to make up the numbers, so I can take Baxter with me. Emblyn Gribble even brings her cat, Mr Pibs, though I have noticed he smells a little off these days. That is ever since Elvira Wyvern and her apprentice brought him back from the dead."

"So how is Baxter?" interrupted Trumper, who really wanted the old lady to tell them about the night the mooners first struck. And of course, answer some more questions regarding the Dragonbutt Witch's Institute. "We haven't heard of any more vampire attacks in the village, so I guess your blend number thirteen must be working."

Old Mrs Dingle told the boys that her new blend had not simply worked; it had been an unbridled success. Thanks to Bingo, once she had started using rabbit blood to replace the hard to find kangaroo blood in her blend number twelve, the little vampire never dared to reappear. As long as she fed Baxter a pint of her peculiar concoction once a day before sunset, he was, according to the old lady, back to his former sweet self with not a bad bone in his entire doggy body.

Whether it was the effect of the tasty bacon or simply her insatiable desire to gossip, Old Mrs Dingle did not have to be asked about her unpleasant encounter with the mooners. Though instead of getting straight to the point, she rambled on about who had attended that evening and who had not; how Bucktooth Tom Blewitt had an all too familiar look about him which could only have meant one thing, that he was about to call bingo. And if Emilia Baggot hadn't been so much of a busy body and opened the door to Dragonbutt Victory Hall, then none of them would have been any the wiser, but someone could have been fifty pounds better off.

"What about the mooners, Old Mrs Dingle? Did you or any of the other bingo goers see anything that would identify them? I know nothing was reported in the Dragonbutt Smoker, but someone must have noticed something," urged Trumper, somewhat impatiently.

"No, they looked like your run-of-the-mill mooners to me, just like the ones from years ago," responded the old lady, as she popped another two slices of bread into the toaster to make herself another bacon sandwich. "I had all but forgotten about them until I read Detective Huntress's statement in the Dragonbutt Smoker. And as I recall it took a whole year before Dragonbutt police could catch them."

"I know it has been a long time, but can you remember anything about those mooners?" probed Trumper, who had just finished eating his bacon sandwich. And unlike Bingo, who had already started on his second, had wisely decided that one was more than enough for him. "You never know, it may just help us discover the identity of these new mooners."

"As a matter of fact, I do," chuckled Old Mrs Dingle, while handing a rasher of the salty bacon to Baxter. "But it's not me you should speak too, it's Angus Hogswood. Now, who would like another bacon sandwich?"

To the old lady's surprise, both of the boys declined, knowing that in a few short hours they would be eating Flanna Dooley's famous all-you-can-eat buffet at the Dragonbutt Arms. Trumper was also conscious that time was marching on and if they were going to make it to the snowball fight by ten, then they would only have enough time to ask Old Mrs Dingle a few more questions. And those, he knew, should really pertain to the Dragonbutt Witch's Institute.

"So have you attended another meeting of the DWI since we last met?" inquired Trumper, as he gave Bingo a sly wink while the old lady was feeding Baxter yet another rasher of bacon.

Shaking her head, she revealed that once Barry Beasley had broken the story in the Dragonbutt Smoker about the capture of the little vampire and the existence of the DWI, then all hell broke loose at Dragonbutt Victory Hall. The Reverend Pinkerton had such a hoo-ha with the DWI's Grand Witch, Elvira Wyvern, that all the other witches thought it would surely end in carnage. And it could well have done so if it had not been for the intervention of her young apprentice.

Elvira told the Reverend in no uncertain terms it was Wyvern money that built the original Victory Hall, and it was the continued support of the Wyvern family that had maintained it over the centuries and even re-built it from time to time. The Reverend Pinkerton though was to have none of that. Dragonbutt Victory Hall, he said, was built to remind the residents of the village that their ancestors had defeated and driven out all the monsters during the dark days. And, as he put it, only over his dead body would he allow Elvira and her fellow witches to resurrect them during one of their unearthly meetings in that very hall.

Despite that threat, Elvira said the DWI intended to continue holding their meetings at Dragonbutt Victory Hall every Sunday evening. And if the Reverend was to drop dead, she would appreciate if he could do it quietly and preferably not in full view of her fellow witches. It was at that moment her apprentice took the Grand Witch to one side and whispered something into her ear. Astonishingly, she looked at the witches gathered before her and clapped her hands together before announcing, change of venue ladies.

"Where does the Dragonbutt Witch's Institute hold its meetings now?" questioned Trumper, rather urgently, as he had just noticed the time was nearly nine-thirty. And this meant both he and Bingo had better leave soon and return to the Bovington house to muster their fellow snowballers, Bertie Bovington and Flitcher Jenkins.

"Wyvern Manor," replied Old Mrs Dingle, who was just finishing her bacon sandwich. "And that really surprised us all because it is not like Elvira to back down against anyone, especially not the Reverend Pinkerton. Our first meeting of the new year will take place a week from tonight."

"Well, thank you for the bacon sandwiches and bottles of Braithwaite's, Old Mrs Dingle. Bingo and I have an appointment that we simply cannot miss and so we have to leave now," disclosed Trumper, who had already stood up from the kitchen table and was walking towards the hallway. "Come on, Bingo, we need to go to Bertie's house right now if we are to make it to the snowball fight on time."

"Oh, of course, boys. You know, I was having so much fun with the two of you that I simply lost track of the time," admitted Old Mrs Dingle, as she quickly gathered up everyone's plates and placed them in the kitchen sink. "Baxter and I need to leave shortly as well so that we're not late for the Sunday service. Although to be honest, we'd both love to join you for a snowball fight as I can't remember the last time I had one. Unfortunately, the Reverend Pinkerton is a bit of a stickler for punctuality. And so ten-thirty really does mean ten-thirty and not a quarter to eleven, as he often likes to remind the few of us that make up his dwindling congregation."

In no time at all, the boys were dressed in their warm winter outdoor clothing and had pulled on their wellington boots once again. Prior to their departure, Trumper and Bingo patted Baxter on the head and said their goodbyes to the old lady before stepping out into the soft and refreshingly clean snow.

"Dragonsbutts! I never thought that Old Mrs Dingle would be up for a snowball fight," laughed Bingo, happily trudging through the snow. "And why did she tell you to speak with Angus Hogswood? What would he know about mooners?"

"I have no idea, Bingo," said Trumper, thoughtfully. "But if I know Angus, and I think I do, then there is more than a good chance he will be at the Dragonbutt Arms for Sunday lunch, even if it's just for a liquid one. And that is when I will ask him to reveal everything he knows about the mooners that plagued the village some two and a half decades ago."

Standing at the front door of the Bovington house, it was Trumper's turn to knock on the door. And according to Bingo, this was just fine by him as he had no desire to repeat his unpleasant experience from earlier that morning. Just as he raised the heavy cast-iron knocker, the imposing front door abruptly and by the look on the boys' faces unexpectedly opened to reveal a smiling Bunty Bovington. She was dressed in her favourite and by all accounts rather expensive new velvet winter dress, which could best be described as a shade or two darker than cherry red.

"Happy New Year, Trumper," greeted Bunty, grinning from ear to ear. "If I had only known that it was you who called earlier, I would have opened the door sooner. Although by the time I managed to climb down the stairs, you had unfortunately gone. Come in, and I will make you some hot chocolate."

"Thank you, Bunty, but we are in quite a hurry and just wanted to know whether Bertie can join us?" answered Trumper, quite sternly.

"Well, yes, he's upstairs with that Flitcher Jenkins," confirmed Bunty, who by now was looking somewhat disheartened. "Would you like to wait inside?"

"No, we'll be fine right here, but you can tell Bertie and Flitcher to get a move on," stressed Bingo, as he was eager for the snowballers to be on their way.

"Oh, you're here as well, Bingo. I didn't see you lurking in Trumper's shadow," hissed Bunty, not at all happy she wouldn't be able to spend time with her classmate from Dragonbutt Primary School. "I heard all about you mistaking Bertie for a vampire and how you captured him and Flitcher in that trap of yours on Pigswill Alley. You know it would not have bothered me in the slightest if you had chopped both of their heads off with that battleaxe you keep harping on about. As far as I'm concerned they're both such a nuisance and just an annoying thorn in my side."

And with that, Bunty walked down the long hallway to the foot of the stairs and yelled her brother's name at the top of her voice a good half a dozen times. Soon after, the heavy clonking of footsteps could be heard, and that was when Bertie and Flitcher appeared. They were dressed just like Trumper and Bingo, in their winter coats, DPS emblazoned woolly hats and warm woollen gloves. Without saying a word to Bunty, they pulled on their wellingtons before brusquely barging passed her and running outside. Immediately, the two of them plunged their cupped hands into the plentiful snow, pressed firmly to form a good solid snowball, and then threw them with all their might at Trumper and Bingo.

Flitcher's snowball merely clipped Trumper's left shoulder. While Bertie's would certainly have struck Bingo squarely in the face if it had not been for his lightning-fast reflexes. Luckily, this allowed him to duck and therefore avoid being hit, which meant the snowball found

Bunty before exploding all over her nice new dress. After hearing her deafening scream, all four boys decided it would be wise to forego the formality of saying their goodbyes and so they simply cut and ran.

It was not until they had left Counting House Lane and were halfway to Dragonbutt pond that the four boys breathlessly came to a halt. Gasping for air, Trumper was the one who spoke first, "Hey, you two, the snowball fight is not against Bingo and me. We're all supposed to be on the same side."

"Dragonsbutts! We know that, but Bertie and I wanted to get you back for the trap you set for us on Christmas Eve," retorted Flitcher, while looking at Bertie and hoping his best friend would let him know if he should throw another snowball.

"Fair enough, Flitcher," chimed in Bingo, who was not surprised in the least and had been expecting some kind of retaliation from his two friends ever since that now-infamous night on Pigswill Alley. "Even so, I don't think Bunty will look at it that way."

"Yes, I know, she always reckons I do these things intentionally," shrugged Bertie, thinking he would be well-advised to avoid his sister over the coming days. Although that would be quite a challenge as regrettably, both of them lived in the same house. "So do you know who will be with Chugher and Chomper Junior in this snowball fight? I just hope it's Mad Maddox because Flitcher and I haven't forgotten the kicks he gave us that night. They left both of us black and blue all over."

"And don't forget the wedgie he gave me," interjected Flitcher, remembering the uncomfortable and all too embarrassing incident in the back of the Dragonbutt police van. "That's the second time in my life I have had a wedgie, and on both occasions, it was by Mad Maddox."

"Alright, that's enough talking you three. It's nearly ten, and so we need to hurry if we are to arrive at Dragonbutt pond on time," declared

Trumper, as he led the way by making large strides in the snow-laden Hunnickle Drive with the others following close behind.

By the time they reached Dragonbutt pond, the four of them were only two or three minutes late. Almost at once, they spied three boys that appeared to be around their own age throwing snowballs and yelling excitedly at the top of their voices. As Trumper and the others moved closer, they saw that two of the boys were Chugher Harris and Chomper Baverstock Junior. And the other, who alas for him seemed to be at the receiving end of most of the snowballs, was Mad Maddox, much to the delight of Bertie and Flitcher.

"We were thinking you weren't going to turn up," grumbled Chomper Junior, who, even though his characteristic shiny gelled chestnut hair was obscured by the DPS woolly hat he was wearing, was easy to recognise because of his rather small amber coloured eyes and always well-fed body with its distinctive short stumpy legs. "Anyhow, you're here now, so let's make some rules before we start."

"But we have four on our side, and you only have three on yours," stated Trumper, pointing out the obvious. Notwithstanding, as a stickler for fairness, he felt it necessary to call attention to this glaring imbalance.

"Don't worry about that, we have one more coming. Chomper Junior and I invited Flynabillie Braithwaite," confirmed Chugher, with a wicked grin and one of his hyena-like laughs. "She's great in a fight, but like all the Braithwaite's, being on time is not really her thing."

"Dragonsbutts! No one mentioned anything about inviting a girl," lamented Bingo, though it was not only the fact a girl would be joining the seven boys in their snowball fight that had perturbed him. Rather, it was because the girl in question was Flynabillie Braithwaite. She was Dragonbutt born and also a well-known tearaway at Dragonbutt Primary School. And not only that, Flynabillie was the only girl in the school that could give the short-tempered Bunty Bovington a run for her money.

As the oldest, it was Trumper who came up with the rules and reiterated them to everyone present. Each team would build a snow fort at opposite ends of Dragonbutt pond, and these would act as their base. The aim of the game was to capture the opposing team's base and this would be achieved when at least one of them steps foot in the other's snow fort. Only snowballs could be used, which meant no punching, kicking and biting were permitted. And, stressed Trumper to Mad Maddox, absolutely no wedgies would be allowed.

Impatient to start their snowball fight and not wishing to waste any of their precious time on more chatter, they all agreed with Trumper's rules. Each team then chose a good spot to build their snow fort, and within the hour two seemingly impregnable forts had been completed. Both of these were erected using a dozen or so large snowballs that must have measured at least three feet in diameter, and then lots of smaller snowballs had been stacked on top. This ensured each team had defences that rose nearly four feet from the ground with an opening in the back to allow the snowballers to come and go.

Just as they were finishing, Flynabillie Braithwaite was seen coming from the direction of Pigswill Alley. She was in the same year as Trumper and stood nearly as tall as him. Her proud mother claimed that this was the result of all the nutritious apple juice she had drunk throughout her childhood. Despite that, her father, Typsy Braithwaite, insisted that the impressive height of all their children was the product of his acclaimed Butts Batch cider. This, unbeknown to his wife, had been mixed with their milk from the minute each of them was born until they were just about old enough to leave home.

"I'm here, so we can start the snowball fight now," bellowed Flynabillie, as she strode up to Trumper. He spent a minute or two explaining the rules to her and then pointed towards Chugher Harris and the others at the far end of Dragonbutt pond.

"To think, we were waiting for her," hissed Bingo, though wisely out of earshot. This was because Flynabillie Braithwaite, with her mass of long wavy blond hair, blue eyes and thickset athletic body, was more than a match for even the hardiest of boys. "So, team, what's our plan?"

"Let's charge straight at them and take Mad Maddox down first," proposed Flitcher, who was looking forward to getting his revenge on the Dragonbutt Primary School bully.

"I second that idea," confirmed Bertie, as he was also yearning to humiliate Mad Maddox, something that was undeniably long overdue.

"No, they'll be expecting that, and besides, I think with Flynabillie on their side they are simply too strong for a head-on attack to work," warned Trumper, believing he had a better plan. "We should surprise them and split their forces by using a pincer movement. So Bertie and Flitcher will circle around one side of the pond, while Bingo and I will attack from the other. If we are lucky, in all the confusion, one or two of us may be able to break through and get a clear run all the way to their snow fort. But remember, we need the element of surprise on our side if this is to work, and that means everyone needs to be silent. Understood?"

Each of the boys nodded their heads and agreed that the older boy's plan just might work. And so they rolled as many snowballs as they could fit in the pockets of their coats before advancing on their enemy with a snowball in each hand. It was Bingo, the fastest runner amongst them, who was the first to emerge on the right flank with Trumper close behind. Bertie and Flitcher were then seen a second or two later charging forward from their assigned position on the left flank.

No one ever really knew whether the plan could have succeeded because unfortunately Chugher's team was tipped off by the forgetful and somewhat slow-witted Flitcher. Failing to understand the meaning of the word 'surprise', and in all the excitement of the moment, he had run around the pond chanting, "You're going down, Mad Maddox".

And so on hearing Flitcher's furore, Chugher Harris and his teammates were duly alerted and well prepared by the time the main attack began.

While Trumper and Bingo were intercepted by Flynabillie and Chomper Junior resulting in a ferocious exchange of snowballs, Bertie and Flitcher were quickly pushed back by another merciless barrage from Mad Maddox and Chugher. Even though Bingo was eager to fight on, Trumper saw that it was a hopeless cause and reluctantly called out, "Retreat". Relentlessly pursued by their enemy and failing to dodge the never-ending salvo of snowballs, all four boys were forced to fall back to the comparative safety of their snow fort.

Once the boys were standing behind the substantial four walls they had built, Bingo, who was not willing to succumb to an embarrassing defeat, roared, "Counterattack". With a snowball in each hand, he bravely but rather recklessly ran out of the snow fort and threw them as hard as he could. And as luck would have it, he hit both Chugher and Flynabillie in the face. Taking advantage of this stroke of luck, his teammates scrambled out of the fort and pelted Chomper Junior and Mad Maddox with a multitude of snowballs. This time it was Chugher's turn to call for their retreat, to the cheers of Trumper and the others as they watched their enemy withdraw to the far side of Dragonbutt pond.

As the snowball fight was not as yet decided, it was Bingo who came up with what he termed his brilliant grand plan in which Trumper, Bertie and Flitcher had to noisily charge at the enemy from one side of Dragonbutt pond. They would then have to engage Chugher and the others, fooling them into thinking they were fighting four boys and not three. And that is when Bingo planned to perform a classic flanking manoeuvre. Whereby, he would discreetly sneak around the other side of the pond and run for all he was worth to the vulnerable enemy snow fort.

Before Chugher and his teammates knew what was happening,

Trumper, along with Bertie and Flitcher screaming at the top of their lungs, emerged from the near side of the pond. Just as Bingo had envisaged, all four of the enemy quit their snow fort and ran towards the three boys, both sides pummeling each other with snowballs. By the time Flynabillie noticed Bingo was not with them, it was ten seconds too late, and this was all the time it had taken for the triumphant young boy to run to the undefended fort. He then climbed to the top of the closest wall and shouted, "Winner" while waving his arms in a round of rapturous glee.

"Dragonsbutts! That was sneaky of you, Bingo," groaned Chugher, who, as the leader of his team, was forced to declare their defeat. "Anyway, it's got to be close to lunchtime by now, and I'm going over to Chomper Junior's house for the Baverstock Sunday meat fest."

This reminded Trumper that in the heat of battle, he had all but forgotten his own lunch plan and the promise made to his aunty that both he and Bingo would be home by twelve. As it was now five past twelve, their promise was already broken, but as Old Mrs Dingle often liked to say, it's better to be late than never turn up at all. So the boys swiftly said their goodbyes, knowing the very next day they would see everyone again as it was the start of the new school term. And then, with all the energy they could summon, Trumper and Bingo ran back to Counting House Lane as fast as their weary legs could carry them.

Four

A Full Moon

⚜

"Late, as usual," called out Aunty J, who had been staring at the clock on the kitchen wall as the thoroughly bedraggled boys, whose clothes were now sodden and quite dirty, entered the kitchen of the little old house. "Well you are not going out like that, you're both filthy. I want you to wash yourselves in the bathroom and change into some clean clothes before we go to the Dragonbutt Arms."

"That's impossible, these are my buffet running bottoms," retorted Bingo, knowing that with the buffet lunch to come a regular pair of trousers simply would not do. "How about we just go as we are, I'm sure Trumper doesn't mind, and I know I don't."

"Bingo, go upstairs now and change your clothes or there will be no buffet for you," ordered Aunty J, in a tone of voice that meant this subject was not up for further discussion. "But before you go, give me your running bottoms, and I will plonk them in the dryer for ten minutes which should do the trick."

Washing and changing into clean clothes were two of the things that Bingo knew he had to do from time to time, though usually only when his aunty absolutely insisted. He was never happy about it and was known to use a variety of excuses to avoid what he believed to be unnecessary and wasteful undertakings. But considering his tummy was now starting to rumble, and he was going to be able to wear his running bottoms to the buffet anyway, he decided it was best not to grumble, and without another word, the young boy followed Trumper upstairs.

"Ah, Trumper, I'm rather looking forward to a good lunch as I seem to have overslept and missed my breakfast," exclaimed Uncle P, who was sitting in his favourite armchair in the living room when the older boy entered wearing a new set of clean clothes. "I think I deserve it after the shock we all had last night."

"Why, what happened last night?" inquired Trumper, curious to know what had occurred at the Dragonbutt Arms that could have distressed his uncle so much.

"Mooners, Trumper. It was three of them, just like last Wednesday evening at Dragonbutt Victory Hall," revealed Uncle P, while shaking his head as if he was still a little traumatised by what he had witnessed. "Boosey Dooley was absolutely furious as half his customers were so shaken they went home an hour before closing time. And that's unheard of on a Saturday night."

"Dragonsbutts!" uttered Trumper, thinking this mooning problem was definitely getting out of hand. "Did you recognise any of them?"

"I'm afraid not. Although after five or six pints of Dragonstone Fire, my vision is a long way from twenty-twenty if you know what I mean. And most of the other customers were no better off than me," admitted Uncle P, who was looking a little sorry for himself because as the editor-in-chief of the Dragonbutt Smoker he could not be more helpful. "I was drinking my pint and chatting to Boosey Dooley when we were startled by three deafening blasts of an air horn. Almost everyone ran out of the Dragonbutt Arms to see what all the commotion was about and that's when we saw them. Three bare butts staring at us from the opposite side of Dragonbutt High Street and giving us a full moon. Then all of a sudden, they just vanished into the darkness."

"What was that about mooners?" demanded Bingo, on entering the living room wearing a new jumper and the running bottoms with the all-important elasticated waist that while still quite dirty were for the most part dry.

Before either Uncle P or Trumper had a chance to answer, Aunty J walked into the living room to remind everybody that their table had been reserved for twelve-thirty, and it was already a quarter to one. Not wishing to arrive any later than they already had too, everyone quickly dressed in their winter coats and woolly hats, and for those that had dry gloves, they wore them as well.

Once they had left Counting House Lane, all four of them briskly trudged through the snow to Dragonbutt pond. From here they chose to take the shortcut by way of the narrow path to Pigswill Alley that led to the opening between the two old willow trees. From here they walked up Bristletooth Lane and past Dragonbutt Victory Hall, then onto Dragonbutt High Street and into the always warm and welcoming Dragonbutt Arms. This gave Trumper time to fill Bingo in on the latest development with the irksome mooners and the deplorable spectacle of their full moon.

"Greetings," boomed the voice of Boosey Dooley, as they entered the Dragonbutt Arms. "Boys, I haven't seen you since our merry band of vampire hunters captured that little vampire, the one who was causing all the trouble before Christmas."

Even though Boosey Dooley was not one of the six vampire hunters who had set out from the Dragonbutt Arms on that cold winter's evening to capture the little vampire, the boys and their uncle were just too hungry to argue with the boastful landlord, and so they simply smiled and allowed him to escort them to their favourite table. In actual fact, their brave band of vampire hunters had been made up of Trumper and Bingo, their Uncle P, along with Barry Beasley from the Dragonbutt Smoker and Angus Hogswood. Oh yes, and one should not forget Mad Maddox. However, he had been more of a hindrance than actual help.

After everyone was seated, Boosey Dooley announced that Flanna had prepared her rather extravagant 'Triple Seven Buffet'. This comprised a choice of seven delicious roasts, seven scrumptious side dishes and seven yummy desserts. And naturally, everything was all-you-can-eat, which according to Bingo was always the best part of any buffet.

"So what are you all drinking," asked Boosey Dooley, knowing they would surely get thirsty eating his wife's generously salted roasts. "It's all-you-can-drink as well, and that includes the Dragonstone Fire and Butts Batch, and of course Braithwaite's for the kids."

Seeing her husband's eyes light up at the mention of Dragonstone Fire, without a seconds delay, Aunty J ordered four bottles of Braithwaite's. It was then left up to Bingo, whose tummy was by now rumbling quite loudly, to lead the way to the buffet with Trumper and Uncle P in tow.

Where to start first is always a dilemma for many an amateur buffet goer, but luckily for Bingo, he was definitely not that. A bit of everything and then some more was his approach, a strategy that had on many an occasion proved successful. This had always allowed him to eat absolutely every dish on offer, which meant he had never left a buffet disheartened with the thought; I wish I had eaten a little more.

Beef, lamb, pork and chicken were all there, along with duck and goose, and what turned out to be three plump rabbits. All of which, of course, were supplied by Baverstock's the Butchers. Bingo placed a slice of each onto his large oval plate and then moved on to the seven tempting side dishes.

First came his favourite, mixed sausage casserole, containing five different types of sausage from the Hogswood Piggery. Then there was the Yorkshire pudding, which was smaller than usual but still filled a sizeable part of his plate. Seeing that his first plate was nearly full, he sensibly took a second for the remaining five side dishes. And as might be expected, the young boy was careful not to drop even a single morsel of the tasty food he had already amassed on his plate.

Though he was certainly not what you would call a fan of vegetables, Bingo was quite fond of Flanna's cauliflower cheese. And so he helped himself to a generous portion along with a good dollop of her garlicky mashed potatoes. Moving on, he threw caution to the wind and took four buttered asparagus spears that had been wrapped in Hogswood bacon, which made them taste more than alright by him. Last but not least were the devilled lamb's kidneys that smelled simply delectable and so he piled them high on his plate, and then there was the boiled tripe and onion stew he knew would go down a treat.

Back at the dining table with his two overfilled plates, Bingo did not hesitate to dig in right away, and so by the time the others joined him he had all but polished off his first plate. And after draining his bottle of Braithwaite's in no time at all, Boosey Dooley made sure there was no delay in getting him a second, which made it easier for the hungry boy to devour his remaining food and even go back for one more plate.

"Fancy meeting you here," announced Barry Beasley, as he walked over to Uncle P, and patted him on the shoulder. "I just came in for a spot of lunch but can see it's a full buffet today. Hello, Jemyma, and you too, Trumper and Bingo. You boys must be going back to school tomorrow."

"Yes, we are," sighed Trumper, thinking the Christmas holiday had come and gone far too quickly for his liking. But at least he and Bingo had been part of a real adventure for once, and he had written his first journal. "Did you hear about the mooners giving a full moon last night, right outside the Dragonbutt Arms?"

"Dragonsbutts! Not again," replied Barry, who sounded disappointed he had not been at the Dragonbutt Arms on Saturday night to cover the story. "According to Doris Clutterbuck, Dragonbutt police have absolutely no idea who these mooners really are, and Detective Huntress has yet to find even a single lead. Perygrin, did you see them?"

"Of course he did, Perygrin was here last night and as usual so was I," bellowed Boosey Dooley, because after overhearing them talk about mooners, the Dragonbutt Arms landlord wanted to be sure the young reporter listened to what he had to say on the subject. "If it's not one thing, then it's another. First, that Ogglejay woman opened her fish and chip shop across the street, and now it's mooners driving away my good paying customers. Pies orders are down, and Flanna is beside herself. At this rate, I'm going to be forced to bring back 'Free Pie Friday'. That's the promotion I ran two years ago where you get a free pie if you drink two or more pints, and that's really going to eat into my profits."

"What if I drank two bottles of Braithwaite's?" queried Bingo, thinking free pies sounded like an outstanding idea to him.

"Absolutely, Bingo," confirmed Boosey Dooley, mindful that as a family establishment, the Dragonbutt Arms needed all the customers it could get. "If you drink at least two bottles of Braithwaite's then you can have the pie of your choice for free."

"Then count me in," yelped Bingo, never one to miss out on the opportunity to eat a free pie. Or for that matter any type of food he could readily get his hands on.

"Ogglejay. Morweena Ogglejay!" exclaimed Barry, with a faraway look in his eyes. "Now that's a name I haven't heard in a long time."

"Do you know her, Barry?" inquired Trumper, guessing that Morweena and the young reporter must be around the same age.

"Well, I used to know a girl called Morweena Ogglejay during my early years at Dragonbutt Primary School, although that was obviously quite some time ago. And besides, she left Dragonbutt with her family, and I never saw her again," explained Barry, wondering if it could really be her.

At that moment and without warning, the front door of the Dragonbutt Arms swung open. This was followed by the thunderous voice of Angus Hogswood roaring, "A pint of your finest ale, please landlord." Then the huge bearded figure of Boosey Dooley's best customer could be seen strolling towards them. Without hesitating, he propped himself up against the bar in a spot that was reserved just for him. Conveniently, this was only a few feet away from the table where Trumper and the others were eating their Sunday lunch.

"Now this is the man you should talk too if you want to know about mooners," chuckled Boosey Dooley, as he pulled Angus his first pint of Dragonstone Fire.

While Uncle P nearly fell off his chair laughing, Trumper, Bingo, Barry and Aunty J all looked quite bemused. This was because they had no idea why the hulking Angus Hogswood, who they all loved and knew so well, would know anything about mooners. Trumper though, being rather astute in these matters, guessed his uncle and the Dragonbutt Arms landlord knew something about Angus that everyone else at the table was unaware of. However, he suspected this was about to change.

"Oh yes, I was a mooner," disclosed Angus, somewhat nonchalantly as he downed his first pint and requested a second. "But that must have been twenty-five years ago. I wasn't much older than Trumper in those days and was still attending Dragonbutt Primary School at the time. Mooning used to be more than a hobby for me, it was a passion, and I must say we had a good run at it. Dragonbutt police took nigh on a year to catch us, and in that time we must have mooned everyone in the village at least half a dozen times."

"Dragonsbutts!" cried Aunty J, quite taken aback by Angus's shocking confession and doing everything she could to picture something altogether more pleasing. "I think it's dessert time, boys."

When it came to dessert, Bingo was not the sort of person who had to be asked twice. And therefore he was the first one at the table to help himself to a plate of Flanna's sugary but always heavenly desserts. While he knew it would be a squeeze to fit all seven desserts onto what was now his forth large oval plate, the young boy was more than reassured by the fact he could always go back for seconds.

He started by taking a Coddington clanger, made of locally made beef suet that had been rolled with a good helping of strawberry jam and then wrapped in muslin and boiled. Next came the crumble, apple of course, then rich custard tart, a lardy cake made with an ample quantity of Butts Batch infused dried fruit, creamy bread and butter pudding, and a large portion of Flanna's much-loved family recipe of the quintessential English trifle. And not to appear too greedy, he limited himself to two brandy snaps, and then covered everything in a generous layer of luscious Dragonbutt cream.

"So in your day how many mooners were there, Angus?" probed Trumper, who following Bingo's lead had returned to the table with a plate that was all but overflowing with a bountiful selection of the delightfully appetising desserts.

"Mooners always come in threes, Trumper," divulged Angus, as he placed his second empty pint glass on the bar and gestured to Boosey Dooley that he was now ready for a third. "Aside from me, there was Typsy Braithwaite and Chomper Baverstock Senior. We were all best friends at Dragonbutt Primary School, and so when I had the idea of mooning, naturally, they became mooners as well."

"But why three mooners, Angus?" asked Bingo, while slapping his tummy. Feeling grateful Aunty J had allowed him to wear his elasticated running bottoms so that he could return to the buffet table for another Coddington clanger.

"It's just one of those things, Bingo. For as long as anyone can remember, mooning has invariably been done in threes. Not more and never less," stated Angus, who was tapping his fingernails on the bar while impatiently waiting for his pint of Dragonstone Fire.

With everybody engrossed in the topic of mooners, someone else had entered the Dragonbutt Arms and was walking in the direction of the boys' table. This time it was not a customer, who stood before them, instead, it was the imposing five-foot-ten figure of Heather Huntress. As Dragonbutt's one and only police detective, she had helped Trumper and Bingo, albeit begrudgingly, capture the little vampire in their first adventure.

"Ah, good afternoon everyone," announced the detective, looking very stylish yet neat and respectable in her black leather jacket and dark blue jeans. "Trumper and Bingo, I hope you have stayed out of trouble since we last met. Anyhow, it's actually Angus I have come here to see and would like to ask him a few questions."

"Well hello, Detective Huntress, what have I done to deserve a visit from Dragonbutt police? And on a Sunday at my place of worship I may add," laughed Angus, and unable to contain himself, Boosey Dooley joined in too. "If you buy me a pint of Dragonstone Fire I'll tell you anything you want to know."

"This is official Dragonbutt police business, Angus," countered the detective, who was looking very serious as she spoke. "I'm here to investigate the recent outbreak of mooning in the village and understand you have quite the police record regarding that despicable crime. What I want to know is where you were between the hours of nine and ten last Wednesday evening and around the same time last night?"

"Let me think, detective. Now last Wednesday evening I was at the piggery looking after old Bess. She's my prize sow who gave birth to a dozen piglets that night," responded Angus, while sipping his pint. "And last night I was having a bit of a shindig with Typsy Braithwaite and Chomper Baverstock Senior over at the Dragonbutt Cider Mill. Typsy doesn't get out a lot, not with all the cider he's been making lately and of course those kids of his take up much of his spare time. You know he has eleven of them now, enough to form the cricket team he always wanted."

"Do you have anyone who can corroborate your claim that you were at the Hogswood Piggery on Wednesday night?" questioned Detective Huntress, sounding unconvinced by Angus's story. "And do you typically spend your Saturday evening's at the Dragonbutt Cider Mill with your two friends?"

"It was just me and old Bess that night, and you're welcome to talk to her anytime," howled Angus, as the palm of his large right hand hit the top of the bar resulting in some spilt beer and a roar of laughter from Boosey Dooley. "And to tell you the truth I'm usually standing at this very spot every Saturday night. You see I'm more of a Dragonstone Fire drinker than Butts Batch, but friends are friends, and Typsy is always very generous with his hospitality."

"So your alibi as to your whereabouts during the two mooning incidents is that you were with a pig during the first occurrence, and last night you were in the company of two other known mooners," declared the detective, as she wrote something that must have been important in her official Dragonbutt police notepad. "I will be speaking with Typsy Braithwaite and Chomper Baverstock Senior, and make no mistake, I'll be keeping a close eye on you in the future. Good day gentlemen, and of course you too, Mrs Entwhistle."

Just as she had entered, Detective Huntress discreetly and almost noiselessly negotiated her way between the tables full of diners and exited through the front door of the Dragonbutt Arms. This left Trumper deep in thought, while Bingo, discovering he still had some space in his tummy to fill, was crunching on a plate of brandy snaps that were swimming in Dragonbutt cream.

"I think we have had enough talk of mooners for one day," asserted Uncle P, who was the first to break the uncommon silence that had enveloped their table. "What I would like to know is how your investigation into the DWI is coming along, Barry? This is immeasurably more important than chasing after three delinquent mooners. No offence, Angus."

"That's alright, Perygrin, none taken," grinned the big man, as he began to chat with Boosey Dooley who was still lurking behind the bar.

Frustratingly, the young reporter confessed he had discovered precious little since learning about the existence of the mysterious and rather secretive society that called themselves the Dragonbutt Witch's Institute. Even though he had known many of its members for much of his life, he found they were a thoroughly tight-lipped bunch when it came to revealing information about the goings-on at their weekly meetings.

He added that the Reverend Pinkerton had not helped one bit by barring the witches from using Dragonbutt Victory Hall. Where they would meet now, Barry had yet to establish. And then, of course, there was Elvira Wyvern who was difficult to deal with at the best of times. One thing he could confirm is that she was definitely the Grand Witch of the DWI and Elvira always cast her spells with the help of a young apprentice. The identity of whom the young reporter still had not been able to ascertain.

"According to Old Mrs Dingle the DWI will now meet at Wyvern Manor, and their first meeting will take place next Sunday," blurted out Trumper, pleased to be able to help Barry with his investigation. "So we really aren't any closer to learning the truth about the DWI than we were before Christmas."

"That's true, but thanks to you, Trumper, I now know where and when the DWI will meet next. And unknowingly, Boosey Dooley has given me one more important lead," divulged Barry, with an unexpected glint of excitement in his eyes. "You know what? I have a craving to eat fish and chips for lunch."

"Dragonsbutts!" exploded the exasperated landlord, after overhearing the young reporter. "I thought you were eating here. Don't tell me I'm losing another customer to that Ogglejay woman?"

"Next time, Boosey, I promise," shouted Barry, who had said his goodbyes and was hurriedly making his way out of the Dragonbutt Arms.

Trumper had no idea what that was all about; notwithstanding, if Boosey Dooley had given Barry a new lead, then he was clueless as to what it could have been. As their tummies were now full, it was time to say their goodbyes to Angus and the Dragonbutt Arms landlord. So, as usual, their aunty paid the bill, while Uncle P left a tip of two pounds, one pound for the waiter and one pound for the chef. 'Just enough to show appreciation, but not too much to make it look like you are showing off', words the boys had heard on many an occasion.

As the four of them walked back home, Trumper thought long and hard about the DWI and how Sherlock Holmes would have dealt with a formidable case like this. Naturally, the answer was obvious, both he and Bingo must go to Wyvern Manor to learn what they could from the Grand Witch. This, of course, would have to wait until Saturday, as he knew all too well that witches and monsters, or even the Entwhistle Oath, would never be a good enough excuse to allow the boys to miss any of their classes, especially during the first week of a new term at Dragonbutt Primary School.

Five

The Head Boy

Monday started rather early with a hurried breakfast consisting of porridge drenched in plenty of Botters honey, two slices of white bread toast covered in a thick layer of creamy Dragonbutt butter, and a large mug of hot chocolate. A somewhat measly spread deliberated Bingo and entirely inadequate for two young boys with a long day of learning ahead of them. However, to be polite, he accepted everything with a smile and instead focussed his thoughts on what he would be eating for lunch.

By a quarter past eight, it was time to leave as their schoolday always started promptly at nine and tardiness was not something their headteacher, Dr Wimbish, had ever been inclined to tolerate. Each boy wore a maroon coloured sweatshirt that clearly displayed the letters DPS embroidered in an eye-catching golden-yellow thread. Along with clean blue jeans, which were only allowed if they were not ripped, and a pair of black lace-up trainers. And so dressed in their winter coats, DPS woolly hats and warm woollen gloves, and holding their backpacks, the boys headed out of the front door of the little old house into one of those typically dreary-looking January days.

To their disappointment, the snow that had fallen only a day or so ago and had allowed them to enjoy a momentous snowball fight was now all but melted with only a few small patches still visible here and there. Although this was quite common for a drab Dragonbutt winter, it did mean their walk to school along Pigswill Alley would be a wet and muddy one.

Dragonbutt Primary School was located at the end of Firedrake Lane, not far from Old Dragonian Way and just a short walk from Upper Dragonbutt High Street. This wasn't the same Dragonbutt Primary School attended by Uncle P and so many residents of the village. That was usually referred to as the 'Old School' and was burnt to the ground by Mad Tolly Butterworth during a failed science class experiment. To no one's surprise, this ultimately led to her expulsion, which was not such a bad thing for her because, like all the Butterworths, she was never any good at school in the first place.

As was his habit, Dorcas Wimbish stood at the main gate of Dragonbutt Primary School with his pocket watch in one hand and a clicker in the other. This was to ensure all his students were present and accounted for and to confirm they had all arrived on-time. He was as thin as a pencil and bald as a billiard ball with a somewhat prominent and decidedly pointed nose, which conveniently propped up his pair of antiquated round wireframe glasses. And as he was often seen wearing an unfashionable and quite poorly fitting blue pinstripe suit, this rather short middle-aged man of fifty-two was never what one would call hard to miss.

Trumper and Bingo arrived at school with a good fifteen minutes to spare, to the obvious approval of Dr Wimbish who gave them a nod and two firm clicks on his clicker. Once in the school grounds, the boys were greeted by two of Bingo's boisterous friends, Bertie

Bovington and Flitcher Jenkins, shouting, "A pinch and a thump for the first school day of the month."

This was a ritual Trumper had participated in during his younger days, but now he was in year four he left that type of thing to the less mature kids. After two or three minutes of pinching and thumping each other, yelping and yowling, and rubbing their bruised arms, Bingo and his friends finally got bored. And thinking that was enough of that, they slowly walked back to where Trumper was standing.

"Hey, did you hear that the Begbys sold their house and moved out of Dragonbutt because they weren't going to live in a village full of witches and monsters," broadcast Bertie, a little breathless from all the pinching and thumping. "That means the head boy position held by Trenton Begby is up for grabs."

"Are you going to put your name forward, Bertie?" teased Bingo, who along with Flitcher, was laughing at the thought of their friend becoming the new head boy.

"No, of course not, but I heard Bentley DuPont is going to be nominated, and no one else wants to run against him," continued Bertie, irritated that Bingo and Flitcher were making fun of him. "None of us can stand the sight of Bentley, especially Trumper, so maybe we should nominate you for the position, Trumper."

It was certainly true that Trumper did not like the most spoiled kid in the school, Bentley DuPont, one little bit. His family was considered new money, having earned a fortune in the big city, yet they chose to retire in the country at the grand old age of thirty-two. Like his mother and father, he was not Dragonbutt born, and because his parents had a penchant for exotic travel, they had a habit of leaving their only child at home for much of the time. Even though he had a nanny named Endolyn to look after him, she was far too easy going and allowed the young boy to do as he pleased with a bucketful of cash to spend on anything he liked.

"I agree with Bertie, we can't let Bentley stand uncontested. It'll be a nightmare if he becomes head boy," affirmed Bingo, who disliked the DuPont boy nearly as much as Trumper did. "Bentley is not going to be able to win by throwing his parent's money around like he usually does. If someone runs against him, we're going to have to decide the winner by the traditional DPS way, and that means Trumper is the only one here who has a chance of beating him."

Trumper knew what Bingo had said was true. The only way to stop Bentley DuPont becoming the new head boy of Dragonbutt Primary School was for him to run too. Although because it was already a minute past nine, he understood things like that would have to wait until later. And so he urged the other three boys to run as fast as they could into the school to avoid being late for Dr Wimbish's morning assembly and the start of his beginning of term speech.

As with most of their headteacher's speeches, the first ten minutes were not only incoherent and rambling but tediously boring as well. Bingo, noticing Flitcher was wearing a pair of stylish new trainers, whispered, "Are they new, Flitcher?" And on seeing Flitcher smile and nod his head, he loudly uttered a single word, "Stamps!" Whereby everyone within earshot rushed to jump on Flitcher's new trainers. "Now they're no longer new," the young boy roared, laughing hysterically and all the boys and girls in the assembly joined in too.

This outburst did not go unnoticed by a red-faced Dr Wimbish, who being rather short-sighted was unable to identify and vent his ire on the disruptive student responsible. And so he chose to continue with the rest of his lengthy and much-practised speech. Only at the mention of witches and monsters did Trumper and Bingo's ears prick up. Though to their frustration, it was just their headteacher informing his students that any such nonsense was not to be discussed during school hours.

Moving on, his remarks about mooners and the recent outbreak of mooning in the village resulted in a chorus of giggles. Nevertheless, he soon put an end to that by glaring at a handful of carefully chosen students, and not surprisingly Bingo was one of them. It was not until the end of his speech that he brought up the now vacant post of head boy. This was one of two prestigious positions (the other being head girl) given to only the most deserving of students, to represent all the boys at Dragonbutt Primary School.

Dr Wimbish formally asked for the nominations, and to Trumper and Bingo's astonishment, it was Chugher Harris who raised his hand to nominate Bentley DuPont. The surprise was not that he had been nominated because they already knew this was going to happen. Instead, it was that Chugher was the one to nominate him as the DuPont boy was no friend of his. Not wanting to waste any time, Bingo raised his hand high and shouted, "Trumper Gallant." And all at once, the assembled students erupted in a round of enthusiastic cheers to the obvious displeasure of the other nominee.

With the nominations now confirmed and no other boy willing to enter the race, Dr Wimbish reminded the boys they had until Friday to decide who would be the victor. As he knew Dragonbutt Primary School had its own peculiar rules and traditions to choose the winner, he elected to leave those details to the boys standing before him. And then without further ado, the headteacher closed the assembly and instructed each and every student to go directly to their assigned classes.

While the boys and girls filed out of the hall in a more or less orderly manner, they chatted about the reason Trenton Begby had left the school and whether the next head boy would be Trumper or Bentley. In the meantime, Dr Wimbish had already climbed down from the stage and was standing by the exit. With his beady eyes scanning the hordes of noisy children, the headteacher singled out the two boys he wanted to have a word or two with.

"Ah, Trumper and Bingo, I'd just like to bend your ear for a minute or two," announced Dr Wimbish, who, as the boys knew all too well, was not Dragonbutt born. "You know that I run a tight ship here and so I don't want you encouraging any of the other students with foolish talk of witches and monsters. I read all about that so-called adventure of yours in the Dragonbutt Smoker, and I didn't believe a word of it. It's just tabloid journalism, and I'm very disappointed in Barry Beasley for writing it. You know he was a student here, but of course, that was a little before my time. Nonetheless, may I remind you that I expect a lot more from the students at Dragonbutt Primary School than my predecessor ever did."

"But it's all true, every word of it," pleaded Bingo, getting a little hot under the collar with his headteacher. "I captured the little vampire with Little MO, and the Dragonbutt Witch's Institute really exists. Elvira Wyvern is their Grand Witch, and she brought Emblyn Gribble's cat, Mr Pibs, back from the dead. And we believe the Dragonbutt prophecy has come true and just like back in the dark days there are going to be monsters galore. However, there's no need to worry, Dr Wimbish, Trumper and I have taken the Entwhistle Oath, and so we're going to protect everyone, and that includes you."

"Hogwash, that's exactly the type of ludicrous talk I will not tolerate at Dragonbutt Primary School," snapped Dr Wimbish, whose glasses were now sliding down his nose upon being ruffled by what he had heard. "Trenton Begby was just the kind of head boy we needed here. Not once did he ever question my authority, and he was always a good student that never got into any trouble. So I am none too happy that his family has left the village because of all this silly talk of witches and monsters that you two are largely responsible for. If you become head boy, Trumper, then you are going to have to set a good example to the other boys, particularly the younger ones. Furthermore, I hope we are not going to have a repeat of what happened during the last school term, Bingo. Don't forget that detention is for you to reflect on the error of your ways. And if I have any reason to believe that you haven't, then you will be back on my detention list faster than you can say Dragonsbutts! Now off to your classes, the both of you."

Since the two boys never attended the same class, as Trumper was in year four and Bingo in year two, it wasn't until lunchtime that they had a chance to talk again. The younger boy was already sitting at a table in the school canteen with Bertie Bovington and Flitcher Jenkins on either side of him. They were all drinking bottles of Braithwaite's and tucking into a large plate of pigs in blankets. Each of these had been made using an enormous Hogswood sausage that was lovingly wrapped in a savoury English pancake and topped with a rich Red Dragon cheese sauce.

With just enough room on their plates for the vegetables, Bingo and his friends had also helped themselves to a generous portion of mashed potato dotted with butter sautéed leeks. These were the nutritious green things that all students were told they must eat and then the boys had doused everything in a river of tangy onion gravy. And as no meal is ever complete without something sweet, each of them jealously guarded their dessert, a hefty bowl full of steamed jam roly-poly covered in lots of delicious creamy custard.

Just as Trumper took a seat at Bingo's table, with a sturdy plastic tray containing his main course, dessert and a bottle of Braithwaite's, Bunty Bovington appeared from nowhere and sat down beside him, to the trepidation of every boy present.

"Hello, Trumper," she said spiritedly, while ignoring the other three boys at the table. "I was so pleased to hear your name called at the morning assembly, and I'm sure you're going to be the next head boy. Even though he is in year five, Bentley DuPont is no match for you, and as you know, I'm the head girl this year. So when you become head boy, it will be just like we're married. It's so exciting, isn't it?"

Exciting was not the word that came to Trumper's mind as he

remembered, a tad too late in the day, that Bunty Bovington was indeed the head girl. That meant if he became the head boy, Trumper would undoubtedly have to see a lot more of her, more than he would ever have wished for. Once her name was put forward at the beginning of the last school term, everyone knew it was a foregone conclusion that Bunty would win the head girl contest. As the favourite child of Henley and Hildy Bovington, she could often get her hands on the celebrated Choco Bombs she loathed so much. And so because the head girl was always chosen by a single vote from every girl in the school, a gift of a Choco Bomb here and there ensured Bunty had an easy victory against the other three nominees.

"Oh well, Trumper, I must be off now. I always have lunch with the most popular girls in the school, and I'm sure they are wondering where I am by now," explained Bunty, as she rose from her chair and scowled at the other three boys who had been winking at each other and sniggering as she spoke.

"Trumper, my darling Trumper, it will be just like we're married," mimicked Bingo, who was laughing hysterically after Bunty Bovington's departure, and naturally Bertie and Flitcher were in stitches too.

"Why didn't any of you remind me Bunty was the head girl?" demanded Trumper, looking none too happy that on Friday he could be the new head boy. "Dragonsbutts! How am I ever going to get out of this mess?"

"Too late, Trumper, you need to take one for the team, or in this case, nearly every boy in the school," chimed in Bertie, who was actually thinking if his sister spent more time with Trumper, then she would have less time on her hands to bother him. "You can't think about backing out now, there are only two nominees, you and Bentley, so you absolutely must go through with this and win."

While Trumper knew that Bertie was right, he also felt he had gotten himself into an utter pig's breakfast as they say. This was something he was sure Sherlock Holmes would have been able to resolve. Yet regrettably, try as he might the young boy could not think of an easy way out of this dilemma.

"Boys, I hope you don't mind if I join you," exclaimed Puffer Hendrick, Dragonbutt Primary School's head of sports. As he sat down on the chair previously occupied by Bunty Bovington with a tray containing a mountainous portion of pigs in blankets and mashed potatoes. "Dr Wimbish caught me vaping behind the school gym, and so I am in his bad books once again. It's best to avoid him for a few days when that happens, and so here I am."

Percy Hendrick, or Puffer, as he was better known due to his fondness for vaping, was not born in the village; rather, he was a native of Merman Island. This was the small island connected to the mainland by a causeway and was regarded as the easternmost limit of the district of Dragonbutt. As such, the popular sports teacher had always been considered Dragonbutt born.

Puffer was not a tall man, as his height was barely five-foot-eight. And he certainly did not look much like an athlete carrying three stones more than his doctor would have liked. When it came to his eyes, they were best described as a dullish grey-blue, which is one of those unfortunate characteristics of many a heavy vaper. It was the colour of his hair though that was often a topic of much discussion, yet remained somewhat of a mystery to most. This was because, with the aid of one of those exceptionally sharp disposable razors, he shaved it every morning giving his head the appearance of a hard-boiled egg.

Despite the fact he was now forty-one, Puffer still remembered the dream he had in his younger days to become an Olympic champion. And if that failed, to be the highest goal scorer of the Dragonbutt Flamers, the village's popular and occasionally successful football team. Sadly, that dream had come to nothing because of his unwholesome habit of vaping. Instead, he had to make do with teaching sports, and during his spare time, coaching the junior team of the Dragonbutt Flamers.

"So Trumper and Bingo, I read in the Dragonbutt Smoker all about your escapades over the Christmas holiday and how you captured that little vampire," remarked Puffer, as he hungrily tucked into his lunch. "Most of the teachers here are not Dragonbutt born and don't believe in such things, but I have no doubt in my mind that it's true. Don't forget I'm from Merman Island and so I know a thing or two about monsters. Back in the dark days, the whole island was ravaged by those awful crabbers; frightful brutes they were."

"I was the one who caught the little vampire with my battleaxe, and the DWI is likely to bring back more monsters unless we can stop them," blurted out Bingo, who was prone to excitable outbursts every time the topic of monsters was raised. "That's why Trumper and I have formed MAOS. It stands for MONSTERS ARE OUR SPECIALTY. We're going to rid Dragonbutt of these monsters once and for all. I tried to tell Dr Wimbish, but he simply refused to listen."

"That Dragonbutt Witch's Institute sounds like an unsavoury bunch to me, and if I were you, I would stay well away from Elvira Wyvern. I never did like the Wyverns; they have a dark and troublesome history as you may well know. And Dr Wimbish is not Dragonbutt born, so even if a monster walked right up to him and bit him on the butt he would probably still deny their existence," chuckled Puffer, thinking he would gladly buy a round of Dragonstone Fire for everyone at the Dragonbutt Arms to witness that. "And how are you, Trumper? Looking forward to the head boy contest on Friday? Between you and me, I hope you win. I simply can't abide that DuPont boy and the same goes for his big city parents."

Needless to say, Trumper was not looking forward to Friday due to the very real possibility he could end up being the next head boy and the knowledge of what that position would entail. Despite this, he was all too aware that choosing the head boy at Dragonbutt Primary School was nothing like picking the head girl. As custom dictated, the head boy was never selected by a simple vote, but a rather peculiar kind of contest. And because this was Dragonbutt, the contest had its own unique set of rules and had been held the same way every year for generations.

"Well, I've finished my lunch, and so I must be on my way now. The Dragonbutt Flamers junior team is practising this afternoon, and I need to repair one of the goalposts. You know people do the strangest of things. I came to school this morning only to find someone had taken down one of the nets over the Christmas holiday. To be fair, they had put it back on the goalpost again, but it's now upside down. Who in Dragonbutt would be crazy enough to do something like that?" sighed Puffer, not noticing that the four boys were smirking at each other while thinking of Mad Maddox. "Have a good afternoon studying, boys. And Bingo, the junior team is in dire need of some speed, and you are the fastest runner in the school. Why don't you come for a tryout sometime? All the top Dragonbutt Flamers attended DPS, and the junior team is the best way to start."

"I might just do that, Mr Hendrick, when I have enough time that is. I'm pretty sure the next few weeks are going to be taken up with MAOS business. And of course this week I need to prepare Trumper for the head boy contest," acknowledged Bingo, happy that Puffer Hendrick thought he was good enough for the Dragonbutt Flamers junior team even though he had not yet reached his seventh birthday. "But don't worry; I'll definitely let you know."

Once Puffer had left, the boys got down to the serious business of the Dragonbutt Primary School head boy contest. In time-honoured tradition, the contest was held at least once a year in what was politely called the little boy's room. In point of fact, it always took place against the wall situated between the cubicles and the washbasins, an area reserved for the deplorably named urinal.

The rules were quite simple, 'How high can you pee and it's the best of three'. Some used to say the contest was rather vulgar and thoroughly distasteful, but this of course was the sort of thing young boys were often known to do. And so the rules of the contest stuck, and the head boy of Dragonbutt Primary School was chosen this way year after year.

It was Bertie who underscored the old saying 'practice makes perfect' as he was eager for Trumper to beat Bentley DuPont and become the new head boy. And it was Flitcher, who ordinarily was not the sort to have a good idea, that said Trumper should drink at least three bottles of Braithwaite's before attempting the daunting challenge.

After three arduous days of preparation drinking bottle after bottle of Braithwaite's and an awful lot of peeing, the big day finally arrived for Trumper. Chugher Harris was there to act as Bentley DuPont's second, and to supply him with copious amounts of ridiculously expensive imported sparkling mineral water. Every bottle of which had been stamped with an absurdly fake DuPont family crest.

Bingo was Trumper's second, looking well prepared he firmly held onto a bottle of Braithwaite's in each hand that had been chilled to just the right temperature. These were to be used as a last-minute top-up, or so he told the older boy, convincing him it was better to be safe than sorry as the three bottles he had just drank might not be enough to do the trick.

In typical DuPont style, Bentley arrived fashionably late, believing his vast family wealth allowed him that privilege. Although to the rest of the boys at Dragonbutt Primary School, it was simply a sign of his intractable uppishness. A characteristic that had made him the least popular boy in the school.

He was just as tall and slim as Trumper, though that was where their similarity abruptly ended. Everything about him screamed of money, from his expensive big city hair cut to the twenty-four-carat gold braces he wore to straighten his crooked teeth. His designer clothes were always custom made in Chelmsford, and if that was not bad enough, he never wore the same pair of underpants twice. Instead, it was rumoured he donated every used pair to needy underprivileged boys residing in far-flung parts of the country.

Trumper and Bentley were the first to enter the little boy's room, with their seconds holding the refreshments by their side. Then as many of the boys as could fit crammed in behind them. Each one chanting how high can you pee and it's the best of three, to the cheers of those standing outside.

Naturally, no girl was ever allowed in the little boy's room, as this was the only place in the school where girls were expressly prohibited from entering. But that did not stop them from congregating outside with the boys, and of course, an overly exuberant Bunty Bovington was one of them.

While Trumper apprehensively guzzled the two bottles of Braithwaite's that Bingo had handed him, a suspiciously confident looking Bentley DuPont casually sipped on a bottle of sparkling mineral water using a long bendy straw. This was because, regrettably for Trumper and to every unsuspecting boy present, the DuPont boy planned to cheat by wearing a pair of pump-up trainers. These had been made specifically for this very occasion and were the insurance policy he believed would assure his victory. And so in his right pocket, the pump lay hidden with a tube that ran down the inside of both trouser legs all the way to his seemingly innocuous trainers.

Before the contest could begin, the two contenders had to decide who would go first. By chance, it was Bentley who won the coin toss, and so with everyone standing a good six feet behind him he took his first turn and peed a very respectable four-foot-six. Trumper, looking a little nervous, was not so lucky and mistakenly peed at a diagonal that barely attained three feet in height.

After Bentley's second attempt reached an impressive one inch shy of five-foot, all the pressure was now on Trumper, and the shouts of support from the boys in the crowd proved it. Bingo, knowing Trumper only had two more chances, wisely gave him some words of wisdom on how to improve his technique. Whatever they were seemed to work as the older boy took another pee and achieved the splendid height of five-foot-three. This resulted in the little boy's room erupting into a chorus of Trumper! Trumper! Trumper! How high can you pee and it's the best of three.

It was during this timely distraction that Bentley determined the time had finally come to cheat. Discreetly, he proceeded to squeeze the pump in his pocket no more than half a dozen times. Luckily for him, not a single boy noticed his height had increased a good two inches since he had entered the little boy's room, and this was all it took for him to pee to the unheard-of height of five-foot-eight. A record at Dragonbutt Primary School and one that every boy knew would be a tall order for Trumper to better.

Disillusioned, Trumper tried his utmost to win, yet sadly his valiant effort only managed to gain him another inch on his personal best. And so with the triumphant DuPont boy clearly gloating, it was left to his only two supporters, Chugher Harris and Chomper Baverstock Junior, to declare Bentley the winner.

As soon as all the boys vacated the little boy's room and had communicated the outcome of the contest to everybody standing outside, they walked to their respective classes; downcast in the thought Bentley DuPont had won. Trumper, though, had no time to dwell on his defeat and was already thinking of MAOS and the trip he and Bingo were planning to make the following day. To Wyvern Manor, the new meeting place of the Dragonbutt Witch's Institute and the ancestral home of the Grand Witch herself, Elvira Wyvern.

Six

Wyvern Manor

~~~

Sausage Saturday was not something Aunty J was particularly fond of. And for that reason, she only ever held it for the boys at the end of their first week of a new school term. With the exception of Cumberland sausage, which by tradition should never be eaten before midday, it entailed a sumptuous breakfast of every type of sausage you could conceivably imagine. This meant there was always a good ten pounds of them, and naturally, they were all handcrafted using only the finest ingredients at the Hogswood Piggery.

It was not only the two boys and their aunty who sat at the kitchen table, as Uncle P was eagerly waiting for a plateful of sausages as well. While the adults each had a cup of good strong English breakfast tea, Bingo drank from a bottle of Braithwaite's. And Trumper, unusually for him, was unhurriedly sipping on a large glass of warm milk.

Once Aunty J had placed the enormous platter of sausages on the table, Bingo did not hesitate even for a moment and dived straight in. He considered sausages to be his favourite food and at first focused his attention on the regional varieties. Gloucester, Lincolnshire and Manchester all tasted simply great, and then came the Marylebone, Suffolk and Oxford, which he thought were absolutely top-notch. As a matter of fact, the only one that was not to his liking was the chilli seasoned Yorkshire, and that was because as everyone knew all too well, the young boy didn't like anything too spicy.

With room in his tummy for more, he drained the remaining apple juice from the bottle of Braithwaite's and then helped himself to the rest of the sausages. These were the foreign types that the Hogswood Piggery termed 'specialist'. And though they were not as popular as their English cousins, for those with a flair for the exotic, there was still quite a market for them.

Bingo almost managed to put away one of each, the Polish, Italian, French and even the Hungarian and Slovenian. But alas he could not manage the last one, a large German sausage that Aunty J said she would put aside for Baxter. While giving away his favourite food, especially to a dog, was not something the young boy was known for, he was comforted by the fact that when it came to sausages, in Dragonbutt, there were always plenty more to be found.

"I guess you won't be drinking Braithwaite's for some time to come," chuckled Uncle P, after noticing Trumper was avoiding Dragonbutt's most popular non-alcoholic beverage. "You know that back in my DPS days, I was the head boy for three consecutive years, and it was drinking several bottles of Braithwaite's before each contest that got me there. I simply can't understand how you lost to Bentley DuPont, he's not even Dragonbutt born."

"Why the head boy of Dragonbutt Primary School is always the one who can pee the furthest up the urinal wall is beyond me," shrugged Aunty J, who was not at all impressed with this so-called school tradition. "Anyhow, don't fret about it Trumper as there is always the next school year, and hopefully by then, Dr Wimbish will insist the boys vote for their head boy. And if that happens, you're bound to win."

"Yes, cheer up, Trumper. It's not all bad," interjected Bingo, while sitting back on his chair and grinning from ear to ear. "Did you see Bunty Bovington's face when she heard the news that Bentley had won? It was priceless. I thought she was going to cry, and while Bertie wanted you to win, he's apparently having a whale of a time teasing her about it. You know she absolutely loathes Bentley DuPont and was even talking about standing down as head girl until Dr Wimbish told her she couldn't."

During the past week, Trumper had quaffed more than his fill of Braithwaite's and had no desire to drink another bottle of the local favourite for the foreseeable future. In truth, he was also quite relieved he had not won the contest the day before. Bentley DuPont's victory meant that not only would Bunty Bovington be out of his hair, but he could also focus on MAOS and their investigation into the DWI. This, he was sure, was a whole lot more important than becoming Dragonbutt Primary School's latest head boy.

"What I don't understand is not only how Bentley was able to pee that high, but also the reason Chugher and Chomper Junior supported him? And to think of it, why did Chugher nominate him in the first place?" questioned Bingo, who was not really expecting an answer to his intriguing questions. "I know that neither of them like Bentley, and he's nearly three years older than they are, so why all of a sudden are they hanging out together?"

"I think we have all heard enough about this head boy contest for today, and there's nothing you can do about it now anyway. Bentley DuPont is your new head boy, and so that is that," affirmed Aunty J, as she stood up from the kitchen table. "I'm going to be working at the dental surgery this morning, and Azalia Blenkinsop will take over from me around one this afternoon. That means your uncle will be preparing lunch for you, and if you need to get in contact with me then call Wenna Loopey; she's going to be staffing the reception all day. Do you have anything planned for today, boys?"

"Dragonsbutts! I completely forgot to tell you. This morning I have arranged to meet Barry Beasley at the Smoker, and I probably won't be home until after lunch," recalled Uncle P, while peering at the clock on the wall and then abruptly jumping up from his chair. "There was another mooning incident yesterday afternoon, and this time it was outside Fanshaw's the Baker's. Wilimina Fanshaw had just served her last customer of the day, Emilia Baggot, and was about to lock up when it happened. As she helped Emilia out of the store, the two ladies were startled by a blast from an air horn then confronted by three bare butts on the other side of Dragonbutt High Street. Without a thought for her own safety, Wilimina took hold of the French baguette that Emilia had just bought and chased after the mooners. She nearly caught up with them on Bristletooth Lane, but it was already quite dark, and they finally managed to elude her on Pigswill Alley."

"Did Mrs Fanshaw manage to see their faces?" probed Trumper, hoping the mooners had finally made a mistake so that their true identity could be revealed.

"No such luck, they are always careful to moon under the cover of darkness, and so the only thing their victims ever see are the mooners gleaming white butts," disclosed Uncle P, who was hastily placing the dishes and cutlery in the dishwasher. "So you boys can either occupy yourselves here and eat whatever leftovers you can find in the fridge, or come with me and sit in my office at the Smoker."

"That's alright, Uncle P, Trumper and I will probably spend our morning doing some research at MAOS headquarters," replied Bingo, while giving the older boy a sly wink with two fingers crossed behind his back. "But we could meet you around midday and go for lunch at the Dragonbutt Arms. I know I could eat a pie or two and I'm sure

Trumper would be happy to do the same."

"Fine, but mind you behave yourselves when we're gone because I don't want you getting into any trouble," responded Aunty J, as she and Uncle P pulled on their winter coats and gloves. "I'll also tell Old Mrs Dingle you are home alone, so don't hesitate to go over to her house if you need anything."

After their aunty and uncle had left the little old house, the boys wasted no time in readying themselves for the adventurous day that lay ahead of them. Uncharacteristically, Bingo was the first to brush his teeth and wash his face. Not as thoroughly as Aunty J would have liked, still, he was somewhat passable, and that was all she could ever have wished for. He then quickly dressed himself in a clean set of warm clothing before stomping down the stairs. It was a good ten minutes before Trumper joined him, looking eager for the two of them to be on their way. Yet to his dismay, the younger boy was standing in the hallway with his Dr Who backpack slung over one shoulder while excitedly waving his two-headed battleaxe in the air.

"Bingo, there is no need to bring Little MO with you to Wyvern Manor," rebuked Trumper, a little incensed the younger boy always thought that brute force was the solution to everything. "Investigating the DWI will take a far more subtle approach than simply threatening everyone you meet with a deadly weapon. We have to think more like Sherlock Holmes, and I don't remember him ever using a battleaxe in his investigations. While you return your Monster Obliterator to MAOS headquarters, I will wheel our bikes out of the garage and around to the front of the house."

Though Bingo was clearly not in agreement with the older boy when it came to visiting the home of a supposed dark witch armed with nothing more than their wits, he knew it would be pointless to argue. And so without a word passing his lips, he traipsed down the long garden path to MAOS headquarters. By the time he got back, Trumper was already wearing his helmet and sitting on his bicycle, which meant the only thing left to do now was for Bingo to wear his.

As it was another cold winter's day, Trumper and Bingo were glad of their winter coats, warm woollen gloves and of course the two pairs of socks they both wore inside their wellington boots. Without delay, they left Counting House Lane and cycled along the pavement that bordered Hunnickle Drive and then rode past Dragonbutt pond and onto the narrow path that led to Pigswill Alley. Thankfully Jack Frost had been out and about early that morning, and so the ground was as hard as iron which made it more or less perfect for riding bicycles.

Conveniently for the boys, Pigswill Alley went all the way to the Hogswood Piggery, and from there, they had been told, Wyvern Manor was no more than a five-minute ride down an ancient and little-used lane. Because they were always quite competitive, the two boys peddled their bicycles as fast as they could and arrived at the piggery in no time at all. And as usual, Bingo stubbornly declared himself the winner even though he was barely a tyre length ahead of Trumper.

"Good day to you, boys," greeted Angus Hogswood, who, with a squealing piglet under each of his massive tree trunk-like arms, was walking across the courtyard that separated his home from the huge structure housing the piggery. "What brings the two of you all the way up here?"

"We're on our way to Wyvern Manor to investigate the Dragonbutt Witch's Institute," spluttered Bingo, a little out of breath after his impromptu race with Trumper. "And how are you, Angus?"

"I'm doing well, but no one ever goes to Wyvern Manor unless they have too. And in the past I've heard some of those that did, never returned," declared Angus, looking a little concerned. "It wasn't a surprise to me to hear that Elvira Wyvern has been meddling in witchcraft. The Wyverns always had one too many witches in their family, ever since the dark days when Eradorn Wyvern was around. I would stay clear of that place if I were you. They may be neighbours of mine; nonetheless, I have never set foot in Wyvern Manor and have no intention of ever doing so."

"Don't worry Angus, this is MAOS business, and we know what we're doing. Bingo and I have taken the Entwhistle Oath, so if Elvira Wyvern is really using dark magic in her DWI meetings then we have to do something about it," stated Trumper, unwilling to be deterred by Angus Hogswood and his grim warnings. "So did you hear that there was another mooning yesterday afternoon, outside of Fanshaw's the Baker's?"

"Oh yes, I was at the Dragonbutt Arms last night and heard all about it from Boosey Dooley. It looks like Emilia Baggot has now been mooned twice," chortled Angus, looking downright amused. "Good luck to them is what I say as a bit of mooning never hurt anyone. I just wish Detective Huntress would leave Typsy, Chomper Senior and me alone. She seems to have gotten it into her head that we are responsible. I don't mind telling the two of you that although I still dream of mooning, it's a young person's game and I'm simply too old for it now. My mooning days were twenty-five years ago. That was my year of fame, and sadly I don't see it ever coming back."

"Thank you for telling us, Angus," commented Trumper, who was trying not to laugh and signalling to Bingo to do the same. "It was good speaking to you again, but we really must be off to Wyvern Manor now."

"Well if you insist on going up to the manor then be mindful while you are there," cautioned Angus, as he shook his head. "By the way, what are you doing for lunch? My housekeeper always cooks up something tasty at the weekend, and you are welcome to join me."

"Will it be sausages?" beseeched Bingo, who, needless to say, was tickled pink at the thought of eating more sausages.

"Oh no, I never eat anything made of pork when I'm at the Hogswood

Piggery. You see pigs have an awfully strong sense of smell and if they ever got a whiff of something piggy in my vicinity then they would never forgive me," replied Angus, while shaking his head once again. "Shall we say twelve-thirty? And I'll call your uncle to let him know you are having lunch with me."

"Thanks, Angus, we'll be there. But don't mention anything about Wyvern Manor to Uncle P," winked Trumper, knowing the big man would understand and not give them away.

Pleased as punch they would be eating lunch with their friend, even though it would not include any of the piggy creations the Hogswood Piggery was famous for, the boys said goodbye and continued on their way. Having never visited Wyvern Manor before, once they emerged from the old and somewhat overgrown lane that had only taken them a matter of minutes to navigate, they were a little surprised by what they saw. Instead of a grand old house standing before them, Trumper and Bingo faced a towering brick wall. The seven-hundred-year-old wall soared a good twelve feet into the sky, and unbeknown to the boys it encircled the whole of the expansive Wyvern estate.

"Dragonsbutts! It looks like the Wyverns don't like visitors," called out Bingo, who was a little over a bicycle length ahead of Trumper.

"Maybe, but the purpose of a wall is never to simply stop people from getting in. It's almost always built to ensure people, or something, cannot get out!" answered Trumper, quite astutely.

Because Trumper and Bingo could not see any obvious way in, they rode their bicycles in a clockwise direction around the foot of the impenetrable wall. Eventually, the boys came to a large opening that was conveniently located at the end of Witches Brew Lane, only a short distance from the main road leading into Dragonbutt. Two sturdy looking wooden gates barred the way, which left the two of them scratching their heads, stumped as to how they could enter.

Bingo, who was never one to give up easily, banged with all his strength on the heavy wooden gates. And as you might expect, they did not budge even an inch. So he made it known to Trumper, that if the older boy had only allowed him to bring Little MO, he would have been able to smash through the gates quite effortlessly. While Trumper could well believe this, he was quite obviously at a loss as to how they were going to gain access to Wyvern Manor.

"You're early," a lady's shrill voice could then be heard, that must have originated from the other side of the gate, or so the boys assumed. Though in actual fact, it came from a cleverly concealed intercom in a section of the wall that bordered one of the wooden gates. "Oh well, you better come in, but make sure you use the tradesmen's entrance at the side of the house. You can't miss it; it's the black door with a sign that says 'Tradesmen Only.'"

It took no longer than the time it would take for a dog to wag his tail for the troublesome wooden gates to creak and then swing open, allowing an appreciative Trumper and Bingo to enter. With no one on the other side to greet them, the boys set off and rode their bicycles along a wide gravel path, and it was then that the majestic sight of Wyvern Manor came into view.

With no less than twenty bedrooms and countless rooms for entertaining, Wyvern Manor was unquestionably the most impressive house the boys had ever seen. At least in Dragonbutt, that is. Not wishing to waste any of their valuable time, they speedily rode around to the side of the house, then propped their bicycles up against the wall and hung their helmets from the handlebars. It was then left up to Trumper to ring the doorbell of the only black door they could see.

After two or three minutes of ringing the doorbell at least half a dozen times, the boys heard the slow but ominous thud-thud-thud of someone who must have been exceedingly heavy and probably uncommonly large. Having seen Elvira Wyvern a couple of times in the village, albeit at some distance, Trumper's only recollection of her was of a tall yet rather skinny lady. A far cry from the ponderous sole on the other side of the tradesmen's entrance.

Just as the weighty footsteps abruptly halted, it was Bingo, who, remembering where he had heard a sound like that before, alerted the older boy to the likely identity of the mystery person. And so Trumper, somewhat taken aback, hastily took two steps backwards a split second before the door was finally opened.

"Mumford!" they both exclaimed, as the gigantic and unnerving figure of Morweena Ogglejay's manservant stood before them at the doorway. After staring at the two boys for just a moment or two, he gestured at them to come inside. And then, with his characteristic thud-thud-thud, he slowly walked back down the hallway.

The boys warily followed with the older boy taking the lead. Mumford then pointed to a small and rather austere looking waiting room on one side of the hallway. And so Trumper and Bingo cautiously stepped inside. Being unable to speak, the giant of a fellow pointed his right index finger into the air before continuing with his slow thud-thud-thud down the hallway. Not sure if this meant one minute, one hour, or even one day, the two of them, knowing it was MAOS business they were on, elected to take a seat and wait for what was to come.

It did not take a day let alone an hour, in-fact not even a minute went by before the lady of the house appeared in the doorway of the waiting room and marched straight in. Although this had not given the boys enough time to discuss what Mumford was doing at Wyvern Manor, they were confident everything would reveal itself in due course.

"Ah, the help," said Elvira Wyvern, somewhat brusquely as she sat down on a chair directly opposite Trumper and Bingo. "So you boys are from the village and are here to lend a hand. You were supposed to arrive at twelve, but never mind, the early bird catches the worm as they say. Now I can't promise you the work will be easy, and I absolutely cannot guarantee it is entirely safe. However, I can assure the two of you will be well paid for your time."

Even though the boys had no idea what 'work' the Grand Witch was referring too, they were both shrewd enough to smile, nod their heads and of course, keep their mouths shut. This was just the break they needed as it would allow them to undertake their investigation without drawing too much attention to themselves. Trumper, therefore, was more than a little pleased, and the watchful Bingo could see it.

Elvira Wyvern was just as Trumper had remembered her, although she was perhaps a little taller and not so skinny now that he could see her up close. And as all the Wyverns were Dragonbutt born, he assumed, naturally, that Elvira was as well. She was a dowager in her late fifties with no children of her own and had long grey hair and rather small blue eyes that gave her a somewhat harsh and autocratic look. What unnerved the boys the most about her though was the fact she wore black from top to toe.

"Witch," whispered Bingo, into Trumper's ear, who just smiled at the younger boy for stating the obvious.

"Why thank you," acknowledged Elvira, after inadvertently hearing what Bingo had said and smiling as if she had been given a great compliment. "I'm no ordinary witch you know; I'm actually the Grand Witch of the Dragonbutt Witch's Institute."

Trumper and Bingo just looked at each other in astonishment. Surprised that Elvira Wyvern had been so open about her involvement in the very organisation they had come all the way to Wyvern Manor to investigate. Although sensing this candidness might simply be a trap, Trumper chose to feign ignorance. And so he pretended to have never heard of the Dragonbutt Witch's Institute, and fortunately, Bingo played along with this artful ruse too.

"I have to say, you boys are not quite what I imagined," remarked Elvira, while carefully examining each of them with her inhospitable looking eyes. "My niece told me that one of you was a Choco Bomb or two shy of portly. Now, where is she? Meow!"

While Trumper and Bingo felt a little uneasy listening to the Grand Witch point out the lack of meat on their bones, it was not this that worried them the most. What had really shaken the boys was that she was calling for her cat. And knowing all dark witches own a fiendish black cat, which they invariably use when casting only the very worst type of spells, they knew no good would come of that. So with the thought of being boiled alive in a witch's cauldron at the forefront of their youthful minds, they said a hasty goodbye to their creepy host.

As the two boys reached the waiting room door, Mumford silently stepped from the hallway and used his enormous body to block their exit. And then the Grand Witch called for her cat again, not just once but three more times, "Meow! Meow! Meow!" Needless to say, by this time they were both in a bit of a panic, and even Trumper now regretted preventing Bingo from bringing along Little MO.

With no alternative open to them other than to return to the sofa they had been sitting on, Trumper and Bingo waited for what seemed like an eternity to learn the ghastly fate the Grand Witch and her cat had in store for them. As Mumford stepped to one side, to their utter amazement, it was not a black cat that entered the room. Instead, it was the proprietor of Oh My Cod!, Dragonbutt's newly opened fish and chip shop.

Seven

Meow

Morweena Ogglejay was casually dressed in a dark-platinum coloured woolly jumper and a pair of tight-fitting faded blue jeans. Despite the fact her jeans were almost new, they had that worn type of look with holes visible around the knee and upper thigh. Although this was known to be exceptionally fashionable in the big cities such as Chelmsford, it was not so much in Dragonbutt, and that was the reason Trumper and Bingo were drawn to them. Seeing the boys sitting on the sofa, she stopped dead in her tracks and her welcoming smile momentarily vanished, to be replaced by a look of outright surprise.

"Oh, you're not the boys from the village I hired," she asserted, while taking a seat next to the Grand Witch and smiling once more.

"And you're not a black cat," retorted Bingo, stating the obvious, yet again.

"Yes, of course, but w-w-where are my manners," stammered Morweena, struggling with the letter W as always. "W-W-Welcome to

W-W-Wyvern Manor."

"If these are not the boys, then who are they?" interrupted Elvira, looking none too pleased she had been wasting her time entertaining the wrong village boys.

"Apologies, aunty, I'm sure you remember the daring young boys you read about in the Dragonbutt Smoker who captured that little vampire. W-W-Well, these are the very same boys, Trumper Gallant and Bingo Malloy," announced Morweena, while trying her best to avoid using too many words where she would have to pronounce the dreaded letter W. "And may I ask the purpose of your visit, gentleman?"

"We didn't know that you were related to the Wyverns, Morweena. But it's like this, we happened to be passing by and thought we could ask the Grand Witch a few questions regarding the Dragonbutt Witch's Institute," admitted Trumper, because as the cat was now mostly out of the bag, he thought it was best to come clean, or thereabouts, regarding the real reason they were at Wyvern Manor. "If that is alright by you, Mrs Wyvern?"

"No, it is definitely not alright with me. I'm a busy lady, and I am not in the habit of squandering my precious time on two young ruffians who have nothing better to do than chase after poor unfortunate creatures. Whose only crime, I may add, is that they are a little different than most," fumed Elvira, as she stood up and started to make her way out of the waiting room. "And my title is not Mrs! You may address me as Lady Wyvern or your Ladyship, and if I am wearing my official DWI hat and robe, it's Grand Witch. Good day to you."

"Unfortunate creatures!" repeated Bingo, while staring at Morweena and grumbling rather loudly after Elvira Wyvern had left. "That little vampire wasn't innocent you know, he attacked and drank the blood of the Reverend Pinkerton, Roly Poly and Mad Tolly Butterworth. And he would have done the same to me, if I had not taped a protective layer of holy water-soaked nappies around my butt, and been carrying

Little MO of course."

"You're an audacious boy, Bingo; I knew that the moment I set eyes on you in Oh My Cod!," conferred Morweena, as she watched the young boy smile, even though he was not entirely sure what the word 'audacious' actually meant. "Now, I think hot chocolate and some cake is in order. Mumford, inform cookie I would like three mugs of hot chocolate and a cake to be served in the drawing room in fifteen minutes."

Mumford did not have to be asked a second time and simply nodded his head before setting off to the kitchen with a slow thud-thud-thud. Once there, he selected the items requested by Morweena using pictures the cook had conveniently pasted into a large and well-organised scrapbook. The only thing he had to do then, was select the right quantities and the time everything should be served, which he managed with the aid of his gorilla-like fingers.

At the mention of hot chocolate and cake, Bingo's tummy began to rumble, and so he happily accepted Morweena's kind invitation without bothering to consult Trumper. Fortunately, the older boy also thought it was a splendid idea and one he was grateful for on a cold winter's day. After noticing Morweena's beguiling green eyes staring at their wellingtons boots though, he hastily slipped out of his and motioned to Bingo to do the same.

By the time Morweena had led them down the hallway to the elegantly appointed and, as the boys noted, luxuriously carpeted drawing room, their hot chocolate and cake were already waiting for them. With Mumford standing motionless at the far end of the room, Bingo helped himself to an overly generous slice of lemon drizzle cake. This, as it turned out, tasted even better than it looked. For the most part, because of the decadent sugary lemon syrup that had slowly seeped into the sponge, creating a wonderfully moist cake.

When offered a second slice, Trumper and Bingo simply could

not resist, but like their first, sadly, it all too quickly disappeared. Once the cake was all gone, the boys started on their mugs of hot chocolate. And although it had been made using Bovington's chocolate, disappointingly, there were no marshmallows. So they had to make do with a large dollop of fresh whipped cream served to them by Mumford.

"Morweena, we're so glad you turned up because when Lady Wyvern started calling for her black cat, I thought me and Trumper were both goners," confided Bingo, as he finished drinking the last of his hot chocolate. "I have to say though, Meow is a funny name for a witch's cat."

"Oh no, my aunty has many cats, and not one of them is called Meow," she laughed heartily, and then took a few seconds to compose herself. "I'm Meow, it's the family nickname given to me when I was a child, and it just stuck. Though it's only my aunty who calls me by that name these days, but I would be delighted if you boys call me Meow too."

"And why the name Meow?" asked Bingo, who was using the sleeve of his coat to wipe the remains of the chocolate and cake from the edges of his mouth. A habit he was all too aware Aunty J had repeatedly told him never to do, especially when he was in polite company. Be that as it may, he thought, his aunty was not here, and so she was hardly in a position to grumble this time. "Is it because you have green eyes like a cat?"

"No, of course not," she giggled, before responding to Bingo's question. "M-E-O-W are my initials, and they stand for Mor-w-w-weena Eradorn Ogglejay-W-W-Wyvern. However, for the sake of brevity, I usually shorten my name to Mor-w-w-weena Ogglejay. And I am sure I don't have to remind you both that my middle name, Eradorn, comes from my famous ancestor, the Lady Eradorn W-W-Wyvern."

"Dragonsbutts! So that means you're a Wyvern. I thought that when you called Lady Wyvern, 'aunty', it was like our Aunty J is to Bingo and me. We're foster kids you know," imparted Trumper, glad they had discovered the Grand Witch was not the only Wyvern currently living at the manor. "I guess you are the niece she alluded to earlier, but why do you use the last name Ogglejay?"

Meow confirmed that she was indeed Elvira Wyvern's niece and had been born at Wyvern Manor and happily lived there until the tender age of eight. It was not until nine months ago that she had reason to return following the untimely deaths of her mother and father. They had both perished in an unfortunate diving tragedy off the Great Barrier Reef after being eaten by a terribly hungry and by all accounts awfully large shark.

Although she had some regret not accompanying them on what would be their last dive, Meow knew if she had, then another Wyvern would have been shark bait that fateful day. So in her grief, she came back to the only home that remained to her, Wyvern Manor and her beloved Aunty Elvira. To live with the Grand Witch of the DWI, and she hoped, rebuild her life in the village of her youth, Dragonbutt.

Her mother was born a Wyvern and her father an Ogglejay, and because her mother's family name was such an eminent and influential one, her parents used the surname Ogglejay-Wyvern. After they left Dragonbutt, Meow spent most of her childhood at an exceptionally elite and extraordinarily expensive boarding school in Switzerland. During the holidays though, she travelled the world with her mother and father to all sorts of exotic, and to the most part thoroughly captivating places in wondrous but far-flung regions across the globe.

In the course of her extensive travels, Meow encountered an incredible number of peculiar creatures as far away as the undiscovered rainforests of Amazonia and the hard to reach Indo-Tibetan plateau. And during treks along umpteen ancient trails that uncannily all seemed to lead to the always hot and dusty city of Timbuktu. This is where she acquired a passion for the strangest and rarest of animals which culminated in the achievement of a double first in animal psychology and zoology at Cambridge.

While this encouraged her to study further, just two years into her doctoral studies, she was unexpectedly expelled. The reason for this, Meow claimed, was an altogether too conservative and intellectually limited faculty that could not grasp the merits of combining zoology with the almost forgotten art of magic. Something that Trumper, on hearing the word 'magic', took note of.

"When Bingo and I first arrived, we were surprised to see Mumford, but now I understand why he's working at Wyvern Manor," stated Trumper, with a smile. "Has he always been with you?"

"Mumford has lived at the manor since before anyone can remember, and after I was born, he became my manservant. He has always looked after the w-w-witches of W-W-Wyvern Manor," explained Meow, while smiling back at the boys. "He can never leave Dragonbutt, and so w-w-when my parents took me away, Mumford remained here. Though he had plenty to do mind you, w-w-what w-w-with all his other duties."

"Does that mean you're a witch as well?" inquired Trumper, a little hesitantly as he was not sure it was the right time to ask such a direct and profoundly revealing question.

"Naturally, all the female line of my family has w-w-witch's blood flowing through their veins. Ever since Lady Eradorn lived in Dragonbutt during the time you villagers call the dark days. Although to us W-W-Wyverns it w-w-was a progressive period of advanced learning called the enlightened times," confessed Meow, who looked noticeably proud she had been born into a long line of witches. "My mother didn't have time for such things, but w-w-witchcraft always fascinated me. And after my aunty discovered Lady Eradorn's old books on magic, it became all the more spellbinding, if you know what I mean."

"But why is it that only the females in your family are witches?" probed Trumper, wanting to get as much information out of the seemingly receptive Meow as he possibly could. "Or should I say, wizards, because I believe they are the male equivalent of a witch."

"Yes, that's correct, the proper name is w-w-wizard," struggled Meow, looking quite vexed Trumper had brought up that particular name. "Nevertheless, there are none of those accursed pretenders of magic in our family. They are all just sleight of hand tricksters, the lot of them."

"I'm sure that you're a good witch, Meow," declared Bingo, who had been unusually quiet while listening to the young lady's bewitching story. "Are you a member of the Dragonbutt Witch's Institute too?"

"As a matter of fact, I am. However, I have only been a member for about six months as my ancestors always practised their w-w-witchcraft alone. My aunty w-w-was the one who dreamt up the idea of the DWI, and she invited some of the ladies from the village to join. Each and every one of them are very enthusiastic, though I'm afraid that is all they are. None of them has the gift my family inherited from Lady Eradorn," disclosed Meow, and then she gave the boys an enchanting smile. "You may not know this, but I'm the Grand W-W-Witch's apprentice."

"Dragonsbutts! So you're the apprentice we have been hearing about," remarked Trumper, a little too excitedly. "I imagine you'll be attending the next meeting of the DWI tomorrow night and we understand it is going to be held right here, at Wyvern Manor."

"Um, you boys seem to be exceptionally knowledgeable regarding the affairs of the DWI. I hope that none of our loyal covern has been loose-lipped because my aunty w-w-would hate to discover she has a Judas amongst her brethren," snapped Meow, somewhat more sternly than Trumper and Bingo were expecting. "And the Grand W-W-Witch doesn't like the term, 'meeting'. Instead, she insists on using the more w-w-witchlike expression, 'gathering.'"

Unwilling to give Meow the name of their source, Trumper just nodded and did his best to change the subject by asking, "If you are a zoologist, what I can't understand is why you run a fish and chip shop in Dragonbutt. Wouldn't it be better for you to work in something more closely related to your profession, like a zoo?"

"W-W-Well, for your information, I do have a job in a zoo, although it's a rather extraordinary kind of zoo that is closed to the general public. Until I get access to my trust fund in a little under five years, fish and chips are simply a means of earning a living. Moreover, Oh My Cod! is only open during the evenings from Monday to Saturday and at lunchtime every Sunday. So this allows me time to do as I please throughout much of the day," professed Meow, as she suddenly stood up and clasped her hands together. "Now enough of talking about little old me, I do believe you have never been to the manor before so it's time I took you on a special guided tour."

Trumper and Bingo both agreed that Meow's offer to give them a tour of Wyvern Manor was a marvellous idea and one in which they cheerfully accepted. And so with no shilly-shallying around, the boys followed the benevolent young lady out of the drawing room. Just a few steps behind them though, a distance deemed polite by most, they could hear the slow thud-thud-thud of Mumford.

At first, Meow led them upstairs to take a look at some of the more extravagant bedrooms that were as large as the boys' little old house, but of course, far more elaborately furnished. Then they returned to the ground floor to view the extensive and much talked about Wyvern library. This was the place where Elvira Wyvern had discovered Eradorn's legendary collection of books, 'The Dragonbutt Witch's Guide to Witchcraft and Spells from beginner to the more advanced'. These were the books that had transformed the DWI from a harmless bunch of ladies having a bit of fun on a Sunday evening to a gathering of witches dabbling in real magic, including the dark kind as practised by a nefarious Grand Witch.

Stretched out on one of the shelves, presumedly to safeguard Eradorn's irreplaceable magical books, was an exceedingly well-fed black cat with evil-looking green eyes. Not wanting to dally in the airless and rather musty smelling library, the tour then moved on. Though not before Bingo noticed their comfortable group of four had now grown by one to a decidedly unwelcome five.

"That must be one of the Grand Witch's cats," warned Bingo, while whispering into Trumper's ear to alert him to the presence of the frightful animal following them out of the library. "If only I had Little MO with me."

"Thank goodness you don't," uttered Trumper, in a subdued tone of voice to ensure Meow and Mumford could not overhear. Nonetheless, to be on the safe side, he still kept one eye on the menacing-looking black cat. "This won't take much longer, and we will be able to talk more freely once we're on the other side of the wall that surrounds Wyvern Manor."

They continued their tour by visiting countless other rooms with each new one seeming to be grander than those that had come before. To their dread, every time either Trumper or Bingo turned around, they saw the black cat was still trailing after them. Yet curiously, Meow, who was tirelessly giving the boys a running commentary on seven-hundred years of Wyvern family history, seemed not to notice.

The final leg of their jaunt around Wyvern Manor included the largest and undoubtedly most impressive room in the grand old house. It was a banqueting hall so vast it could easily seat two-hundred around an inordinately long and these days rarely used dining table. The most notable feature in the whole room though was its paintings. These must have numbered well into their hundreds and covered each of the four walls, leaving precious little room for anything else.

"Ah, I see you're looking at the portraits of my ancestors," commented

Meow, as the boys gazed at what must have been a painting of every Wyvern witch there had ever been. And as one might expect, over seven-hundred years, that amounted to a whole lot of witches. "The one at the end is of me, and the oldest is hanging over the main entranceway. It's our most prized painting, and I have been led to believe it's a very real likeness of Lady Eradorn herself."

Perhaps it was the sight of all those witches with raven coloured hair and cat-like green eyes, or maybe it was because of the sinister-looking black cat's watchful stare. Either way, the boys missed something that should have been there but was not, and this had everything to do with the Grand Witch. What did catch the older boy's eyes though was something in Eradorn Wyvern's portrait that looked very much out of place. As Trumper took a closer look, he discreetly signalled to Bingo to examine the painting as well. Slowly, both of the boys turned around to gaze at Mumford, and then they studied the painting one more time.

"Dragonsbutts! That looks like Mumford," exclaimed Bingo, as quietly as he could while pointing at the painting. "Do you think that's his ancestor standing behind Eradorn Wyvern?"

"No, it is Mumford," responded Trumper, his voice barely a whisper. "But why is he in a seven-hundred-year-old portrait of the most famous witch in Dragonbutt history?"

"Now that about completes our tour of the house, can I take you to see the zoo before you go?" called out Meow, in a matter of fact sought of way, as if it was quite common to have a zoo in one's home.

"You have a zoo at Wyvern Manor!" spluttered Bingo, who was just as astonished as Trumper. "Where is it?"

"Yes, though for hundreds of years it's been called the menagerie, and it has always been located at the back of the house," replied Meow, while clicking three fingers to summon her manservant. "Mumford can escort you to the entrance, and I'll meet you there after collecting my coat as the air has a bit of a nip in it today. He's been looking after the menagerie for a very long time. But since I opened Oh My Cod! it's been a little too much for him. That's the reason I hired two boys from the village to help with cleaning the enclosures and feeding some of the less troublesome creatures."

Even though time was marching on, Trumper and Bingo believed this was something they absolutely could not miss. And so they followed Mumford with his slow thud-thud-thud back to the waiting room to retrieve their wellington boots. With the black cat tagging along behind them, a little too close for comfort in the boys' opinion, they left the foreboding house for the Wyvern family menagerie and who knows what!

Eight

The Cryptid Menagerie

By the time Mumford had led the boys around to the back of the house, Meow had been as good as her word and was standing at the entrance to the menagerie with a large rusty key in one hand. Along with her signature congenial smile, she was wearing a well-fitting and stylish jet-black leather jacket and a pair of slender ebony suede gloves to match.

All that Trumper and Bingo could see at this time was a sky-blue coloured door in the middle of an ivy-covered brick wall. This must have stretched a hundred feet in either direction but was not as tall as the one they had come through when entering Wyvern Manor. Built into the wall was a rather grand looking stone doorway in the shape of a gigantic eight-foot baroque arch. Just to the right of this and set into the brickwork was a visibly tarnished brass plaque that looked extremely old. And written on the plaque were the words, 'The Menagerie', followed by, 'ENTER AT YOUR OWN PERIL!'.

With both hands outstretched, Meow placed the key in the keyhole and gave it a long clockwise turn. The door, which had been constructed using two pieces of locally grown willow, opened in the centre with a loud creak to allow everyone present to enter. Knowing they were still being followed, Bingo, who was the last of them to step inside, wisely slammed the door shut before the black cat could make his way in too.

Once they were on the other side of the door, the boys could see they were standing in a dark and spacious room. The only illumination came from a gas lantern that Mumford had only then just lit and hung from a hook on the far wall. Covering the whole of the closest wall was rack after rack of all sorts of weapons, and of course, these garnered the attention of Bingo right away. Some of them resembled the butt sticks he had read about in the Entwhistle journal about the great shug monkey incursion and were innocent enough. Yet others on closer inspection were manifestly more lethal.

There were several awfully heavy and unwieldy-looking mallets that only someone the size of Mumford could have managed. Then there were numerous long wooden sticks with sharp metal spikes, boomerangs that must have been all of four feet long, and lots of metal chains with a large iron ball at one end. Although these were all quite fascinating to Bingo, it was the two-headed battleaxes which looked all too like Little MO that interested him the most.

"I'll take the battleaxe," beamed Bingo, as he picked up the nearest one to feel its weight. "This is going to be more fun than I thought."

"No," called out Meow, who swiftly backed away from the young boy and the battleaxe he precariously held above his head. "Those old things haven't been used in ages. I prefer something more akin to this century that is a little less destructive than those barbaric things my ancestors used." She then pulled from another rack an inoffensive looking rubber handled metal stick that was around two feet long. "It's called a 'punisher', and it can deliver up to a hundred thousand volt electric shock to anything that gets on the wrong end of it."

"Wow, can I have a go?" shrieked an overexcited Bingo, as he handed the battleaxe to Trumper and grabbed another punisher from the rack before Meow had a chance to stop him. The young boy then opened the door they had just come through and stepped outside where he promptly zapped the waiting black cat. This not only left the unsuspecting animal stunned with its legs pointing upwards into the air, but its fur was also noticeably singed. "Well, it definitely works. Can I take this one to school? I would love to try it out on Mad Maddox and Bentley DuPont."

"I think not," admonished Meow, who quickly retrieved the punisher from Bingo's hand and returned it to the rack, while Trumper did the same with the battleaxe he was holding. "There are many untamed and a few quite savage creatures living in the menagerie, but you'll be perfectly safe as long as you do everything I say. Oh, and stay close to Mumford. To my knowledge, he has never lost a guest, not one."

Meow led Trumper and Bingo to another door that was painted a bright shade of red and had a large iron bolt running its entire width. And written on the door in bold black letters were the words, 'WHETHER COMING OR GOING ALWAYS ENSURE YOU BOLT THE DOOR!'. As the Grand Witch's apprentice slid the bolt to one side, the door swung open and she turned around to smile. Without delay, Meow stepped through to the other side, and the boys impatiently followed. This left Mumford, who had been slowly bringing up the rear, to bolt the door behind them.

On the other side, the boys could see the menagerie was much larger than they had first thought. Although it was about two-hundred feet wide, its length must have been as much as ten times that distance with the ivy-clad brick wall enclosing the whole area. Presumedly, to keep whatever was inside from getting out. Many of its occupants, though certainly not all, were considered harmless enough, but if they ever became unruly the punishment had always been 'off with their head'. This was an unwritten rule at the manor, yet one that many a Wyvern witch had on occasion been reluctantly required to carry-out. Most commonly with a weapon more than suitable for that purpose, the two-headed battleaxe.

The menagerie comprised not just one but two compounds, with a convenient well-worn cobblestone walkway running alongside each. The main compound had been built some seven hundred years ago and was by far the larger of the two. The second and smaller one had only been constructed in the last six months and was reserved for only the most exceptional and dangerous of creatures. And these were the ones that Meow had a heartfelt professional interest in.

From the very beginning, it was intended that the creatures living there should have plenty of room to roam around and mingle with their neighbours. And so the only condition of their entry was for each and every one of them to get along with all the others. There were never any cages within the walls of the menagerie, only strong metal fencing surrounding each compound and a door to each that used the same solitary key. As you might expect, this key was always held by Mumford, who zealously guarded it and ordinarily would never permit it to leave his possession.

"So what makes the menagerie different from any other zoo?" inquired Trumper, who was the closest to Meow as the four of them ambled along the walkway. "And what did you mean by 'savage creatures'?"

After a brief interval, she explained to the boys that nowadays every zoo you come across contains the sort of animals that can be found almost anywhere. At the menagerie, you simply would never find any of those kinds of animals, which is what made it such an interesting place. And this was because it was founded to protect only the rarest and the most unusual creatures that had ever been known to inhabit the planet. All of whom, Meow added, are now very much extinct outside the walls of Wyvern Manor.

It was actually the brainchild of Eradorn Wyvern, who during the dark days acquired the first of the unconventional creatures to be brought there, which were the ones the residents of Dragonbutt liked to call 'monsters'. And then after her passing at the tender age of a hundred and seventy-two, it was left up to successive generations of Wyvern witches to add those a little less maleficent to her uncommon collection. Soon after that, a wall was built around their compound to ensure they could never run away, which has proven successful right up to the present day.

In the years that followed the dark days, Eradorn's favoured creatures, whose lives had been extended by her powerful spells, all died out. With the discovery of the Grand Witch's books on witchcraft and spell making, Elvira Wyvern and her young apprentice found that dark magic could actually bring them back to life, or thereabouts! The only downside to this, they learnt, was that the reincarnated creatures often had quite a craving for blood and the distasteful habit of devouring the living.

This was the reason Mumford had recently constructed a second compound that Meow dubbed the cryptid menagerie. And out of an abundance of caution, it was enclosed by an exceptionally deep moat, which contained a particularly monstrous variety of flesh-eating piranha. Initially, there had only been two of them that in typical Dragonbutt fashion were named Forbes and Willougby. Although with the aid of one of Eradorn's old spells, their number rapidly swelled to the hundreds.

"But don't the creatures that live in the cryptid menagerie try to eat each other?" questioned Trumper, who was relishing the thought of meeting a bunch of monsters that had been around during the dark days. "And what about you and Lady Wyvern, aren't you worried they will eat the two of you as well?"

"Yes, and don't forget Mumford," added Bingo, thinking Meow's oversized manservant would be quite a banquet for some of those bloodthirsty creatures. "If they ate him, it would be like eating half a dozen regular people."

"Oh no, it has only been a few months since my aunty and I discovered the spell to bring these creatures back from the dead, and so there are just three success stories so far. Moreover, they only have an appetite for those that have always been living. And though the reincarnated creatures are now mostly alive, in the past they had been every inch dead," disclosed Meow, rather enthusiastically. "Naturally, real w-w-witches have nothing to fear because no creature in the cryptid menagerie could ever bite the hand that brought them back to life."

"So how did Old Mrs Dingle's dog turn into a bloodsucking vampire?" probed Trumper, noting Meow had failed to mention Mumford in her lengthy but illuminating explanation. "He wasn't brought back from the dead, yet he still became possessed by the spirit of a monster that had been alive during the dark days."

"Quite true, though I consider that incident no more than a trifling accident. Albeit a fortuitous one because it allowed such an interesting creature to live amongst us once again," stated Meow, looking caught up in her own thoughts. "That potion had been specifically brewed to bring a recently departed animal back from the dead, in this case, Mr Pibs. And it did just that, but it also enabled a bygone spirit to inhabit Baxter's living body after he inadvertently drank some too. I can only assume that because the potion had been meant for the dead and not the living, the unexpected must have happened, an all too common occurrence amongst w-w-witches that dabble in the more advanced forms of magic. Obviously, it takes a very different kind of magic to reincarnate the distant departed and of course the possession of their preserved body."

"Do you mean to say you still have the bodies of creatures that were alive during the dark days?" beseeched Trumper, somewhat aghast with his mouth wide open.

"Oh yes, all of Eradorn's creatures from that time are stored in a special vault beneath the menagerie. It's located so deep underground that the cold temperatures down there act as a freezer to preserve the bodies," shared Meow, who seemed to be delighted with this fact. "That's the reason they can now be brought back to life again."

"Dragonsbutts! Where is this vault?" cried out Bingo, as he was eager to take a look at these long-dead creatures. "And how many of them are stored there?"

"I imagine there are dozens and dozens of them, though to be truthful I don't think anyone really knows except Mumford, and he could never tell anyone," professed Meow, while momentarily making eye contact with her lumbering manservant. "He's the only one that ever journeys into the vault, and needless to say guests are strictly prohibited from entering. Now here is the main compound. The two creatures you see on the hill are sidehill gougers."

Trumper and Bingo excitedly ran over to the first enclosure which contained not exactly a hill, more a steep mound that reached a height of a little over thirty feet. The two creatures Meow had pointed out certainly looked quite odd and were both the size of a medium-sized dog, but with legs on the left side of their body that were quite a bit longer than their right. This meant the sidehill gouger could live on the side of steep hills and run after its prey, though only ever in one direction. If it foolishly tried to run the other way, then assuredly it would tumble down the hillside. And not being able to stand on the flat ground below due to its uneven legs, the helpless creature would be stranded there and without doubt, just wither away.

"I'm sad to say there are only clockwise sidehill gouger's living here these days. Long ago my ancestors mistakenly placed into the same enclosure some of their anti-clockwise relatives too, that happened to be smaller and had longer legs on their right side than their left. But as they can both only run in one direction, they ultimately had to meet, and that resulted in the untimely demise of the anti-clockwise sidehill gouger," expounded Meow, who was slowly shaking her head. "Naturally, their bodies have been preserved in the vault so they can always be brought back to life again. But of course next time they need to be placed in the cryptid menagerie to avoid the blunders of the past."

As the group moved onto the second enclosure, the boys could see what appeared to be a much more ferocious type of creature. Beyond the confines of the fence was a pool of exceedingly muddy water that was little more than half the size of Dragonbutt pond with a lush array of trees and bushes on the far side. And in the water was an enormous and truly ugly looking reptile that was neither a crocodile nor an alligator, but what Meow eloquently termed a crocogator.

It was a creature that had long been extinct, and even when it had been alive, it was known to be extraordinarily rare. The crocogator came about by crossing a crocodile with an alligator, which even back then was one of those things that hardly ever happened. This was because not only did each species believe the other to be rather unsightly but always utterly disagreeable as well. And that is why crocodiles and alligators are never found in the same location and instead choose to live in entirely different parts of the world.

"Elequtia W-W-Wyvern brought the last crocogator to the menagerie nearly three-hundred years ago, and my ancestors have been able to keep it healthy and thankfully alive ever since. Out of interest, the key to its longevity is to ensure it can never look upon its own reflection. So Mumford always keeps the pool exceptionally muddy or else it might realise how dreadfully ugly it is. The almost certain shock of seeing itself can arrest the heart of a crocogator, and that is the reason all the others are now extinct," disclosed Meow, who looked noticeably proud of her family accomplishments. "Now there's plenty more to see, so let's not dawdle."

Acutely aware that the morning hours were rapidly slipping away, Meow picked up the pace and hurried along the cobblestone walkway to the other enclosures. While Trumper and Bingo easily matched her stride, Mumford, with his slow thud-thud-thud, dropped back somewhat, only catching up with them when his mistress stopped to point out another of the strange creatures.

There was a family of Cornish devils that were far worse than the Tasmanian kind, and the once common and downright scary looking wolpertingers. These had the body of a rabbit but with horns, fangs and bird-like feet, and clipped feathered wings to prevent any of them from flying away. And hidden in a patch of trees were three or maybe four timid Lilliputian sasquatches that were just as hairy as their larger cousins, though they could not have been more than three feet in height.

After almost an hour they came to the end of the main compound and saw a large flock of doodos. These had disappeared centuries ago because they had short-sightedly eaten the entire population of their distant relative, the legendary dodo, which was the only kind of food the greedy doodo liked to eat. Following a great deal of trial and error, Elga Wyvern, another of Meow's more notable ancestors, discovered that doodos, who were only marginally more intelligent than the dim-witted dodo, could be fooled into thinking a chicken was really a dodo. But only if the doodo drank at least one bottle of Butts Batch first, and this is what had guaranteed the survival of the doodo species.

The boys must have seen three dozen or more of these bizarre creatures before they reached the moat that encircled the new compound housing Meow's cryptid menagerie. As a safeguard to ensure no one would fall in and be devoured by the perpetually hungry piranhas, Mumford had erected a solid safety rail. And this had proven its worth because none of the malicious fish had so far gotten the chance to eat even a morsel of human flesh.

While Bingo leaned over the railing to get a closer look at the piranhas swimming beneath him, Mumford carefully lowered a heavy wooden drawbridge. Prudently, Meow pulled out her punisher and switched it on to its minimum setting, just in case she had a need to use it. With Trumper barely two steps behind her, the Grand Witch's apprentice then sauntered across the drawbridge to the first enclosure to take a look at whatever was inside.

"What do they eat?" called out Bingo, as he inspected the forbidding looking moat brimming with piranhas.

"Anything that has meat on its bones and if they are hungry enough they'll eat the bones too," laughed Meow, who was eager to show off the newly reincarnated creatures in the cryptid menagerie. "Now come along Bingo, these creatures haven't been seen since Lady Eradorn's time, and they are my personal pride and joy."

Bingo followed the others across the drawbridge and gazed into the enclosure. Although as far as he could see it appeared to be empty except for the many trees and bushes that occupied about three-quarters of its area. Meow informed the boys that this section of the cryptid menagerie was reserved for the much-feared bugaboo. This was a creature whose body looked quite like a bear, yet was smaller and had short spindly legs and a face that resembled a rather ugly goblin with a long pointy nose. Unfortunately, the solitary bugaboo was seldom ever seen during the day, choosing instead to come out at night to feed and do whatever bugaboos like to get up to.

"And what do bugaboos like to eat?" asked Bingo, sounding disappointed that he could not see the frightful creature.

"As I mentioned earlier, every occupant of the cryptid menagerie hungers for the living. So everything Mumford feeds them has to always be alive and kicking," reiterated Meow, who was looking towards the next enclosure in the hope of spotting the macabre creature that resided there. "However, I do recall Bugaboos favourite food is actually naughty children, especially mischievous young boys. But of course, Mumford never feeds it anything like that here."

"Dragonsbutts! I'm glad that we are on this side of the fence," exclaimed Trumper, as he took a step back from the bugaboo enclosure and signalled to Bingo to do the same. "So why did you call this compound the cryptid menagerie?"

The Grand Witch's apprentice explained that while her university degrees were in animal psychology and regular zoology, her doctoral studies concentrated on cryptidzoology. This is the little known study of creatures that are commonly believed to have never existed. Although in reality, just like during Dragonbutt's dark days, they really had. Not only did Meow study these creatures with fervour, but she also wanted to bring them back to life with the aid of a little magic. And that was the real reason she got herself into so much trouble at Cambridge, which eventually led to her unceremonious and rather abrupt dismissal.

"Ah, so you're a cryptidzoologist," uttered Trumper, thinking everything was now getting a little bit clearer. "That explains your interest in helping the Grand Witch bring these creatures back from the dead and the reason you became her apprentice."

Without saying a word, Meow simply smiled at Trumper and then ushered everyone on to the next enclosure. This time the boys could clearly see its occupant, or at least its head, peering out from behind a particularly grandiose and remarkably vibrant coloured purple rhododendron.

"That's not scary, and it doesn't look very dangerous," scoffed Bingo, as he pointed to what appeared to be the head of a chicken looking directly at him. "I've seen plenty of chickens before, and none of them has ever frightened me."

Just as Bingo finished speaking, the creature he had assumed was an everyday inoffensive chicken turned out to be something altogether different. All of a sudden, it emerged from its hiding place and charged headlong towards the fence at the very spot where the boys were standing. Fortunately, Meow stepped forward and promptly zapped the strange looking thing with her punisher. After a tumultuous screech it was thrown into the air and landed feet upwards on the ground, a little dazed yet none the worse for wear. It was at that moment Trumper and Bingo could see no ordinary chicken occupied this enclosure. Instead, it was a creature that had the head, claws and wings of a chicken, but the body and tail of a terribly scaly and hideous-looking lizard. And if that was not distressing enough, it had a long forked tongue with a set of razor-sharp gleaming white teeth.

"That's a chizard. Chizards are not the most sociable of creatures, and as you have just witnessed this one really doesn't like strangers very much," declared Meow, who cautiously kept one eye on the stunned chizard. "Now let's move along to the final enclosure and then I will escort you out of the menagerie so that you can return home."

Before the four of them reached the last of the enclosures in the cryptid menagerie, Trumper and Bingo could hear a great deal of shrieking and howling going on as if a pack of raucous baboons were throwing a wild party. Obviously, this enclosure could not have contained only one inhabitant like the previous two. On the contrary, there must have been a multitude of creatures in this one.

"Dragonsbutts! They're shug monkeys," yelled Bingo, as he peeked into the enclosure and immediately recognised the dreadful creatures from the pages of the Entwhistle journal he had all too recently perused.

As a matter of fact, there must have been at least two dozen shug monkeys drinking from a couple of large wooden barrels that had the words 'Butts Batch Cider' stamped on their side. While the boys watched in disbelief, the shug monkeys continued with their disorderly and somewhat boisterous behaviour. And though most of them were very much aware they had visitors, the self-centred and entirely wayward creatures just chose to go on with their rowdy partying.

"So you know about shug monkeys," remarked Meow, who had to raise her voice due to the awful din the roguish creatures were making. "It's only been a fortnight since my aunty and I brought one back from the dead, and look at them all now. To keep their numbers down Mumford has started to substitute much of their food for Butts Batch. He now uses a regimen of one day of food and then six of cider. That's how my ancestors used to manage their numbers, and it seems to do the trick, more or less."

"But I thought all the shug monkeys were driven out of Dragonbutt during the dark days," insisted Trumper, still a little shaken after seeing so many of the detestable creatures he had been led to believe were long gone and very much dead. "It was Fannie Entwhistle who drove them out, and in her Entwhistle journal she wrote they never returned."

"Yes, that's mostly accurate. Although the truth is that one of them never actually left Dragonbutt," revealed Meow, with one of those 'I know something you don't know' types of looks on her face. "You see a solitary shug monkey had fallen asleep in the Dragonbutt Cider Mill after drinking more than its fair share of Butts Batch that fateful day. Luckily, Lady Eradorn found it cowering under an empty crate, and so she brought the poor sozzled creature back to the manor to live in the menagerie."

"Well at least shug monkeys are all vegetarian," chimed in Bingo, thinking this was probably their only saving grace.

"I'm afraid these shug monkeys are not. Once reincarnated, they are just like the other creatures in the cryptid menagerie and so they only eat the living," answered Meow, as she casually checked the time on

106

her wristwatch. "Now it's time for Mumford to feed the bugaboo and chizard. I'll take you back to the house because feeding time can be quite an unpleasant experience, especially if you get queasy at the sight of blood."

Even though the boys did not have a problem with seeing a little blood, they knew that lunchtime was nearly upon them because Bingo's tummy had just then begun to rumble. So they accompanied their host, walking in the direction the four of them had come earlier that morning, all the way to the bright red door with the large iron bolt. At that point, Meow strode into the weapons room and returned her punisher to its rack. Then, on hearing the Grand Witch call out her nickname, she hurriedly opened the blue door and stepped outside with Trumper following close behind.

"I just have to tie my shoelace," shouted Bingo, who had remained inside the weapons room. "I'll only be a minute and will catch up with you."

This did not seem at all out of the ordinary to Meow who understood that laces can sometimes come untied and this was especially true with shoes worn by rambunctious young boys. Trumper, on the other hand, knowing Bingo was wearing a pair of laceless wellington boots, knew the remark was definitely out of place. While this meant the younger boy was probably up to no good, he believed it was best to question him later, after they had taken their leave from Wyvern Manor.

When Bingo finally emerged from the weapons room, he could see Elvira Wyvern standing in a doorway at the back of the house. It looked like she was talking to Meow, though the distance was simply too great for him to clearly make out the words. Trumper stood next to her, and so with his left arm pressed rigidly against the side of his coat, he marched swiftly over to where they were gathered.

"What was that all about?" demanded Bingo, who had just reached the spot where Meow and Trumper were standing when the Grand

Witch stepped back into the house and abruptly closed the door.

"Lady Wyvern said the two boys hired to help out in the menagerie have just arrived at the main gate and will be here shortly," conveyed Trumper, while noticing Bingo was hiding something under his coat. "Anyway, it's lunchtime, so we need to be on our way."

"Don't forget that Oh My Cod! is open tonight," implored Meow, as she escorted the boys around to the side of the house to collect their bicycles. "Thank you for visiting W-W-Wyvern Manor and do call again next time you are passing by."

Feeling the pangs of hunger in their tummies, Trumper and Bingo promptly pulled on their helmets and then waved goodbye to Meow after thanking her for the tour. Not wanting to be late for their lunch with Angus Hogswood, the boys sped up the gravel path they had cycled along earlier that morning. However, as they turned a corner, another pair of bicycles ridden by two familiar boys came careering towards them.

"Dragonsbutts! What are you two doing here?" snarled an indignant Chugher Harris, who along with Chomper Baverstock Junior had been forced to brake rather suddenly to avoid crashing into Trumper and Bingo.

"We've been visiting our friend, Meow, and she gave us a tour of Wyvern Manor and the menagerie," snapped Bingo, as he was none too pleased with Chugher's hostile tone of voice. "I see that you two have new bikes as well. Ours were Christmas presents from our aunty and uncle, but I'm sure yours were gifts from Bentley DuPont for services rendered."

"So what of it? Bentley is not as bad as everyone makes out," retorted Chomper Junior, who with his chubby right hand was reaching for an air horn that had fallen out of his coat pocket onto the gravel path below. "Come on Chugher, we've got work to do at the menagerie, and we're not only getting paid for it, but we get free fish and chips to boot."

While the mention of free fish and chips certainly made Bingo more than a little jealous, his tummy rumbles told him it was not the time to linger. So without uttering another word to his DPS classmates, he and Trumper set off again to ride the short distance to the Hogswood Piggery. To tell Angus Hogswood all about what lay hidden behind the walls of Wyvern Manor, and of course, eat lots of yummy food.

Nine

Telling Angus

"Hey, Bingo, I've been meaning to ask you something. What were you doing in the weapons room?" questioned Trumper, who with the younger boy by his side had just passed through the open wooden gates at the entrance to Wyvern Manor. "Obviously, I know you were not tying your shoelace, and I can see you have something hidden under your coat."

"I just wanted to borrow something," sniggered Bingo, while pulling out the object he had been so careful to conceal. "It's not as deadly as Little MO, but still, I think it could come in very handy for MAOS."

"Dragonsbutts! You stole a punisher from the menagerie," fretted Trumper, who was quite taken aback by Bingo's audaciousness. "There are two witches at Wyvern Manor and don't forget that one of them is a dark witch. What do you think they'll do when they find out you took one of their punishers? Maybe Meow will send Mumford after us to retrieve it."

"Don't worry Trumper, they have plenty of them in the weapons room, so I doubt they'll miss this one," assured Bingo, feeling confident his little indiscretion would likely go undiscovered. "Besides, Meow is our friend, and she is not a dark witch, like Elvira Wyvern. She's a good witch, so I'm sure she will understand."

Trumper was certainly not convinced of that but believed if the two of them tried to return the punisher now, they would more than likely get caught. Therefore the best course of action would be to keep Bingo's recklessness under wraps. And to ensure the younger boy avoided any foolhardy behaviour like bringing his new weapon to school, or worse, zap an unsuspecting resident of the village.

As he thought about all the strange creatures they had come across in the course of the morning, Trumper was a little concerned that he and Bingo may have bitten off more than they could chew. The bugaboo, chizard and shug monkeys who resided in the cryptid menagerie were some of the very monsters that had wreaked havoc in Dragonbutt during the dark days. And though they were the very reason for the creation of MAOS, it was one thing to read about these monsters in the pages of the Entwhistle journals, but an entirely different one to meet them up-close.

It occurred to Trumper that Sherlock Holmes never had to contend with witches and monsters during his time, yet still, both he and Bingo had taken the Entwhistle Oath. As such, it was their duty to rid Dragonbutt of any monster that posed a threat to the residents they were sworn to protect. But that would have to wait as they had already arrived at the Hogswood Piggery and could smell something truly tantalising coming from the kitchen. So they leaned their bicycles against the wall of the house, hung their helmets from the handlebars and then sprinted to the kitchen door.

Bingo managed to get to the door first, which was green in colour and had a shiny brass knocker in the shape of a pig's head at a height that was just within the young boy's reach. Without hesitating, he grasped hold of the knocker and gave three thunderous raps on the door to make certain the occupant of the house was sure to hear. It did not take more than a moment or two before the boys could hear the heavy footsteps of Angus Hogswood, and then the door noiselessly opened.

"Ah, there you are. I was beginning to think you weren't going to turn up," boomed Angus, using his customary loud yet always welcoming tone of voice. "My housekeeper has just laid the table so we might as well dig in. What would you like to drink? I have plenty of bottles of Braithwaite's in the fridge."

"That's fine for me, but I don't think Trumper is in the mood for Braithwaite's just yet. Not after the number of bottles that he went through while competing in the head boy contest," chuckled Bingo, as he pulled off his wellingtons. And then placed the punisher inside one of the boots and hung his coat on a hook by the door.

"Oh yes, I heard all about it last night at the Dragonbutt Arms. Along with the exploits of the mooners, pretty much the whole village has talked about nothing else. So Bentley DuPont is now the head boy," sighed Angus, who was shaking his head with disappointment. "You know during my DPS days everyone thought that I would be the head boy one day, what with my height and all. Unfortunately, it just wasn't to be, and I lost to little Arlo Nethercott. It's funny, but I can still remember all the chanting on that day, how high can you pee and it's the best of three. Those were the good old days, long gone though never forgotten."

Angus ushered the boys over to a long kitchen table that was located in the centre of his generously sized and thankfully warm kitchen. Its top was made out of a single piece of wood that had come from an exceptionally old oak tree. This had stood in the grounds of the Hogswood Piggery for nearly five hundred years until one night around a century ago a random lightning bolt split the tree in two.

One of those pieces went to construct the new alter at Dragonbutt Village Church, and the other was used to make the kitchen table and a dozen sturdy chairs.

While Trumper accepted a chilled glass of milk, Bingo and Angus thirstily drank from their bottles of refreshing Braithwaite's. On the table before them, the now famished boys could see that Angus's housekeeper had not disappointed them in the least. In a large cast iron casserole dish at the centre of the table was more than enough hotpot to feed half a dozen or more starving souls. Or in this case, two hungry boys and Angus Hogswood.

The hotpot was not the more common type consisting of lamb, onion, carrot, turnip, leeks and lots of potatoes that people typically associate with the county of Lancashire. Instead, it was the Dragonbutt variety, which, though quite like the better known Lancashire hotpot, used rabbit rather than lamb. And of course, it had been stewed overnight in a gallon of Butts Batch.

Next to the hotpot was a heavy glass bowl containing a mountain of rumbledethumps. This was made by sautéing onion and cabbage in plenty of Dragonbutt butter then adding mashed potatoes and a little salt and pepper. After that, it was covered in a liberal sprinkling of Red Dragon cheese before being baked in a moderately hot oven. Although it was somewhat like bubble and squeak, one of the boys' favourites, by and large, it was ordinarily only eaten by those living north of the border. And this meant that in Dragonbutt it was considered to be quite a treat.

"Thanks, Angus," said Trumper, on behalf of the both of them. Because Bingo was preoccupied with eating a slice of the still-warm bread that their host had placed on the table. "I thought you would have been drinking something a little stronger than Braithwaite's."

"Oh no, I never drink alone. If I did, then people in the village might get the idea I'm a bit of a booser, and that just wouldn't do. I have my reputation to think of you know," maintained Angus, who was looking almost serious for once. "Although Dragonstone Fire is my favourite tipple, for the most part, I reserve that harmless pleasure for those times when I patronise the Dragonbutt Arms."

"Is that fish I can smell?" asked Bingo, while chewing a juicy piece of rabbit meat that he had just popped into his mouth. "I have a nose for this sort of thing, and I'm sure it's coming from the oven."

"Dragonsbutts! I completely forgot about the pie," cried out Angus, as he jumped up from the kitchen table and grabbed a pair of worn oven gloves. Then he darted over to his expansive oven to retrieve its somewhat overbaked contents. "No harm done, just a little sunburned around the edges. It's my housekeeper's speciality you know, so you have to try some."

It was no ordinary pie that Angus placed on the table; rather, it was the peculiarly named stargazy pie. So-called because it had eight singed pilchard heads peering out from its dark brown crust in an attempt to gaze at the stars. In addition to pilchards, it contained another six types of seafood that included sand eels, horse mackerel, herring, dogfish, ling and a handful of Dragonbutt saltwater prawns. The only non-seafaring ingredients in this unusual but remarkable dish, was milk, eggs and even more of Angus's favourite homegrown potatoes.

As Bingo was invariably adventurous when it came to unfamiliar types of food, he accepted an extra-large serving with two flavourful yet slightly salty pilchards. Trumper took a more cautious approach and requested a smaller piece of the pie. And although this contained only one lonely pilchard, he knew that if it tasted as good as it looked and smelled a second helping would always be there for the taking.

"I'm glad to see that you made it back from Wyvern Manor in one piece. But tell me, what did you get up to while you were there?" implored Angus, who was also helping himself to a sizeable portion of stargazy pie. "You were gone for so long I got to thinking that old witch

Elvira Wyvern had turned you both into toads, or maybe something even worse."

Trumper revealed to Angus how they had not only met Elvira Wyvern but her niece, Morweena Ogglejay, as well. He then went on to say that it was the niece who had given them a tour of the vast manor and its eye-opening menagerie. When the big man was told of her colossal manservant, Mumford, he slowly nodded his head and then shook it more vigorously on hearing about the Grand Witch's devilish black cat. And then his eyes grew larger as he learnt of the outlandish creatures that inhabited the main compound, particularly the bloodcurdling wolpertingers and the decidedly odd-looking doodos.

By the time Trumper had gotten to the bit about the cryptic menagerie, Angus was silent, though strangely his mouth was wide open. He could hardly believe his own ears after listening to the young boy's account of the long-dead creatures that resided only a stone's throw away from the Hogswood Piggery. And while he was not so familiar with bugaboos and chizards, like everyone Dragonbutt born he had heard all about the terrible shug monkeys.

"For as long as I can remember, there have been strange sounds coming out of Wyvern Manor, but I was repeatedly told by my parents not to kick up a fuss. It's never wise to mess with the Wyvern family you know, particularly their women. As I told you earlier, they are all witches, the lot of them. I always assumed those noises were from common livestock such as cows and sheep and the like. Come to think of it, I've recently heard quite a racket coming from the manor, though I put that down to some exuberant Christmas partying. It never crossed my mind that they have shug monkeys living there," grumbled Angus, while mopping up the last of his hotpot with a thick wedge of bread. "And this Mumford, you say he's a big fellow and is even taller than me?"

"Yes, he must be seven-foot-tall. And that's not all, he can't talk and looks even older than Old Mrs Dingle," interjected Bingo, who was just finishing a second helping of stargazy pie but with only one pilchard this time. "Angus, do you know him?"

"Well, I've never heard of anyone called Mumford. Although during our mooning days, my fellow mooners and I once climbed to the top of the wall that surrounds Wyvern Manor. There were a lot more Wyverns living at the manor in those days, and Elfrida Wyvern was still alive and matriarch of the family. During that year we had mooned everyone we could think of in the village, and so naturally the Wyverns were next on our list. It was Chomper Senior's idea to stand on the section of the wall next to the main gate, and then I let off an air horn to get their attention. While we mooned in unison, Typsy, being the most athletic amongst us, peered between his legs and saw a mountain of a man slowly stomping in our direction," divulged Angus, while shaking his head as he recalled the events of that day. "As you can imagine, we couldn't pull up our trousers quick enough, and then we just hotfooted it out of there as fast as our legs would carry us. Mind you, I managed to get a good look at him, and he must have been something like a hundred years old with only one badly mangled cauliflower ear. But it couldn't possibly be the same person because that was twenty-five years ago."

"That's interesting. Mumford only has one ear as well, and it's definitely exceedingly mangled," remarked Trumper, who was deep in thought as to how that could possibly be. "And this morning, while we were touring Wyvern Manor, Bingo and I saw an old portrait of Eradorn Wyvern. The strange thing about it was that we could see an enormous oafish looking old man standing behind her in the painting, and he looked just like Mumford."

"Trumper, I don't recall exactly when she died, but Eradorn Wyvern lived in Dragonbutt during the dark days. If it was really him you saw in the painting, then either Eradorn was recently alive and kicking or this Mumford must be about seven centuries old. And that beats Emilia Baggot's age by a good six hundred or more years, which is not going to please her at all. I think the old grouch only remains with us to remind everyone she is the oldest person in the village. So news of a resident over seven times her current age would probably send Emilia to an early grave," chuckled Angus, as he did not believe the man in the painting was Mumford at all.

"It was definitely Mumford, I can assure you of that," barked Bingo, who sounded quite offended their host had doubted Trumper's story. "Anyway, I'm just about ready for dessert, so what are we having."

"Oh yes, of course. I have some nice treacle tart and ice cream coming right up," revealed Angus, hoping that a homemade dessert would cheer up the visibly displeased young boy. "You said Mumford works at the new fish and chip shop on the high street, and it's actually owned by Elvira Wyvern's young niece. Naturally, I know Elvira, though I stay as far away from her as I can. But I've never met Morweena Ogglejay, or for that matter, I don't recall anyone with that family name living in Dragonbutt. All the same, I do like fish and chips, so I will make a trip to Oh My Cod! in the next few days, and I'll take a gander at this monstrous manservant of hers while I am there."

"Her full name is Morweena Eradorn Ogglejay-Wyvern. Although her aunty always calls her Meow for short," explained Trumper, who, like Bingo, was eager to taste the treacle tart. "She's a true Wyvern and is Dragonbutt born. However, her family moved away when she was young, and Meow has only recently returned to the village to live at Wyvern Manor again. Frying fish and chips is not her real profession you know; she's actually a cryptidzoologist and is the Grand Witch's apprentice."

"Dragonsbutts! That's all we need, another witch at Wyvern Manor," groaned Angus, while placing the treacle tart in the searing oven. Just

117

as his housekeeper had instructed so that it could be served piping hot. "I think Morweena must be the daughter of Ellora Wyvern, and if I remember correctly, she married some rich fellow who was not Dragonbutt born. They left the village a long time ago, and I have absolutely no idea what became of them."

"Eaten by a shark," stated Bingo, somewhat brusquely as he impatiently waited for the dessert. "Surely the treacle tart must be ready by now."

Frustratingly for the young boy, it took another five minutes before the treacle tart was hot enough for Angus to remove it from the oven. It was made the traditional way with a mouthwatering buttery shortcrust pastry base and needless to say the filling contained lots of sugary golden syrup, breadcrumbs and lemon juice, and a pinch of ginger and cinnamon for good taste. And to give it an opulent crispy finish, it had been finished off with strips of pastry in the shape of the letters 'HP', which as one would expect stood for Hogswood Piggery.

As treacle tart should never be eaten on its own, Angus's housekeeper had churned up a batch of the ice cream he liked the most. It was called Choco Bomb Sensation, and as luck would have it, this was Trumper and Bingo's favourite as well. Not only was it made with delicious Bovington's chocolate, which had to be the best chocolate anywhere in the world, but each serving had at its centre a much prized and always yummy Choco Bomb.

Angus, knowing the boys loved their desserts, cut the steaming treacle tart in half and then half again. Before placing a slice into each of the three enormous bowls sitting on the table. Then from the freezer, he retrieved the basin containing the icy cold Choco Bomb Sensation. From which he scooped out the luscious ice cream, ensuring every one of them received a whole Choco Bomb.

After he was handed his dessert, Bingo dived right in by taking a bite out of the still blistering hot treacle tart followed by a spoonful of the frigid ice cream. Being careful not to break the shell of the Choco Bomb, he continued with this approach until all the tart was gone and there was no more ice cream in his bowl. And then as was his custom, he savoured the Choco Bomb with its lovely white chocolate filling and pleasing fresh raspberry at its centre by devouring the renowned Dragonbutt delicacy at the very end.

By the time the three of them had finished eating their dessert, not even Bingo could contemplate taking another bite. Instead, Angus handed the young boy another bottle of cold Braithwaite's from the fridge, while Trumper accepted a top-up of milk to his empty glass. The only thing to do now, the boys discussed between themselves, was to get down to the all-important business of deciding what they should do next.

"You know I don't usually wish harm on anyone, but if Ellora Wyvern was eaten by a shark, then it means there's one less witch in this world. And I for one reckon that is a good thing," declared Angus, as he banged his large fist on the kitchen table resulting in several spilt drinks. "So what shall we do with these two witches living up at the manor? And more importantly, what are we going to do with those monsters the Wyverns have incarcerated in that cryptid menagerie of theirs?"

"Don't worry about Meow; she's our friend and a good witch. Just like most members of the Dragonbutt Witch's Institute," reassured Bingo, who was awfully thirsty after eating three salty pilchards, which meant he had drained his bottle of Braithwaite's in a record ten seconds flat. "It's Elvira Wyvern we should be worried about. She's not only a dark witch but the DWI's Grand Witch as well."

"Boys, make no mistake, the Wyverns have always been dark witches so I wouldn't trust either of them," warned Angus, as he took a hefty swig of Braithwaite's from his bottle. "Anyone who is Dragonbutt born knows that ever since the days of Eradorn Wyvern, the manor has invariably been the home of the worst kind of witches. Up until now, they have thankfully kept their witchcraft to themselves, and I may add, safely behind that wall of theirs. But Elvira Wyvern has now formed this Dragonbutt Witch's Institute, and if that is not bad enough, the two of you have just found out she is reincarnating monsters from the dark days. We had enough trouble over the Christmas holiday with that little vampire. So the last thing we need is for any of those monsters to escape from Wyvern Manor and run amok in the village again."

"I agree with Angus, Meow is a Wyvern, and if truth be told we really don't know much about her. Bingo, just because she gave us a free sausage in batter at Oh My Cod! and a tour of Wyvern Manor doesn't necessarily mean she is a good witch. After all, she is the Grand Witch's apprentice," cautioned Trumper, who was not quite as susceptible as the younger boy to a friendly smile and a complimentary fried snack. "We can't go to Dragonbutt police about this because Detective Huntress simply won't believe us. You know she is not Dragonbutt born and therefore incapable of considering the possibility of witches and monsters inhabiting the village. Furthermore, she is too busy chasing after the mooners to take on another big case. That means there is only one option open to us, it's going to be up to MAOS to stop Elvira Wyvern bringing back any more monsters from the past. So tomorrow night we are going back to Wyvern Manor, although this time we will be uninvited guests of the Dragonbutt Witch's Institute."

"Well I've never heard of a dark witch giving away a sausage in batter," sulked Bingo, because in his eyes, Meow could only ever be a good witch. "And don't forget that she gave us a lemon drizzle cake and a hot chocolate as well."

"Despite the fact I have witches and monsters as neighbours, sadly my pigs won't feed themselves. And so I'm going to have to push on with my chores before it gets dark," announced Angus, as he stood up from the kitchen table after noting the time. "Although before you go, I have a few rashers of my best Hogswood bacon for your lovely aunty. Just make sure one of you hides it inside a coat pocket so none of my pigs can get a waft of it. I'd likely have a riot on my hands if that happened."

Trumper gladly accepted the bacon, which must have been a good five pounds in weight, and placed it into his coat pocket before leaving the kitchen. After Angus noticed something protruding from one of the boys' wellington boots, Bingo gleefully explained that it was called a punisher and roughly how it worked. He even offered to give their generous host a demonstration in the piggery. But to the disappointment of the young boy, the big man just shook his head to the relief of every Hogswood pig.

Once they were outside, the boys said goodbye and thanked their friend for the outstanding lunch they had just eaten. By the time they were wearing their helmets again, Angus had disappeared into the Hogswood Piggery to feed his horde of perpetually ravenous pigs. So without delay, Trumper and Bingo climbed onto their bicycles and headed towards Pigswill Alley. And not surprisingly, they peddled as fast as they could to see who would be the first one back to Counting House Lane.

Ten

A Monster Escapes

⟨ornament⟩

Upon reaching the narrow path that led to Dragonbutt pond, Bingo was more than two bicycle lengths ahead of Trumper. Without slowing down, the younger boy kept on peddling for all he was worth, and this increased his lead considerably. He would have ridden like this all the way back to Counting House Lane if he had not spotted two boys that appeared to be around his own age. They were sitting on one of the wooden benches that overlooked Dragonbutt pond and happened to be wearing the distinctive maroon coloured woolly hats of Dragonbutt Primary School.

Almost immediately, Bingo ceased peddling and pulled on his brakes before coming to an abrupt halt. This allowed Trumper to quickly catch up with him, and then he too stopped to take a look at the two boys as well. It was not hard to recognise who the boys were, and so they pushed their bicycles over to where Bertie Bovington and Flitcher Jenkins were sitting. By the look of it, Bingo's classmates were enjoying an afternoon feast because the bench was littered with at least six Choco Bomb wrappers and two empty bottles of Braithwaite's. And not only that, each of them had chocolate and raspberry smeared over their hands and grinning faces.

"Can I have a Choco Bomb?" pleaded Bingo, as if he had not eaten one in an awfully long time. "It looks like you have plenty to spare."

"Help yourself, the both of you," replied Bertie, who had just pulled a handful out of his bulging coat pocket and placed them on the bench between himself and Flitcher. "I had to return many of the Choco Bombs we stole to my parents, but they really had no idea how many we took so I managed to keep around three dozen. Anyhow, what have you two been up to this morning?"

"We've been on MAOS business up at Wyvern Manor, and we met the Grand Witch and her apprentice. And while we were there, Trumper and I managed to get a tour of the manor and the Wyverns strange menagerie. It's like a zoo, though it is full of weird creatures and they even have some monsters living there too," blurted out Bingo, as he helped himself to a Choco Bomb and handed another to Trumper. "After lunch at the Hogswood Piggery, we decided to race home, and then I noticed the two of you sitting here. And as you saw, I was in the lead as usual."

"You were only a short distance ahead of me, and only because I was weighed down by the Hogswood bacon in my coat pocket," retorted Trumper, who never liked it when Bingo was being boastful. "Anyway, thanks for the Choco Bomb, Bertie."

"We all know that Elvira Wyvern is the Grand Witch of the Dragonbutt Witch's Institute, but who is this apprentice you mentioned?" demanded Bertie, with an inquisitive look on his face. "It sounds to me as though MAOS may need some help. So if you have any openings, Flitcher and I would be keen to join."

"It's Morweena Ogglejay, but we call her Meow. She's the one who opened Oh My Cod!, the new fish and chip shop in the village. Meow is actually Elvira Wyvern's niece, and on top of that she's a true Wyvern and a witch by birth," disclosed Trumper, as he took the last bite of his Choco Bomb. "And we really don't need any more personnel for MAOS right now. If we ever do, then you and Flitcher will be the first we call on."

"Hey, did you hear that Bertie sent Bentley DuPont an anonymous message saying it's Bunty's birthday tomorrow and he should bring flowers if he wants to get on her good side," laughed Flitcher, who did not appear to be following the previous conversation very closely. "He said the best time would be to come at nine in the morning and to bang on the front door really loudly, so she is sure to hear. You've got to be there to see this because it's going to be hilarious."

"But Bunty doesn't have a good side," exclaimed Trumper, as he knew Bertie's older sister all too well.

"Exactly, and she doesn't have a birthday tomorrow either," cracked up Flitcher, and Bertie and Bingo joined in too. "Bunty always likes to sleep in on a Sunday morning, so when Bentley wakes her, she's bound to go crazy. Bertie and I will be up bright and early, and I will record everything on my phone. At a safe distance and hidden from sight, of course."

"Good one, Bertie, we'll be there," confirmed Bingo, without bothering to consult Trumper. "I can't wait to see Bunty lose her temper with our new head boy. By the time she is finished with him, Bentley DuPont is going to rue the day he managed to pee higher than Trumper."

"Bingo, what's that poking out of your coat?" cried out Flitcher, as he suddenly lunged at the young boy and grabbed hold of the punisher. "Wow, what does it do?"

Before Bingo had a chance to explain the innocuous-looking weapon could deliver a hundred thousand volt electric shock, or even to shout 'NO', Flitcher had turned the punisher on and unwisely pressed it against his forehead. Alarmingly, although it was on its minimum setting, the boys were all too aware that this was still enough power to leave a regular person dumber than a dodo.

"BRAIN FREEZE!" squealed Flitcher, who seemed unaffected by the punishers zap as he held it to his head for a good five or six seconds before Bingo managed to wrestle it away from him. "That was amazing, can I do it again?" And then he pulled off his DPS woolly hat to reveal every strand of his ordinarily curly hair was now perfectly straight and standing on end.

"No, you can't," reprimanded Trumper, as he shook his head. Now regretting he had not returned the stolen punisher to the menagerie's weapons room earlier that day. "Bingo, in the future, keep the punisher hidden, and Flitcher, how are you feeling?"

"Absolutely great, everything appears much clearer to me now," nodded Flitcher, who seemed decidedly less dim-witted than he was only a few minutes earlier. "I'm going to have to get myself one of those."

"Flitcher, it's meant for fighting monsters and not for zapping yourself in the head," lectured Bingo, thinking that if anyone was going to get zapped with this particular punisher, then he would be the one to do the zapping. "Trumper and I need to get along home now, but tomorrow morning we'll meet both of you outside Bertie's house at a quarter to nine."

So Trumper and Bingo climbed onto their bicycles once again and waved goodbye to the other two boys. With only a hair's breadth between them, it was Bingo who arrived at Counting House Lane the victor. And he made sure the older boy would not forget it in a hurry by loudly and quite annoyingly chanting, "Win-ner! Win-ner! Win-ner!" Notwithstanding, Trumper pretended not to hear as he hurriedly pushed his bicycle around to the back of the little old house and leaned it against the kitchen wall. And without causing more of a fuss, Bingo did the same.

"We're home," bellowed Bingo, as he burst through the unlocked back door and into the hallway while still wearing his muddy wellington boots. "Is there anything to eat?"

"Bingo, if I have told you once, I have told you a thousand times to take your boots off when you enter the house. You're getting mud on my nice new carpet," berated Aunty J, as she walked out of the kitchen to place a fresh copy of the Dragonbutt Smoker on the hallway floor. "It already looks like you've been snacking on something because I can see chocolate smeared around your mouth and on the sleeve of your coat."

"That wasn't much of a snack; it was just a Choco Bomb," argued Bingo, who could hear his tummy start to rumble, alerting him of the need for food. "And I think hot chocolate would go down a treat as well."

"Alright, but take those wellingtons off right now, and you too, Trumper," appealed Aunty J, as she pointed to the boys rather muddy looking boots. "Hang your coats and helmets on the hooks in the hallway and then come into the kitchen, and don't forget to wash your grubby hands while you are about it."

It did not take more than a couple of minutes before the boys were seated at the kitchen table with unusually clean hands and the five pounds of Hogswood bacon sitting between them. In that time, Bingo had hidden the punisher in a pile of dirty clothes that were underneath his bed to prevent Aunty J discovering his new and much-treasured weapon. Barely five minutes after that each of them had been handed a mug of steaming hot chocolate. And these, of course, contained a large gooey marshmallow and plenty of fresh whipped Dragonbutt cream.

As for their afternoon snack, Aunty J had bought half a dozen freshly baked Eccles cakes from Fanshaw's the Baker's that she hoped would be more than enough for the two hungry boys. Once she had neatly arranged them on one of her prized porcelain plates and placed it on the table, the boys immediately tucked in. And because it was near impossible to eat just one of these delightful puff pastries filled with currants and just a touch of lemon and nutmeg, Trumper had two and Bingo a little greedily ate three, which left their aunty with one just for herself.

"Oh, I nearly forgot, Angus gave us this bacon to give to you," motioned Trumper, as he handed the heavy package of Hogswood bacon to his aunty.

"Can we have it tomorrow for our breakfast?" appealed Bingo, who believed Hogswood bacon tasted so good, given half a chance he would have eaten it uncooked. "You know it's one of my favourites."

"Bingo, everything appears to be your favourite. Don't you want pancakes for breakfast like we do every Sunday?" implored Aunty J, while examining the substantial quantity of bacon Angus had sent. "And what were you doing at the Hogswood Piggery? I thought you were going to have lunch with your uncle."

"Let's have pancakes and bacon for breakfast?" pleaded Bingo, who was unable to decide which one he liked the most. So in his mind eating them both would obviously be the perfect solution.

"Very well, I'll make a batch of pancakes and cook this bacon for tomorrow's breakfast," agreed Aunty J, as she smiled at the young boy with the extraordinarily large appetite. "But you didn't tell me why you went all the way to the Hogswood Piggery to visit Angus?"

"That was because Bingo is working on a school project about bacon and sausages and where they come from," asserted the quick-thinking Trumper, while nodding his head at the same time as the younger boy. For no other reason than to reassure his aunty that this was the truth, even though it most definitely was not.

"Um, so Bingo, what did you learn during your time at the Hogswood Piggery?" quizzed Aunty J, as she was unconvinced Trumper was telling her the full story. Or for that matter, even a part of it.

"Err, well I didn't have enough time to grasp all the details, but I know that sausages and bacon come from Baverstock's the Butcher's," babbled Bingo, who up until that moment had never really thought about the origins of his favourite piggy treats. Only that they always tasted so yummy.

"I can see that your trip to the Hogswood Piggery was well worth it," she said somewhat sarcastically, while thinking the truth would undoubtedly reveal itself in due course. "Anyway, why don't the two of you go through to the living room. The Dragonbutt Smoker came while we were out and so I left it on the sofa for you to read."

As the boys were always keen to find out what interesting things were happening in the village, they walked over to the living room and sat down on the sofa. Then Trumper picked up the latest edition of the Dragonbutt Smoker in both hands while Bingo tossed a couple of logs into the tired-looking fire. Though before the older boy read even one word, he spent a few minutes explaining to Bingo why the Hogswood Piggery was so famous for sausages and bacon.

Now that the young boy was crystal clear as to the origin of Hogswood pork products, Trumper read the headline on the front page, which stated, 'Mooners Strike Again! Dragonbutt Arms Landlord Incensed'. As this concerned the incident that took place the previous Saturday, something the boys knew all about, Trumper just scanned through the story and confirmed there was nothing to be gained from reading it aloud. In fact, Barry Beasley's article was nothing more than an interview with Boosey Dooley in which he spent most of his time talking about the merits of drinking at the Dragonbutt Arms. And that was not all, unashamedly the landlord even managed to promote Free Pie Friday which was going to start the following week.

Deep in thought, Trumper placed the Dragonbutt Smoker by his side, whereby Bingo immediately snatched it up and began to flick through the pages of their uncle's pride and joy. Nothing much interested him until he spotted an article covering half of page seven that included a photograph of a smiling, and as always well-groomed and expensively dressed Bentley DuPont.

"Hey, Trumper, take a look at this," he excitedly announced, while pointing at the headline. "'Record-Breaking DuPont Boy Wins DPS Head Boy Contest'. That could have been you."

Before Trumper had a chance to say that he was not interested in hearing anything more about Bentley DuPont or the head boy contest, their aunty entered the living room. And though it was a Saturday, she told them that their uncle had just invited her to have dinner with him at the Dragonbutt Arms. While this was highly unusual for a Saturday night, the boys were not disappointed in the least because for the second time in a week they would be eating fish and chips that evening.

Even though Bingo was tickled pink to be visiting Oh My Cod! once again, he knew that Meow's charming fish and chip shop only served savoury foods. So the young boy was more than a little concerned as to what he and Trumper would be eating for dessert. After pointing this out to Aunty J, he was thrilled to hear that along with the Eccles cakes purchased that afternoon, their aunty had also picked up a lovely Bakewell tart. And though this was intended for Sunday, she said that after their dinner the boys could each help themselves to a slice.

While Aunty J spent the next hour dressing for what would be a rare Saturday night out, the two boys played video games in their bedroom until she was ready to depart. It was Trumper who took charge of the money, but only after both of them had promised that they would not get into any trouble. Nonetheless, to be on the safe side, their aunty called Old Mrs Dingle and asked her to drop by the little old house around eight.

No more than ten minutes had passed by since Aunty J had left and the boys were already standing outside the back door, eager to be on their way. As usual, they were wearing their coats, warm woollen gloves and wellingtons, along with their helmets, and Bingo had slung his Dr Who backpack over both shoulders. Just as Trumper was turning the house key in the lock, his phone began to ring, and without wavering, he pulled it from his coat pocket. Because the call was from Bertie Bovington, he instantly handed the phone to Bingo and said that it was for him.

"Dragonsbutts! Are you crazy, we'll take it off your hands. That's great; Trumper and I will meet you at Bovington's Sweets and Chocolates after we drop by Oh My Cod! for some fish and chips. I'll see you in about half an hour," promised Bingo, who by now was sporting a wide grin. "That was Bertie; his mum has baked too many chocolate cakes today, and he asked if we wanted one for free. Mrs Bovington always likes to bake them fresh, and the store doesn't sell cakes on Sundays, so she said why not give one of them to Trumper and Bingo. And naturally, I accepted."

"That's perfect, there is nothing better than a chocolate cake made with Bovington's chocolate," smiled Trumper, knowing that once they returned home, the two of them would be in for quite a feast that evening. "Come on, Bingo, let's get going before Mrs Bovington changes her mind."

So not wishing to linger, they hurriedly retrieved their bicycles and pushed them around to the front of the little old house. As it was already getting dark, the boys switched on their headlamps and set off to ride as fast as they could to Dragonbutt High Street. Spurred on by the thought of fish and chips followed by a Bovington's chocolate cake, Bingo arrived at their destination around ten seconds ahead of Trumper. And then without bothering to take his helmet off or wait for the older boy, he ran over to Oh My Cod! and flung open the door.

"W-W-Welcome to Oh My Cod!," stammered Meow, who did not

realise it was Bingo at first because of the helmet he was wearing. "Oh, hello Bingo, it's you, and I see that Trumper is here too."

"Good evening, Meow. We fancied eating fish and chips again today, so here we are. Can we have cod and chips twice with plenty of chips, and how about a pickled egg each while we wait?" winked Bingo, as he ogled at the jar of pickled eggs sitting on the counter. "I told you last week that Trumper and I are going to be your best customers."

"Cod and chips coming right up," confirmed Meow, while calling for Mumford to start the boys' order. "But I think we can do a little better than pickled eggs for you and Trumper. How about a saveloy each? Mumford has just prepared two of them, and of course, they're on the house."

"That's even better. I would eat a sausage over an egg any day," beamed Bingo, who happily accepted the two sizzling saveloys from Mumford and handed one of them to Trumper. "Thank you, Meow, and you too, Mumford."

"How did your two helpers get along at the menagerie this afternoon?" inquired Trumper, as he thought it would be polite to make small talk with Meow while munching on his saveloy. "You know that they are both in Bingo's class at Dragonbutt Primary School, and we passed them on our way out of Wyvern Manor."

"Those boys w-w-were absolutely terrible and undoubtedly imbeciles," fumed Meow, who was obviously unhappy with the quality of work performed by Chugher Harris and Chomper Baverstock Junior. "I specifically told them to feed the creatures in the main compound only and not to go anywhere near the cryptid menagerie."

"Do you mean to say they went into the cryptid menagerie and were eaten by those monsters?" interrupted Bingo, thinking Chugher and Chomper Junior probably got what was coming to them after siding with Bentley DuPont at the head boy contest.

"No, nobody has been eaten, at least not yet. Mumford left

them alone for no more than thirty minutes, and in that time those irresponsible boys took his key and opened the door to the cryptid menagerie," explained Meow, looking like she would have throttled the both of them if they had turned up at that moment. "Apparently the chizard startled them, and then one of the boys dropped the key before they ran back to the house and rode off on their bikes like the clappers. Mumford has been unable to find the key as of yet, and so he had to use a padlock and chain to keep the creatures inside from getting out."

"Um, that sounds just like Chugher and Chomper Junior. You can never trust them to do anything right," remarked Trumper, while shaking his head. "At least there is one saving grace; none of the inhabitants of the cryptid menagerie managed to get out."

"I'm afraid one did. The chizard is no longer in its enclosure," admitted Meow, who was now looking a little uncomfortable. "However, Mumford is bound to find the poor creature soon enough because it must be hiding somewhere in the grounds of the menagerie. So there is no need to get concerned. As I told you earlier, in seven hundred years, not a single creature has ever managed to escape from my family's menagerie."

Except for the sound of two saveloys being all too hastily consumed, a brief yet uncommon air of silence fell over Oh My Cod!. It was not broken by Meow or either of the boys, but by Mumford placing the two portions of freshly fried fish and chips on the counter. Having taken the last bite of his saveloy, Bingo loaded the fish and chips into his Dr Who backpack, while Trumper promptly paid Meow.

Just as the two boys were making their way to the door after thanking Meow for the tasty and much-appreciated saveloys, Trumper's phone rang a second time. As it was Bertie Bovington yet again, he gave the phone to Bingo without making any attempt to answer the call. But since he could only hear one side of the conversation that ensued, which had something to do with an attack on Emilia Baggot, the older boy was unsure what was going on.

"Is it the mooners again?" beseeched Trumper, imagining Dragonbutt's accursed trouble makers had struck once more.

"No, it's a chicken," answered Bingo, after he had handed the phone back to Trumper.

"Bingo, you're not making any sense. Are you saying that Emilia Baggot has been attacked by a chicken?" demanded Trumper, because he was impatient to find out what had actually happened.

"Yes, according to Bertie, Emilia Baggot had just left Bovington's Sweets and Chocolates with half a dozen Choco Bombs, and that's when she was set upon," shared Bingo, who was trying his best to recall the confusing details of the incident that had just transpired. "I could hear Flitcher in the background shouting at Bertie that it was like a chicken, but it wasn't a chicken. Though, I guess that means the effect of the punisher must have worn off and he is back to his old self again."

"Perhaps, but think about what you just said," cautioned Trumper, as he thought out loud. "When is a chicken not a chicken?"

"Dragonsbutts! Is this one of those brain teasers that Dr Wimbish always likes to ask at the school assembly?" groaned Bingo, and then he suddenly realised what the older boy was getting at. "Of course, I know what you mean now. A chicken is not a chicken when it's a chizard."

"Exactly, so let's head over to Bovington's Sweets and Chocolates as fast as we can," urged Trumper, knowing that time was of the essence if they were going to catch the dastardly chizard who had just attacked Dragonbutt's oldest resident. "Goodbye, Meow, and you too, Mumford. I'm sure we'll be returning to Oh My Cod! soon."

"If we're going to hunt for this chizard then I'll need Little MO, and that means we have to ride back to Counting House Lane first," urged Bingo, as the boys ran over to the spot where they had left their bicycles.

"Bingo, there's no time for that. We'll just have to handle this without your Monster Obliterator for once," hollered Trumper, who was already sitting on his bicycle and raring to go.

In no time at all, the two boys were cycling for all they were worth along the pavement that bordered Dragonbutt High Street. As they headed towards Bovington's Sweets and Chocolates, it did not occur to either of them for even a second to look back in the direction they had just come. If they had, then Trumper and Bingo may have seen someone in the shadows who was slowly following them with a distinctive thud-thud-thud.

Thankfully, it only took a minute or two before the boys arrived at the scene of the horrendous attack. And just as Bertie had described, it was only a few steps away from his family's celebrated store, right in the heart of Dragonbutt High Street. Emilia Baggot was sitting on one of the store's chairs, and Hildy Bovington stood holding her hand. By her side were two of Dragonbutt's finest, Dr Hari Banjani and Staff Nurse Bone Cruncher Trudy Fanshaw, who appeared to be examining the cantankerous old lady.

On the opposite side of the street, Trumper and Bingo could see that Bertie and Flitcher were leaning against the Dragonbutt police BMW M5. Standing next to them was Detective Huntress, and she was holding a notepad and pen in her hands. Without hesitating, the boys slid off their saddles and dropped their bicycles on the pavement before running across to the other side of Dragonbutt High Street.

Surprisingly, Trumper got there first and saw that Emilia Baggot's walker was lying on its side only two feet away from the curb where the Dragonbutt police car was parked. As he glanced over his shoulder to find out what had happened to Bingo, he saw that the younger boy had stopped to grab hold of something sticking out of the old lady's handbag. Seeing him slip whatever it was unseen into his coat pocket,

Trumper merely sighed and made a mental note to ask him what he had been up to once they were away from prying eyes.

A few seconds later, Bingo joined Trumper to listen to what Bertie and Flitcher had to say about the attack that had taken place no more than fifteen minutes earlier. The boys already knew that within seconds of Emilia Baggot leaving Bovington's Sweets and Chocolates, she had been attacked by a rather unsavoury assailant. However, what occurred next was unquestionably an eye-opener considering the victim was supposed to be a frail old lady of ninety-seven.

Having been mooned not once but twice over the past week and a half, the old lady had decided enough was enough. And so when she was confronted by a new adversary, Emilia Baggot flew into a rage that astonished both Bertie and Flitcher and left Hildy Bovington quite aghast. This was because she not only used every swear word under the sun and then some, she also picked up her walker and charged at her attacker. After relentlessly beating her assailant half senseless, she finally threw the walker at the strange-looking creature who wisely retreated before hastily scurrying away.

"So what you two boys are telling me is that an errant chicken startled Emilia Baggot as she was leaving Bovington's Sweets and Chocolates. And then in a moment of frenzy, she violently attacked the poor thing, and it eventually ran off," smirked Detective Huntress, while rolling her eyes and casually closing her notepad. "This is not really a detective matter you know; it's more a job for our uniformed police. I'll tell them there is a stray chicken on the loose in the village and to put the word out that if anyone comes across it, they should inform Dragonbutt police without delay."

"Bertie, which way did it go?" implored Trumper, with a sense of urgency in the tone of his voice.

"I know! I know! I know! It was heading in the direction you just came from but on the other side of Dragonbutt High Street," chimed in

Flitcher, while jumping up and down with his hand in the air as if he was volunteering to answer a question at school. "Did you not see it? I can tell you this for nothing; it was an awfully scary looking chicken."

"No, we didn't, which means it must have turned down Bristletooth Lane and is probably heading towards Pigswill Alley right now," concluded Trumper, knowing he and Bingo would undoubtedly have to follow.

"Trumper, this is not one of those mythical monsters that you and Bingo keep harping on about. It's just a regular farmyard chicken," laughed the detective, who was unable to disguise her amusement with the events of that evening. "It looks like Emilia Baggot was just a little shaken and is doing fine now. So I for one will return to the station, and you boys should go straight home and not get yourselves into any trouble by chasing after a silly chicken."

"Naturally, Detective Huntress, whatever you say. Come on, Bingo, we need to leave right now. So let's collect our bikes and be on our way," replied Trumper, knowing that Emilia Baggot had not been attacked by any wayward chicken but something far worse and unequivocally more dangerous.

"Hang on a minute, Trumper, I'm not missing out on a Bovington's chocolate cake because of an escaped monster, even if it is a chizard," muttered Bingo, as he ran over to Hildy Bovington to claim his cake before the older boy could stop him. Happily, it turned out to be one of his many favourites that had no less than six enticing layers filled with chocolate buttercream and redcurrant jam. And to top it off, it was covered from top to bottom in dozens and dozens of white chocolate swirls.

With the Bovington's chocolate cake and two portions of fish and chips safely tucked away in Bingo's Dr Who backpack, the boys were now ready to begin their somewhat reckless and as most would say ill-advised chizard hunt. Once the two of them were on Bristletooth

Lane, Trumper told Bingo to keep his eyes peeled as they rode their bicycles past Dragonbutt Victory Hall and arrived at the willow trees bordering Pigswill Alley. The older boy then cautiously shone his bicycle lamp towards the opening between the two old willow trees that was just about wide enough for a person to pass through on foot. Seeing no sign of the chizard, he propped his bicycle up against a tree trunk and made his way through the narrow opening before beckoning the younger boy to follow.

"What was that?" yelped Bingo, who was now standing next to Trumper in the eerie darkness of Pigswill Alley with only a couple of bicycle lamps to light their way. "Did you hear some footsteps just then; really heavy footsteps coming up behind us?"

"Bingo, a chizard doesn't have heavy footsteps. Moreover, we didn't pass it on our way here so it must be somewhere on Pigswill Alley," snapped Trumper, a little annoyed the younger boy had startled him for no good reason. "You know that this chizard is going to be in a foul mood after being beaten with Emilia Baggot's walker. And so I hate to admit this now, but maybe we do need Little MO."

"There's no need to worry, Trumper, I found this in Emilia Baggot's handbag," grinned Bingo, as he pulled what appeared to be some sort of weapon from his coat pocket. "It's a stun gun, just like the ones you see on the television. It's not the same as Little MO or even a punisher, but I'm sure it will work well enough on a chizard."

"Ordinarily I would be telling you off for taking something that does not belong to you. However, considering this is MAOS business, and we are going up against a particularly nasty kind of monster, then all I can say is good job, Bingo," praised Trumper, believing the younger boy's quick thinking may well have saved their bacon that evening. "Of course our only problem now is to choose which direction we should go. What do you reckon, towards Brimstone Close or Pucclechurch Crescent?"

"Brimstone Close," stated Bingo, while looking oddly confident as he illuminated the ground with his bicycle lamp.

"Why not Pucclechurch Crescent?" questioned Trumper, who was about to toss a coin to determine which direction the two boys should try first.

"Because those tracks look like chicken feet to me and they are heading towards Dragonbutt Vicarage, and that's on Brimstone Close," smiled Bingo, as he pointed to the footprints now clearly visible in the mud.

"Well spotted, Bingo," applauded Trumper, who was pleased the younger boy was thinking like Sherlock Holmes for once. "Then, to Brimstone Close, we will go."

So as not to tip off the chizard, that two fearless monster hunters were on its trail, the boys set off in silence with Trumper taking the lead and the younger boy bringing up the rear. While Bingo firmly held the stun gun in his right hand and one of the bicycle lamps in his left, Trumper shone his own lamp downward so that they could follow the chizard tracks in the muddy ground. From time to time they came to a halt because Bingo believed he could hear the thud of footsteps not too far behind them, yet every time they stopped not a sound could be heard by either boy. Was this simply his overly active imagination, deliberated Trumper, or was there really someone following them. And if so, why?

Just as they neared Dragonbutt Vicarage, the tracks abruptly ended. And even though the two boys shone their bicycle lamps into the darkness, alarmingly, there was absolutely no sign of the chizard. At that moment, Trumper heard the footsteps too, and not knowing who it was, he whispered to Bingo to hide behind the closest willow tree. While they waited, the boys could hear the thud-thud-thud of someone who must have been exceedingly heavy getting closer by the second, until finally the footsteps ceased and there was silence. Except that is for some rather loud breathing close to where Trumper and Bingo were hiding.

Without a moment's hesitation, the plucky boys emerged from behind the willow tree to confront their pursuer. Although before they had a chance to see who it was, the chizard jumped down from one of the overhanging branches that formed the canopy across Pigswill Alley. Rushing straight at Trumper, it took only a heart-pounding split second for Bingo to shoot the stun gun at the terrifying creature. This resulted in a squawk, and then an unrestrained scream before the shocked and thoroughly frazzled chizard fell to the ground.

Only then did Trumper and Bingo see who had been following them as Mumford walked over to the stunned chizard whose feet were now pointing upwards into the air. After a brief examination, he picked it up by the neck in one of his inordinately strong hands and then slowly trudged back the way he had come with a thud-thud-thud. Before Meow's manservant had gone half a dozen paces though, he unexpectedly turned around to face the boys. And while they could not say for sure, in the darkness, it looked as if he gave them a nod and a sly wink before continuing on his way.

"Dragonsbutts! I'm not sure what is scarier; the chizard or Mumford," shuddered Bingo, while returning Emilia Baggot's remarkably effective weapon to his coat pocket. "Trumper, when I saw the chizard lunge at you, I thought you were a goner for sure."

"So did I, if it had not been for you and that stun gun then I dread to think what may have happened," rejoiced Trumper, whose racing heartbeat was only now returning to normal. "It was lucky for us that Mumford came along when he did. So I think the next time MAOS goes on a monster hunt we should be much better prepared."

"I told you so, that's what Little MO is for," taunted Bingo, as he drew his left index finger across his neck. Because if he had his Monster Obliterator with him, then the chizard's grotesque lizard-like body would have been detached from its long feathered chicken neck by now, or so he implied. "Anyhow, it's getting late, and my tummy is rumbling so we should talk about this another time. Don't forget we have fish and chips to eat tonight along with a whole Bovington's chocolate cake, and it's just for the two of us. Let's go back to Bristletooth Lane to retrieve our bikes and then we can race each other back to Counting House Lane. And of course, it goes without saying that the winner gets to eat the first piece of chocolate cake."

Eleven

The Gathering of Witches

Although it was a typical Sunday morning in which Bingo had woken Aunty J and Uncle P at five-thirty, it was certainly unusual and definitely uncharacteristic to see their uncle sitting at the breakfast table by seven. The boys presumed, and rightly as it turned out, that this was most likely due to their aunty's presence at the Dragonbutt Arms the previous evening. And they guessed that it was also the reason their foster parents had unexpectedly returned home at the surprisingly early hour of a quarter to ten.

Only one short night had gone by since the boys had each polished off a portion of fish and chips and a rather large saveloy. And not forgetting a whole Bovington's chocolate cake, which they had no trouble in devouring all by themselves. Nevertheless, Bingo's tummy was already starting to rumble, so he was the one who had urged his aunty to have their breakfast ready by seven. Trumper, who had only put away three slices of chocolate cake to the younger boy's five, could not agree more, though for a wholly different reason. In fact, he was more concerned that time was marching on as they would now have to venture over to Wyvern Manor at a much earlier hour than he had initially planned.

After returning home from their chizard hunt the night before, the boys had learnt from Old Mrs Dingle that the next gathering of the Dragonbutt Witch's Institute was preponed and would last three hours instead of the usual two. This was because the Grand Witch intended to initiate a new member into their covern, and, the old lady stressed, it goes without saying that this would entail plenty of merrymaking. So the next gathering of witches was now going to take place between three and six that very afternoon. And though this meant the boys would be home in time for their dinner at seven, leaving their aunty and uncle none the wiser, Trumper knew he had plenty of reading to do first.

So that they did not have to ride their bicycles in the darkness and through the mud that covered Pigswill Alley, Old Mrs Dingle had kindly offered to take the boys to Wyvern Manor and then return them to Counting House Lane afterwards. Though this was much appreciated by both Trumper and Bingo, it was a bit of a mystery as to how she was going to do this. For no other reason than the old lady did not own a car, or to their knowledge even knew how to drive one. And when asked, she just winked and told them that good things come to those who are patient and they would just have to make do with that.

"Just give me a few minutes while I make you both a hot chocolate. And I noticed that you didn't eat any of the Bakewell tart last night," commented Aunty J, as she placed an enormous stack of pancakes onto the kitchen table. "It's not like the two of you to skip dessert. I guess those fish and chips must have filled you up no end."

"Yes, but don't worry because I can assure you we are going to be hungry for Bakewell tart a little later in the day," replied Bingo, who gave Trumper a wink as he thought about the Bovington's chocolate cake box he had thrown into the recycling bin the previous evening. "Is the bacon ready yet? I'm so hungry I could eat a horse, or should I say a pig."

Happily, Bingo did not have to wait too long because within a minute or two Aunty J handed the boys a large oval plate that must have held about three pounds of Hogswood bacon. And so the younger boy dived right in and placed a generous twelve rashers onto his plate before helping himself to five fluffy pancakes. He then put a sizeable knob of creamy Dragonbutt butter onto the uppermost pancake and allowed it to melt just a little. After which he drenched everything in a river of the sweetest tasting honey one could buy from Botters of Chelmsford.

"You boys missed all the excitement last night," remarked Uncle P, while hungrily tucking into his plate of pancakes and bacon. "Everyone at the Dragonbutt Arms thought those mooners had struck again, but it turned out to be no more than a chicken had frightened Emilia Baggot. You know we laughed about it for the rest of the evening, though it just goes to show how on edge everybody in the village is lately."

"Now dear, as I recall we didn't actually hear this firsthand because you insisted on buying another round of drinks for Angus and Barry," scoffed Aunty J, who thought it was somewhat ironic that the editor-in-chief and the star reporter of the Dragonbutt Smoker were more interested in Dragonstone Fire than what was taking place a little further up Dragonbutt High Street that evening. "And I heard from Hildy Bovington that Emilia Baggot swears she was not attacked by any ordinary chicken."

"I've known Emilia Baggot all my life, and she has always been prone to exaggeration. Moreover, with her eyesight I'm surprised she didn't claim her attacker was a tiger or even a wild bear," chuckled Uncle P, as he helped himself to a few more rashers of bacon before Bingo greedily finished off the rest. "Regardless, even though it's not worthy of the front page, it does deserve a mention. So you will be able to read all about it in next week's edition of the Smoker."

Though their uncle was all too aware the DWI's Grand Witch had been dabbling in dark magic, it had not occurred to him that the attack on Emilia Baggot had any connection to this. While Trumper and Bingo knew different, they both understood that if they told him the chicken was really a monstrous chizard, then he would have insisted on accompanying them to Wyvern Manor. And although he was an Entwhistle and accustomed to almost every kind of monster found in his family's journals, he was not a member of MAOS.

"Well, I'm all done with breakfast," proclaimed Bingo, while slapping his sufficiently gorged tummy with a satisfied look on his face. "We should eat pancakes and bacon together more often and not just pancakes on their own like we normally do."

Trumper nodded in agreement as he wrapped his last pancake around two rashers of bacon and smothered the whole thing in lots of Botters honey. Then he ate the scrumptious creation by taking three gargantuan bites before washing it down with the remainder of his hot chocolate. In the meantime, his aunty and uncle slowly ate their breakfast while savouring a cup of English breakfast tea.

"And what are you boys planning on doing today?" inquired Uncle P, after accepting a second cup of the delicious tea from Aunty J. "Unfortunately, unlike last Sunday there is no snow, and so I imagine we are going to have another cold damp dreary January day."

"We're going over to the Bovington house to play games with Bertie and Flitcher," answered Bingo, which was not exactly the truth, but near enough he thought. "Hey, Trumper, let's go and get dressed because we have to leave soon."

"I know that four young boys can get up to a lot of mischief when left to their own devices. So I want you to behave yourselves while you are there," forewarned Aunty J, who seemed to aim her remark more towards Bingo than Trumper. "And don't forget that lunch will be served at twelve."

"Bingo, I need to do some important research at MAOS headquarters before we go to Wyvern Manor this afternoon. That means you will have to go to Bertie's house on your own, and I'll see you on your return," asserted Trumper, as he ascended the stairs with the younger boy.

"Really, but you're going to miss out on all the entertainment," exclaimed Bingo, somewhat surprised that Trumper was bailing on him. "You know we don't get an opportunity like this every day, so why miss it?"

"I'm aware of that, but I have to read through some of the Entwhistle journals this morning. And besides, this is MAOS business which takes precedence over humiliating Bentley DuPont any day," explained Trumper, who looked a little preoccupied with his thoughts at that moment. "I've been thinking about how the chizard escaped from Wyvern Manor. Meow told us that none of the creatures in the menagerie had ever broken out, yet this chizard not only slipped out of the menagerie unseen, somehow it managed to scale the main wall as well."

Knowing that it was pointless to argue with Trumper, Bingo quickly descended the stairs before pulling on his outdoor clothing and then his muddy wellington boots. Like a flash, he opened the bright red front door and excitedly ran out of the little old house. As Bingo approached the Bovington House, he heard a loud hiss, whereby the young boy turned around to see two DPS woolly hats sticking out from behind a hedge on the opposite side of the street. Seeing that it was Bertie and Flitcher, he walked over to where they were hiding and crouched beside them. After a few minutes of shoving and giggling, Flitcher warned his two friends that the time was now five minutes to nine, and that meant Bentley DuPont was sure to arrive very soon.

Promptly at nine, they heard a bicycle approaching, and then Bentley DuPont came into view. He was dressed in his best and most expensive designer gear and was holding a bouquet of a dozen red roses. As Flitcher recorded everything on his phone, the head boy leaned his bicycle against the nearest lamp post and then walked up to the front door of the Bovington house. With a broad smile on his face, Bentley banged as hard as he could on the door using the heavy cast-iron knocker in the shape of the Bovington letter B. Thinking that Bertie's older sister could not hear him, he continued to bang on the chocolate coloured door until the light in Bunty's bedroom was suddenly turned on.

Instead of racing down the stairs and giving Bentley DuPont an earful of her rage as the three boys were expecting, the window in Bunty's bedroom unexpectedly opened and a bucketful of icy cold water was thrown at the unwary head boy standing below. As its contents came into contact with Bentley, the now water sodden boy took two steps backwards, at which point he unwisely looked up towards the bedroom window. And then without looking down, Bunty proceeded to throw a bag full of her mother's best flour out of the very same window, which hilariously all but covered him.

Still hiding behind the hedge, Bingo and the others fell around laughing just as Bunty poked her head through the open window to see an entirely different boy than the one she was expecting. Flitcher Jenkins was the boy who usually woke her early on a Sunday morning, and so he was the one that should have been soaking wet and drenched in flour. To Bunty's astonishment, it was not Flitcher but Dragonbutt Primary School's new head boy who looked as white as a ghost as he ran towards his bicycle, visibly fuming and calling out to her that she was as mad as a Butterworth.

The boys watched as Bentley DuPont made a hasty retreat by riding his bicycle back the way he had come until he turned the corner at the entrance to Counting House Lane. After seeing Bunty shut her bedroom window and close her curtains, the three of them emerged from behind the hedge, laughing uncontrollably and slapping each other on the back. Then knowing the prudent course of action would be to avoid bumping into his sister for the rest of the day, Bertie handed his friends each a spolly as they slowly walked towards Hunnickle Drive.

"Dragonsbutts! That was so funny and even better than I had hoped for," howled Bertie, whose face was as red as a beetroot from laughing so much. "I'm not sure what was best, watching Bentley DuPont get covered from head to toe in water and flour, or my sister's face after seeing what she had done to the new head boy. Flitcher, I hope you recorded all of that because I want everyone at Dragonbutt Primary School to see it."

"I sure did, including the bit when Bentley said Bunty was as mad as a Butterworth," giggled Flitcher, and the other two joined in. "Hey, Bingo, did you catch the chicken that attacked Emilia Baggot last night?"

"Of course, but it wasn't a chicken, it was really a chizard, which is actually a monster and therefore much worse. Trumper and I caught up with it on Pigswill Alley. And I was the one who downed it with a single shot from a stun gun," boasted Bingo, as he pulled the gun out of his coat pocket to show Bertie and Flitcher. Although this time he firmly held onto his new weapon in case Flitcher felt the need to zap himself in the head again. "What is still a mystery to us, is how the chizard escaped from Wyvern Manor in the first place. There is one wall surrounding the menagerie and an even bigger wall encircling the whole of the Wyvern estate."

"We saw Chugher Harris on Dragonbutt High Street last night, just after the attack on Emilia Baggot and he told us how it managed to escape over the wall of the menagerie. Though he said nothing about it being a chizard, only that it was a crazed chicken," revealed Bertie, who went on to tell Bingo everything he and Flitcher had found out. "And that's not all; he also said that Chomper Junior's dad knows of a secret entrance beneath the main wall of Wyvern Manor. He discovered it during his mooning days with Angus Hogswood and Typsy Braithwaite. So that must be how the chizard got out."

Believing Trumper would want to hear about this right away, Bingo said goodbye to his classmates and then ran back to the little old house as fast as his legs would carry him. After running down the long garden path, the breathless young boy came to a halt upon reaching the white door of MAOS headquarters. This was the door he had written the word MAOS in thick bright red paint, and though it was quite legible, there were drips beneath each of its capitalised letters. It only took a couple of loud knocks on the door before it opened to reveal Trumper and half a dozen Entwhistle journals strewn all over the brown leather sofa.

"I know how the chizard escaped from Wyvern Manor," blurted out Bingo, as he entered MAOS headquarters. "When the chizard slipped out of the cryptid menagerie it did not try to hide as Meow had told us last night. Instead, it ran into the main compound because Chugher Harris and Chomper Baverstock Junior had left that door open as well. In fact, it entered the sidehill gouger enclosure, dug its sharp claws into one of the sidehill gougers and rode the poor creature to the top of its hill at full pelt before launching itself over the wall. Chugher and Chomper Junior saw it all but ran off and didn't bother to tell Meow or Mumford."

"That explains how the chizard got out of the menagerie, but not how it escaped from Wyvern Manor. There is no way it could have climbed over the main wall, it's just too high," broke in Trumper, while shaking his head.

"I was just coming to that," responded Bingo, who was a little irritated the older boy had interrupted his story. "According to Bertie, a long time ago Chomper Junior's dad stumbled across a secret entrance to Wyvern Manor, somewhere beneath the main wall. He couldn't say exactly where it is located, but it's the only way the chizard could have gotten out. Don't you see?"

"Interesting. However, if Chomper Baverstock Senior knows of this secret entrance and he informed his son, who obviously told Chugher, then the both of them blabbed to Bertie and Flitcher, and they revealed this to you, then it's hardly a secret entrance any longer. More a not-so-secret entrance," laughed Trumper, although after Bingo added Angus Hogswood and Typsy Braithwaite to this list, his observation sounded less like a joke; instead, it resonated as exceptionally astute.

As the boys' laughter died down an unexpected knock on the door could be heard followed by the voice of Aunty J calling to them. Bingo was the one to open the door, and he gleefully accepted a flask of hot chocolate accompanied by a couple of large mugs and a plate containing two generous slices of Bakewell tart. While their aunty returned posthaste to the little old house to prepare the family Sunday lunch, Trumper poured the steaming hot chocolate into the mugs. And though the younger boy was unhappy that there was no fresh whipped cream and marshmallow, he cheered up as soon as he tucked into the morello cherry jam filled Bakewell tart.

After Bingo had drained the last of the hot chocolate from his mug and eaten every crumb on his plate, he reached into his coat pocket and pulled out the stun gun. Almost immediately, Trumper told him that the weapon was not his and he would have to give it back to Emilia Baggot. Because he already had Little MO and a pretty powerful punisher in his collection, the younger boy grudgingly agreed to give the stun gun to Old Mrs Dingle so that she could return it to the rapidly approaching centenarian at their next bingo night.

Once he had finished his own hot chocolate and eaten the remainder of his Bakewell tart, Trumper went back to studying the Entwhistle journals. That morning he had begun to read through everything that had ever been written about chizards and bugaboos. And what he had learnt was that while both were thoroughly dreadful and utterly despicable monsters, it was the bugaboo that the younger residents of Dragonbutt should fear the most. Just as Meow had told the boys during their visit to the cryptid menagerie, the bugaboo only came out at night and really did have a penchant for eating children, and preferably boys below the age of twelve because those were the juiciest. The only saving grace with bugaboos, he could make out, was that they never ate their victims straight away. Instead, the bugaboo always chose to feast on a captive child in the comfort of its dark and often dank lair.

While Trumper was completely engrossed in the journals that contained everything a dauntless monster hunter needed to know about chizards and bugaboos, the younger boy told him what had taken place between Bunty Bovington and Bentley DuPont. After a brief bout of hysterical laughter, the older boy returned to his reading and Bingo began to peruse the journals that were mostly concerned with witches. He quickly realised that the stories within these pages were nothing more than a history lesson regarding all the Wyvern women who had lived during Dragonbutt's dark days. And interestingly, every one of them turned out to be a dark witch.

At five minutes to twelve, like clockwork, Bingo's tummy began to rumble so loudly it gave Trumper quite a start. This, of course, meant it was time for the boys' lunch, and so they both lifted themselves off the brown leather sofa to return to the little old house. Bingo was the first one out of the door to run up the long garden path carrying the empty flask, mugs and plate. Meanwhile, Trumper returned the journals to their proper place on the bookshelves and then secured the padlock on the door to MAOS headquarters before running after him.

Sunday lunch was the traditional sumptuous affair that was common in not just Dragonbutt, but almost every home in the land. By the time Trumper and Bingo entered the kitchen, their aunty had already placed thick slices of slow-roasted beef onto each of their plates. And next to the beef were roast potatoes, Brussels sprouts, carrots and peas and not forgetting a huge portion of Red Dragon cauliflower cheese. Once the four of them were seated at the kitchen table, she spooned a liberal amount of horseradish sauce onto their plates and then covered everything in her homemade Butts Batch infused beef and onion gravy.

Even though Bingo had asked for seconds and then returned again for thirds, the young boy insisted he had plenty of room left in his tummy for dessert. So when Aunty J plonked her version of jam roly-poly onto the table, which had lemon curd as a filling instead of the more common jam, he easily managed to eat two whole slices covered in thick creamy custard to everyone else's one.

Afterwards, Uncle P suggested they should all sit around the roaring open fire in the living room and chat for a while to let their heavy lunch subside. Although Bingo thought this was entirely unnecessary because sitting around would only make him feel hungry again, Trumper urged the younger boy to take a seat on the sofa knowing that soon they would have to depart for Wyvern Manor. At one-thirty, the boys said goodbye to their sleepy foster parents and left the warmth of the living room, though they failed to mention where they intended to go and with whom.

Without a word, Bingo ran upstairs to their bedroom to retrieve the punisher and placed it in his Dr Who backpack. By the time he returned, Trumper was already dressed in his coat, along with his DPS woolly hat and warm woollen gloves, and was just then pulling on his wellington boots. Guessing that the younger boy's backpack contained the punisher, he just smiled and winked at Bingo and then shortly after the two boys were on their way.

As they were in no great hurry, Trumper and Bingo slowly ambled their way to the end of Counting House Lane and then walked up the poorly maintained path to Old Mrs Dingle's dilapidated looking house. Seeing that Bingo had pulled the stun gun from his coat pocket and was aiming it towards her faded blue front door, Trumper stepped forward and knocked three times. And then he reminded the younger boy to give the gun to the old lady and to be careful not to shoot anyone, and that included Baxter.

Although her house was undeniably small, it took almost a minute before she opened the door and invited the boys to enter. After the two of them had removed their wellingtons, they followed her to the kitchen where Baxter was enthusiastically lapping up a bowl full of the old lady's blend number thirteen. Though it was earlier than his regular feeding time, Old Mrs Dingle explained that she was still a little fearful he might turn into a vampire again and bite one of the other witches. For that reason, she had decided to give the funny-looking dog one pint now and intended to take another pint with her so that he could drink it before the sun started to set.

Just as he had been instructed, Bingo handed the stun gun, albeit reluctantly, to the old lady and asked her to return the weapon to its owner. While Old Mrs Dingle was noticeably surprised that Emilia Baggot owned a stun gun, she agreed but asked the young boy how it came to be in his possession. Because Bingo was well practised in not always telling the absolute truth, he found it rather easy to concoct a story involving a pick-pocketing circus monkey and a chase that finally ended with him capturing the little blighter on Pigswill Alley.

"Well it was lucky for Emilia Baggot that you were there to witness this incident, and it was a monkey you say. How brave you were to run after him," commented Old Mrs Dingle, somewhat sarcastically as she knew young boys commonly exaggerate such things and from time to time were even known to lie. "I have just made a fresh batch of scones for the gathering and packed two for each of you as a snack. But don't forget that you need to stay hidden or all hell will break loose. Now if you don't have any questions, then let's be on our way."

"I've got a question," announced Bingo, with a sense of urgency in the tone of his voice that suggested it was going to be an important one. "Can we have hot chocolate as well?"

"Certainly, I'll whip up some now, and you can take it with you in a thermos flask," replied Old Mrs Dingle, who like most of the residents of Dragonbutt, always kept an ample supply of Bovington's chocolate on hand in case the need arose for a warming mug of hot chocolate.

"Old Mrs Dingle, I have something to ask you too," uttered Trumper, thinking his question was definitely more far-reaching to them than Bingo's had been. "How are we going to get to Wyvern Manor when you don't own a car?"

"Oh, there's no need to worry yourself about that. I have something much better than a car," chortled the old lady, as she handed Bingo the thermos flask of steaming hot chocolate. "I'll just gather my things and then Baxter and I will meet you in front of the garage in a couple of minutes."

Still none the wiser as to how they would get to Wyvern Manor, Trumper and Bingo pulled on their wellingtons once again and walked around to the garage at the side of the house. The garage had a pair of old fashioned wooden doors that were made to swing open in the middle, but the structure looked far too narrow to fit almost any type of car they could think of. After impatiently pacing up and down in the cold for a good five minutes, the boys heard the yap of an excited dog and someone moving around in the garage. Then without warning, the doors swung open to reveal Old Mrs Dingle pushing a somewhat run-down motorcycle with an attached sidecar containing Baxter. It turned out to be a Mark One 1967 Norton Commando that had, just like the sidecar, been painted an eye-catching rose red by the late Old Mr Dingle.

For a second or two, Trumper and Bingo stared at each other and then apprehensively edged closer to the motorcycle. With a smile on her face, the old lady lifted Baxter out of the sidecar and placed him onto her seat just behind the handlebar before instructing the boys to jump in. They seated themselves with the younger boy in the front holding his Dr Who backpack on his lap and the older boy to the rear of him. And then Old Mrs Dingle handed each of them a pair of vintage goggles and an old crash helmet which they pulled on over their DPS woolly hats.

"Old Mrs Dingle, where is your helmet and goggles?" inquired Trumper, who had noticed the old lady was wearing neither.

"Trumper, I have no need for goggles because as always I'm wearing my glasses. As for a helmet, I prefer to wear this," giggled Old Mrs Dingle, as she placed on top of her head a pointed black witch's hat that had the letters DWI embroidered in a blood-red thread on the front. And to top this off, the old lady threw a matching black robe over her shoulders before securely fastening it around her neck. "This is the uniform of the Dragonbutt Witch's Institute and is worn by every witch in the covern. I made my own robe you know, but the Grand Witch commissioned Bucktooth Tom Blewitt to make the hats. Of course, she made him swear never to tell anyone or else a rather unpleasant spell would be placed upon him."

Now that the four of them were ready to go, Old Mrs Dingle climbed on to her deceased husband's motorcycle and kicked the starter lever three times before the powerful machine roared to life. "Tally-ho!" cried the old lady, while revving the engine and making a sharp left turn onto Hunnickle Drive, which happened to be the opposite direction to Wyvern Manor. "Boys, let's have some fun by riding the entire length of Dragonbutt High Street."

With their hearts pounding, the two boys held on as best they could while the old lady pushed the antiquated motorcycle to its limit. Then as they sped up Dragonbutt High Street, Bingo spotted two familiar figures climbing into an open-top denim blue MG Roadster parked outside of Oh My Cod!. He immediately pointed this out to Trumper who told him to crouch down to avoid being seen by Meow and Mumford. For the simple reason, he knew that both the car and Old Mrs Dingle's motorcycle would be travelling to the very same destination.

"That was unfortunate. The Sunday lunch service at Oh My Cod! must have just ended," shouted Trumper, as loud as he could so that Bingo could hear him over the blare of the motorcycle engine. "Still, I don't think the two of them saw us in the sidecar because they were too busy staring at Old Mrs Dingle in her DWI hat and robe."

"I'm pretty sure that Mumford did," yelled back Bingo, who believed he had seen Meow's seven-foot-tall manservant peering into the sidecar as they rode past. "And it looked as though he winked at me."

After speeding past the Dragonbutt Arms and Gribble's the Grocer's, then Bovington's Sweets and Chocolates and finally, Fanshaw's the Baker's, the unusual sight of a DWI witch riding a motorcycle with a sidecar holding two DPS schoolboys was soon making a hard right turn into Witches Brew Lane. As they rode up to the main entrance to Wyvern Manor, the old lady bellowed, "Keep your heads down, boys." Then with a blast of her motorcycle's horn, the wooden gates set into the almost impenetrable wall swung open.

Hardly needing to slow down at all, Old Mrs Dingle opened up the throttle and tore down the gravel path like a bat out of hell. Upon reaching a clump of trees interspersed with thick bushes, she unexpectedly pulled on her brakes, and the motorcycle and sidecar came to an abrupt stop. On the other side of the trees, at a distance of no more than fifty feet, was an unlit bonfire along with a large cauldron, four long tables and about two dozen ornately appointed chairs.

"Boys, you'll have to lay low here for the next few hours," declared

Old Mrs Dingle, while glancing over her shoulder to ensure that no one was watching them. "Leave your helmets and goggles in the sidecar and make sure you stay hidden behind these bushes because the other witches will arrive soon. Sometime after six when the coast is clear, I will ride over here to pick you up. It will be dark by then, and so nobody will see the two of you."

In silence, Trumper and Bingo removed their helmets and goggles as the old lady had requested and then they ran with all speed to their hiding place. Fortunately for the boys, this was the perfect location for them to spy on the Dragonbutt Witch's Institute without fear of being seen themselves. Barely a minute had passed when hidden in the bushes they saw Meow's sports car tear past them and park directly in front of the house. And though she could only just see above the steering wheel, the Grand Witch's apprentice was clearly the driver, and Mumford, with his head a good foot above the windscreen, sat by her side.

Seeing that the other witches had yet to arrive, and Meow, Mumford and Old Mrs Dingle had entered the house, Bingo lowered his Dr Who backpack to the ground. Feeling the beginnings of a rumble in his tummy, he pulled out the thermos flask containing the old lady's hot chocolate, her freshly baked scones and of course the punisher. And while it was certainly true the young boy had brought the weapon along in case they ran into any trouble, he had never intended to use it so soon. However, he was about to find out it would be one of those days when that was not to be.

Upon hearing a rustling and then a hushed voice in the bushes, Bingo grabbed the punisher and without taking even a moment to think he lunged forward and zapped the lone figure coming into view. Even before the Dragonbutt Smoker's best reporter had landed on the ground, the young boy already regretted his all too hasty decision. And though it was a little too late in the day for it now, he remembered his uncle's often recited words, 'Always take the time to think before you act or else you may regret it later'.

"I can't believe that you zapped Barry Beasley," hissed Trumper, as he examined the young reporter lying on the ground. "Look at him; I think he's gone all doolally. His tongue is hanging out, and his hair is standing on end. What setting do you have that punisher on?"

"It's still only set to low, and Barry always spikes his hair with gel. So that is why it's standing on end," protested Bingo, who couldn't help think that the young reporter should not have surprised him when he was on MAOS business. Therefore, when he thought of it that way, getting zapped by the punisher was really Barry Beasley's fault after all. "Don't worry; I'm sure he'll be right as rain in a few minutes."

Bingo was right about that because hardly five minutes had passed and Barry was sitting up and drinking a cup of hot chocolate, which Trumper had kindly poured for him. As it was particularly cold that afternoon, this perked him up no end. And by the time he had finished eating one of Old Mrs Dingle's scones with her homemade raspberry jam and clotted Dragonbutt cream, he was his normal happy go lucky self once again.

"Dragonsbutts! That was quite a jolt you gave me, Bingo. I think I'm going to have to announce myself more vigorously from now on," proclaimed Barry, after examining the punisher. "So I guess you are both here for the same reason that brought me to Wyvern Manor; the Dragonbutt Witch's Institute."

Before either boy had a chance to answer, in the distance, the three of them could hear a creaky door opening and then closing, followed by the slow thud-thud-thud of Mumford. In an instant, they all leapt to their feet and peered through the bushes to see Meow's manservant walking in their direction with a battered jerrycan in his hand. He then began to douse the bonfire in what must have been petrol before lighting it and walking back the same way he had just come.

While quietly chatting to the young reporter, Trumper and Bingo finished off the thermos flask of hot chocolate and the remaining scones, and then another sound could be heard. This time it was coming from the direction of the main gate and was clearly getting louder by the second. In no time at all a minibus driven by Bucktooth Tom Blewitt, which had been painted a ghostly shade of white, tore past their hiding place and came to a halt next to the now roaring bonfire.

As soon as the door of the minibus opened, a hoard of jostling witches carrying all sorts of Dragonbutt delicacies rushed out and placed them onto the tables. Just like Old Mrs Dingle, each one of them was dressed in a black robe and a pointed hat with the letters DWI embroidered in a blood-red thread. Unaware that there were three uninvited guests at their gathering, the boisterous bunch headed over to the bonfire to perform some sort of strange ritualistic dance. Then they started to sing what could only be described as a rumbustious witch's song that began with the words, 'Round about the cauldron we go, how many times no one knows...'.

Like everyone who was Dragonbutt born, Bucktooth Tom Blewitt had heard many of the old tales about the strange goings-on at Wyvern Manor. And so not wishing to hang around a second longer than he had to, he attempted a woefully inadequate three-point turn that ended up being more like six. Now that he was pointing in the right direction, Bucktooth Tom drove back up the gravel path and headed into the village to calm his nerves at the Dragonbutt Arms before returning for the witches at six.

No sooner than the minibus had departed, Old Mrs Dingle came out of the house carrying a plate of her homemade scones, and Baxter was dutifully by her side. A little way behind her was the hulking figure of Mumford, who was holding a wooden barrel of Butts Batch in his powerful arms. The moment he lowered the barrel onto one of the tables, a raucous cheer went out from the dancing witches. Then one by one they poured themselves a pint of Butts Batch before starting on the food. From the bushes, Barry and the boys watched the witches make merry and then they saw yet another witch leave the house and walk slowly towards the bonfire. She was accompanied by at least half a dozen cats, although to Trumper and Bingo's surprise not one of them was black.

Instead of wearing a plain black robe, this witch had one with gold trim around the edge and a pointed hat with the letters 'GW' embroidered on the front. This, of course, could only mean one thing, that the Grand Witch of the DWI was approaching and this was confirmed by the reception she received from the other witches. Interrupting their singing, they gave a round of unrestrained cheering followed by a clinking of pint glasses and calls of, "Down the hatch for the Grand Witch."

"Witches of the Dragonbutt Witch's Institute, I declare that our first gathering of witches in this New Year is now officially open," announced the Grand Witch, to another round of rowdy but very enthusiastic cheering and even more clinks of half-empty pint glasses. "It is also my privilege to welcome a new witch to our covern. I am sure that most of you already know her and so without any further ado, I would like to introduce Millie Bender. Please step forward, Millie."

"Dragonsbutts! They've managed to rope Ms Bender into this now," exclaimed an open-mouthed Trumper, who was certainly not expecting to see his favourite teacher dressed in a witches hat and robe at a gathering of the Dragonbutt Witch's Institute. "Listen, she's saying something, and it looks like the Grand Witch has given her a wand."

Unbeknown to Barry and the boys, much of what Millie Bender was now reciting could be found in The Dragonbutt Witch's Guide to Witchcraft and Spells from beginner to the more advanced. This was because Elvira Wyvern, following the discovery of Eradorn Wyvern's magical books, had chosen to use the first Grand Witch's revered words in the DWI oath. And needless to say, she insisted that all new witches must recite the oath in front of the whole covern.

"All witches of the Dragonbutt Witch's Institute should follow the teachings of Eradorn Wyvern and for the good of the covern must unfailingly carry out the wishes of the Grand Witch. I, Millie Bender, as a newly appointed witch, affirm that whatever happens at a DWI gathering, always stays within the covern and may never be revealed to any outsider. I swear to this on my wand and the sacred books of witchcraft and spells."

"I've said it before, and I will say it again. Anyone who teaches maths must have a dark side, and that's why I hate Ms Bender's class so much," muttered Bingo, as he watched the witches dance around the bonfire again. "And Trumper, I don't see Meow with the other witches."

"Neither do I, she must still be in the house. And the reason you don't like Ms Bender's class is that you're terrible at maths," retorted Trumper, who disliked hearing anything unflattering spoken about Millie Bender. "Barry, did you get to meet Meow, I mean Morweena Ogglejay? We found out she is Elvira Wyvern's niece, and that's not all, she's also the Grand Witch's apprentice."

"Really, I wasn't aware that she was in the DWI, but it doesn't surprise me in the least as I know quite a bit about Meow. We happened to be classmates together at Dragonbutt Primary School and were the best of friends. Then one day, her parents unexpectedly pulled Meow out of school, and the family moved away from Dragonbutt. I never saw or heard from her again until last Sunday when I popped into Oh My Cod! and there she was, and she still had Mumford with her. Strangely, he hadn't aged a day since I last saw him all those years ago," divulged

Barry, to the two attentive boys. "And Elvira Wyvern is not just her aunty, she's her double aunty."

"A double aunty!" spluttered Bingo, who really had no idea what the young reporter meant by double aunty or its significance.

"Yes, a double aunty. You see Meow's mother, Ellora Wyvern, was married to Elvira Wyvern's brother, Augustus Ogglejay. And she, in turn, was married to Meow's mother's elder and only brother, Edwald Wyvern. So that means Elvira is her aunty on both sides of the family," explained Barry, in a way the boys would understand, or so he thought. However, for Trumper and Bingo, the implications of this had not sunken in just yet. "Unfortunately, Edwald Wyvern passed away some years ago. Eaten by a crocodile I understand, but to my knowledge, he rarely left the grounds of Wyvern Manor so how that happened is quite a mystery."

The boys suspected that no crocodile had eaten Edwald Wyvern. Instead, it had to be the crocogator residing in the menagerie. This would certainly have been an interesting story to tell Barry, if not for the fact that the commotion the witches had been making for the past hour had abruptly died down. After Millie Bender was sworn in as a fully-fledged witch of the DWI, the witches had drank and ate to their heart's content while singing and waving their wands in the air. By now it was rather dark, although the light of the bonfire meant the three uninvited guests could see almost everything. And what they saw was the covern of witches seated at three of the four long tables, and the Grand Witch stood at the head of the fourth.

Due to the uncommon silence, the slow thud-thud-thud of Mumford was clearly audible, and then he came into view carrying a pile of extremely old books. At his side was yet another witch and in her arms was the fearful looking black cat that Bingo had chosen to zap with the punisher only the day before. This witch could not have been more than five feet tall, and therefore the three of them knew she had to be the Grand Witch's apprentice. Once Meow's manservant had reached the tables where the witches were sitting, he handed them every book except one and then gave the remaining book to Elvira Wyvern. Meanwhile, with the arrival of the black cat, Baxter gave a long uneasy growl, and then the other cats hissed before hurriedly running back to the house.

"Fellow witches of the Dragonbutt Witch's Institute, we have now come to the serious part of our gathering. And that is to practise our witchcraft and spells as written down in the Grand Witch Eradorn Wyvern's sacred books," disclosed the Grand Witch, to yet another round of cheers and wand-waving by every witch present. "Wands to the ready ladies, and there is a box of Bovington's chocolates for the witch who casts the best spell of the gathering."

"Dragonsbutts! That must be Eradorn Wyvern's last book, the one that's all about dark magic," pointed Bingo, to the book that the Grand Witch and her apprentice were fervidly studying at their table. At the same time, the other witches read from the rest of the enchanting books and took turns to cast their spells using the heavy cast iron cauldron.

Throughout the next hour or so, all sorts of odd things were thrown into the now boiling cauldron. From toads and hedgehogs to old bicycle tyres and even a curly pig's tail went in. And at one point, Mumford had to bring the ceaselessly chattering witches a second barrel of Butts Batch, which prompted them to sing another frightfully bewitching song. Even though the witches were obviously having a whale of a time, disappointingly, Barry and the boys did not get to witness even a single spell that actually worked.

While all of this was going on, they failed to notice the Grand Witch's black cat had wandered over to the very same clump of trees and bushes where they were hiding. Bingo was the first to spot him, and he immediately pounced into action by zapping the diabolical creature with the punisher. Knowing that the three of them were in peril, he had set the weapon to full power which hurled the black cat a good fifty feet into the air. Landing close to the bonfire with a rather large thump on the ground, only the Grand Witch's apprentice seemed to hear the muffled sound. And then almost at once, a bolt of light resembling a firework flew from the end of her wand to light up the sky revealing Barry and the boys artfully concealed hiding place.

"It seems w-w-we have uninvited guests," whispered Meow, into the ear of the Grand Witch and then she shouted, "Mumford, go and bring them here."

Neither the boys nor Barry had any intention of waiting around for the slow-moving Mumford to catch them. So without uttering a word, Bingo pulled on his Dr Who backpack and then they all ran as fast as they could towards the entrance to Wyvern Manor. Knowing that the wooden gates were sure to be locked, with a sense of urgency in his voice, Trumper called to the young reporter to ascertain how the three of them were ever going to get out.

"I know of a secret entrance, which is how I got into the grounds of Wyvern Manor in the first place," yelled back Barry, who was running ahead of the boys to guide their escape. "Angus Hogswood told me about it last night in the Dragonbutt Arms."

The boys followed Barry to the not-so-secret entrance located less than a hundred feet from the wooden gates they had passed through earlier that afternoon. Concealed behind several overgrown bushes was a passageway at the foot of the wall that according to the young reporter had been constructed when the sturdy barrier was first built. Its purpose was to allow the old open sewer that contained all the foul-smelling mess produced by the residents of the house on an all too frequent basis to flow as far from the grounds of Wyvern Manor as humanly possible. With the onset of modern plumbing though, the sewer had dried up, and over the years most of it had been filled in.

However, the passageway in the wall was simply forgotten.

Holding an exceptionally high powered torch that he had wisely brought with him, Barry led the boys into the old passageway and through the wall before safely emerging on the other side. And then from there, it was only a short dash to the disused dirt track where he had parked his new Mini Cooper convertible with its much-revered racing green trim.

"Come on, boys, I doubt that Mumford knows of the secret entrance, but let's not hang around here to find out," warned Barry, as he jumped into the driver's seat and started the engine. Then Trumper scrambled around to the passenger side and pulled the seat forward so that Bingo could climb into the back. "Dragonsbutts! That was a close call. Fasten your seat belts, and I'll take the two of you back home."

Despite the fact that Trumper and Bingo had planned to return with Old Mrs Dingle and Baxter, they both believed this was a decidedly safer mode of transportation than the motorcycle and sidecar. Unfortunately, this proved to be far from the case as Barry put the car into gear and sped down the dirt track before making a sharp handbrake turn into Witches Brew Lane. Barely missing the minibus driven by Bucktooth Tom Blewitt, who was returning from the Dragonbutt Arms to pick up the now very merry covern of witches, he made another precarious high speed turn and then tore down the main road towards Dragonbutt with his headlights on full beam. Although before they had gotten even a half-mile, the young reporter spotted something in the distance that looked wholly out of place beside the wall that bordered the Hogswood Piggery.

"The moon looks rather low this evening," remarked Barry, while shielding his eyes from the glare.

"That's odd, it looks like there are three moons," said Trumper, who had to squint to get a better look.

"Dragonsbutts! That's no moon; it's the mooners!" thundered Bingo, as he leaned forward on the back seat and pointed at the three bare butts they were just about to pass.

With the speed of a Manx cat, which to those who did not know is a cat that has no tail and can move surprisingly quickly when it chooses too, Barry slammed on the brakes of his car. Following a shrill screech and the smell of burning rubber, the Mini Cooper convertible stopped about fifty feet from where its occupants had seen the mooners.

Trumper was the first to exit the car and then Bingo, who was holding the punisher in his hand and it was still set to full power. Not waiting for the others, he ran back down the road as fast as his powerful legs would carry him. Regrettably, by the time he got there, it was a tad too late as the mooners had already climbed over the wall and were running towards the woods that straddled the Hogswood Piggery.

Once Barry and Trumper arrived, the three of them clambered over the wall, and then the young reporter shone his torch into the darkness. Alas, it was to no avail as not a single mooner could be seen. In fact, the only evidence the three in the car had just been mooned was the sound of an air horn some distance away. And this, as every resident of Dragonbutt now knew, was the telltale sign that the mooners had struck again and pulled off yet another shocking full moon.

"Dragonsbutts! I just can't believe we've been mooned," exclaimed Trumper, who knew it was best to keep this mooning under wraps so that their aunty and uncle would stay in the dark as to what the two boys had been up to.

"Well it's too dark for us to follow them tonight, and besides, they could be almost anywhere by now," shrugged Barry, as he swung the beam of his torch in a wide arc one last time. "It must be close to your dinnertime by now, so let me get you home before your aunty and uncle start to worry and call out Dragonbutt police."

"Excellent idea," nodded Bingo, whose tummy had just begun to rumble after the brief but unexpected shock of being mooned.

"Trumper, I wonder what we're eating tonight? Let's hope it's one of our favourites because I'm absolutely famished."

As Barry drove the boys back to Counting House Lane, unlike the younger boy, Trumper was not thinking of his tummy at all. Since hearing the din of the air horn as the mooners were running away, he could not help but think what Angus Hogswood had told him about how he too used an air horn during his mooning days. And Trumper believed that he and Bingo had recently seen someone else with an air horn, yet he could not for the life of him recollect who.

Twelve

Kidnapped

B right and early on Monday morning, the boys arrived at school to find nearly every student and quite a few of the teachers hunched over their phones in the playground and laughing hysterically. This was because they were watching the recording of Bunty Bovington throwing a bucket of icy cold water followed by a sizeable bag of her mother's flour over the new head boy. Goaded on by Bingo, Trumper pulled out his phone so that he could take a look for himself. And after laughing out loud each of the three times he viewed the hilarious episode, the older boy agreed that Bertie Bovington and Flitcher Jenkins had without question outdone themselves.

"Hey, Bingo," called Bertie, as he and Flitcher walked into the playground with broad smiles on their faces that looked like they had just won the first prize in one of Roly Poly's science quizzes. "It looks like my sister and Bentley DuPont are now an absolute laughing stock. I'm just not sure how I am going to better this, but you know me, I'll definitely give it a try."

"Hasn't Bunty worked it out yet, that it was you who set the whole thing up?" yelped Bingo, while slapping Bertie on the back. "I was half expecting you would come to school all black and blue."

"No, why would she?" shot back Bertie, thinking he had been especially careful not to leave any evidence of his involvement. "Bingo, you forget that when it comes to these sorts of things, I happen to be exceptionally gifted."

"But it's only you that gets up to this kind of stuff. And Bunty is your favourite target," laughed Bingo, who was now looking at a somewhat concerned Bertie Bovington. "If I were you, I'd stay well away from your sister for the foreseeable future, at least until you are old enough to leave home. That goes for you too, Flitcher."

"It wasn't my idea, so she shouldn't blame me," whimpered Flitcher, as he looked around to ensure Bertie's older sister was not lurking close by. "Anyhow, Bingo, we heard that you and Trumper were mooned last night."

"Flitcher, who told you that?" demanded Trumper, who knew that he and Bingo had not spoken to anyone about the shocking scene they both witnessed on their way home from Wyvern Manor. And the only other person there was Barry Beasley.

"We bumped into Chugher Harris and Chomper Baverstock Junior on our way to school this morning. And they said the mooners had given you a full moon," explained Flitcher, who was giggling as he spoke. "But the two of them were laughing so much that Bertie and I were not entirely sure it was the truth."

"I'm afraid it's true. Last night we were returning from Wyvern Manor when the mooners struck again. Barry Beasley was driving, and by the time he stopped the car, they had escaped into the grounds of the Hogswood Piggery. Barry thought it was too dark for us to go chasing after them, but I'm sure that I could have caught at least one mooner," confirmed Bingo, rather immodestly.

"You went to Wyvern Manor again! What were you doing there this time?" questioned Flitcher, while keeping a watchful eye out for Bunty Bovington.

"Flitcher, we were on MAOS business. So if Trumper or I were to tell you then we would need to cut out your tongue before you could blab to anyone else," grinned Bingo, quite naughtily as he winked at Trumper and Bertie. "Let's talk later because it's time for Dr Wimbish's assembly and if we don't get a move on we'll all be late."

Even though the others knew that Bingo was only joking, Flitcher, alas, did not. So he walked to the morning assembly thinking that not only did he have Bunty Bovington to fear, but also if he was not careful, then there was a very real possibility he might lose his tongue.

As Trumper ambled along the school corridor with the other three boys, his thoughts were on Chugher Harris and Chomper Baverstock Junior. In particular, how they had known of the mooning that took place only the night before. And that was not all, it had not gone unnoticed by the older boy that every time there had been a mooning in the village, Boosey Dooley's best customer was nowhere to be seen. Could this mean that Angus Hogswood, Typsy Braithwaite and Chomper Baverstock Senior were the three mooners? That would surely explain the mooning which took place outside the Hogswood Piggery and also the ease of the mooners escape.

If this was true, then Chomper Junior may well have learnt of the latest mooning from his reckless father, and he, in turn, would have told Chugher. Angus Hogswood and his two friends certainly had the means, and without question, they had the opportunity. However, did they have a motive to start mooning again after a break of twenty-five years? Trumper would have continued analysing the facts and coming up with possible answers all morning if it had not been for the unexpectedly stern words coming out of the mouth of Dr Wimbish, who by now was standing behind the lectern on the school stage.

"Mooners!" he proclaimed, looking even more serious than usual.

But before Dr Wimbish had a chance to utter another word, Mad Maddox stood up and turned his back towards the stage. Then he bent over and pulled down his trousers to moon the whole faculty of Dragonbutt Primary School. As a roar of laughter went up from all his fellow students, he was dragged out of the assembly by Puffer Hendrick and Austin Catliter. Though not before strenuously protesting that he was doing no more than his headteacher had asked.

Just like all the teaching staff, Dr Wimbish was all too familiar with the escapades of Mad Maddox. So once the commotion had died down, he returned to his morning speech. "Mooners are an intolerable menace to society, and I would like to remind all of you that mooning is strictly prohibited at Dragonbutt Primary School. If I find out that any of our students are involved in this type of scandalous behaviour, then they will be in a whole heap of trouble. Which I may add, Maddox Butterworth is about to experience."

Mutterings could be heard from all parts of the hall asserting Mad Maddox excelled at this sort of thing. Although nearly all the students and at least half of the faculty thought his antics this time had been irrefutably funny. Thinking Dr Wimbish had finished, everyone began to file out of the hall to attend their first class of the day. That is until they heard a loud slap from the palm of his hand on the wooden lectern which stopped them dead in their tracks.

"Before anyone leaves, I would like to bring up a second yet equally outrageous matter that has been brought to my attention. And that is the video of the assault on our new head boy by the current head girl," disclosed Dr Wimbish, who took his time to peer at the faces of every boy and girl standing before him. "Therefore, I would like to see Bentley DuPont and Bunty Bovington in my office immediately after this assembly. Also, I expect whoever is responsible for recording this video to step forward and identify yourself right now."

While checking out the usual suspects, Dr Wimbish could see that Flitcher Jenkins had turned quite pale and Bertie Bovington displayed what appeared to be an overconfident and rather smug grin. Unbeknown to Bingo's friends, it was not only their headteacher that had taken an unhealthy interest in them at that particular moment. Unfortunately, silently moving from the rear of the hall, someone they had been avoiding was now standing directly behind the two guilty boys.

"It was Bertie Bovington and Flitcher Jenkins," yelled Bunty Bovington, as she grabbed hold of both boys by the scruff of their necks and pushed them to the front of the stage with all the force she could muster. "Dr Wimbish, they set the whole thing up. So if I were you, I'd give them at least ten lashes of the birch."

"Well, thankfully, you are not me, Bunty. And for your information, the birch was banned long before you were even born," replied Dr Wimbish, who was not surprised in the least that Bertie Bovington and Flitcher Jenkins were now standing before him. Though he did feel a little sorry for Bertie as he had no choice but to live with such an overbearing sister. "All of you are to go straight to my office, and Bunty, you still have a lot of explaining to do as to why you attacked the head boy."

What with all the classes they had to attend and the homework many of their teachers liked to assign, Trumper and Bingo had to wait until school was over on Thursday before they could visit Old Mrs Dingle and Baxter again. Not unexpectedly, during this time, the mooners had struck once again. And just like every other mooning in the village, they managed to conceal their identity and carry out a successful escape.

The now ever so common occurrence had taken place on Tuesday evening. After winning another quiz night at the Dragonbutt Arms and celebrating Rector Philipa Dibble's promotion to the much-envied position of Vicar of Fangorn, two of the Dragonbutt Clerics unlucky team members were mooned. Bishop Crankle, who was visiting from his diocese in Chelmsford, and the Reverend Pinkerton were walking back to Dragonbutt Vicarage along Pigswill Alley when the shocking incident occurred. It had been too much for the Reverend, who was still feeling somewhat fragile after being attacked by the little vampire only the previous month, so he simply passed out. This left the fearless Bishop to pull up his cassock and chase after the three mooners until he finally lost sight of them amongst the willow trees that bordered the dark alley.

By the time the boys reached Old Mrs Dingle's house, the sun was already setting, and Baxter had just finished off a bowl of blend number thirteen in the kitchen. Although she suspected that Barry Beasley had been the other uninvited guest at Wyvern Manor, the old lady was a little curious as to how the three of them had escaped. After Trumper disclosed the whereabouts of the not-so-secret entrance and then recounted their run-in with the mooners at the Hogswood Piggery, she just shook her head. And then with a smile on her face, she offered them a plate of freshly baked scones and a mug of hot chocolate, which they happily accepted.

Due to Old Mrs Dingle's disposition to gossip and contrary to her DWI oath, she told Trumper and Bingo that towards the end of the gathering, just after the boys had run off with Barry, the Grand Witch and her apprentice had discovered something rather interesting. According to the old lady, it was one of those eureka type moments when the young apprentice abruptly jumped up from her chair and shouted, "I've found it!" And then she closed the book on witchcraft and spells they had been reading and hurriedly ran back to the house.

"What was it?" pleaded Bingo, as he bit into his third scone, and clumsily dropped raspberry jam and cream onto his crumpled school uniform. "I bet that it was something to do with monsters."

"No, Bingo, I'm afraid it wasn't," confessed the old lady, while shaking her head at the young boy's preoccupation with monsters. "Apparently, she found a spell in the last book on witchcraft and spells, a very dark and complicated one I may add, that could bring Eradorn Wyvern's spirit back from the past. This type of spell can only be cast by a true Wyvern, and naturally, a suitable host would have to be found. That's not the kind of magic I like to practise, and with the exception of the Grand Witch and her apprentice, the same goes for the rest of our covern."

"But why would they want to bring Eradorn Wyvern's spirit back?" asked Bingo, a little naively. "Aren't their enough witches in Dragonbutt already?"

"Boys, only a dark witch born to the House of Wyvern, can cast the really big spells. All of us other witches in the DWI can only pull off the little ones, and that's at a push on our good days," informed Old Mrs Dingle, who was just finishing the last of her hot chocolate. "Eradorn Wyvern was the most powerful witch that Dragonbutt has ever known, and she was the one who wrote the books on witchcraft and spells that have enabled us to become real witches in the present day. Though I don't agree with it myself, the Grand Witch believes that if Eradorn's spirit could be brought back from the past, then the sky really is the limit for the Dragonbutt Witch's Institute."

"Dragonsbutts!" shrieked Trumper, as he dropped his half-eaten scone onto the kitchen table. "If Elvira Wyvern is planning to bring back Eradorn Wyvern's spirit, then I'm willing to bet that she is going to be the host. And that will give her all the powers the first Grand Witch had at her disposal during the dark days. Old Mrs Dingle, when does she intend to cast this spell?"

"As a matter of fact, her apprentice is making all the arrangements to cast the spell during our next DWI gathering on Sunday," affirmed the old lady, with a nod of her head. "It takes quite a bit of preparation to cast a formidable dark spell such as this. Nonetheless, the Grand Witch is quietly confident it can be pulled off."

"Thanks, Old Mrs Dingle. Come along, Bingo, we have some work to do at MAOS headquarters," instructed Trumper, who had leapt to his feet and was ready to leave. "And I mean right now!"

Though Bingo would have been happier if Trumper had allowed him to consume the partially eaten scone that was lying on the kitchen table, grudgingly, he agreed to leave at once and followed the older boy to the front door. After pulling on their outdoor clothes and slipping into their wellingtons, they shouted goodbye to Old Mrs Dingle and Baxter before running back to the little old house. And then not stopping to inform Aunty J of their return, the boys ran down the long garden path to MAOS headquarters.

"Bingo, it's absolutely imperative we stop the Grand Witch before she can cast her dark spell. So that means prior to the next gathering of witches we have to return to Wyvern Manor," declared Trumper, as he began to browse through the Entwhistle journals before choosing to read one of them in more detail. In the meantime, the younger boy spent the next hour fervently sharpening Little MO.

After school had ended on Friday, the boys walked the short distance to the office of the Dragonbutt Smoker, located on Upper Dragonbutt High Street, just a short distance from Dragonbutt Primary School. This was because the night before, their uncle had promised that he would take Trumper and Bingo to Free Pie Friday at the Dragonbutt Arms. And though this pleased Bingo immensely, he had to be assured by Uncle P that a pie was only a snack and his regular dinner would follow at the usual time.

Upon entering the office, their uncle was seen frantically dealing with a multitude of printing issues, which was not an uncommon occurrence at the Dragonbutt Smoker on a Friday afternoon. Regrettably, he literally had to remedy these over the next few hours to ensure the latest edition of the local newspaper was printed and ready for distribution the following day. As Barry Beasley was just about to knock off for the day, he offered to take the boys to the Dragonbutt Arms for their free pie. To which Uncle P wholeheartedly agreed, much to the relief of Trumper and Bingo.

Within a matter of minutes, Barry and the boys were sitting at a table by the bar in the warm and always welcoming Dragonbutt Arms. Boosey Dooley was nowhere to be seen but could be heard arguing with his wife in the kitchen, and by the sound of it, he was on the losing side as usual. It was not long before he finally appeared, red-faced and muttering something that without question would not be deemed repeatable by all but a handful of the ordinarily polite residents of Dragonbutt.

"Well that told her," uttered Boosey, using an unusually subdued tone of voice as he walked over to their table. "You know, sometimes you have to be firm with these kitchen staff to keep them in order. Now gentlemen, what can I get for you?"

"From where we're sitting it sounded like Flanna was keeping you in order," laughed Barry, and Trumper and Bingo joined in too. "I'll have a pint of Dragonstone Fire, and I believe my comrades in arms would appreciate two bottles of Braithwaite's if you please. Oh yes, and can we take a peek at your pie menu when it's convenient."

The pie menu was actually a long blackboard that hung behind the bar on which Boosey Dooley had chalked the names of a dozen sumptuous pies. Consequently, choosing which pie to eat was a tricky decision for the three hungry souls sitting around the table. Being rather conservative in his culinary tastes, Barry chose the steak and kidney pie made with a rich and tangy Butts Batch gravy. On the other hand, Trumper was in the mood for something spicy and a little more exotic, so he went with the curried goat. While Bingo, as to be expected, stuck with his favourite, the wild pigeon and creamy acorn pie.

Because free pies were only given to those customers who bought at least two drinks, the landlord brought Barry another pint of Dragonstone Fire and two more bottles of Braithwaite's for the boys. As he still could not stomach drinking even a drop of Braithwaite's, Trumper asked for a glass of water with three cubes of ice. So once the pies arrived, Bingo had to drink all four bottles of Braithwaite's by himself.

"Barry, is there anything in the next edition of the Dragonbutt Smoker about our visit to Wyvern Manor?" inquired Trumper, while tucking into his pie. "Uncle P and Aunty J have no idea that Bingo and I were at the DWI gathering, and we would prefer to keep it that way, at least for now."

"Don't worry boys, I haven't told anyone about our scrape with the Dragonbutt Witch's Institute and the mooning we witnessed afterwards. This week's front-page story, if your uncle can manage to get the Smoker printed on-time, is about the mooning of Bishop Crankle and the Reverend Pinkerton on Pigswill Alley," promised Barry, who was sifting through his pie to locate the kidney, which he always liked to save until the very end. "You know that we discovered very little at Wyvern Manor, so I decided it wasn't worth mentioning."

"Yesterday, Old Mrs Dingle told us about an alarming development which is going to need our urgent attention," revealed Trumper, and then he went on to explain how the Grand Witch intended to bring Eradorn Wyvern's spirit back from the past. "And so Bingo and I have to return to Wyvern Manor before the next gathering of witches this coming Sunday."

"Interesting, Trumper, and newsworthy as well," agreed Barry, as he finished his first pint of Dragonstone Fire and then started on the second. "However, you said that this spell can only be cast by a dark witch and not only that, she has to be a true Wyvern as well. Elvira Wyvern may be a witch, but I doubt very much she is a dark witch.

And that's because the Grand Witch of the DWI is not a true Wyvern."

"Barry, what do you mean?" chimed in Bingo, who had been busy eating his pie up until that moment and could not quite believe he had heard the young reporter correctly.

"Remember what I told you last Sunday when we were at Wyvern Manor, that Elvira Wyvern is Meow's double aunty. Her husband may have been a Wyvern, but her brother was an Ogglejay, and that means she's really an Ogglejay by birth. The Grand Witch is certainly cantankerous and extremely snobbish, nevertheless, she is no more a dark witch than Old Mrs Dingle," explained Barry, as he finished the last of his pie. "There is only one true Wyvern living in Dragonbutt these days, and that happens to be Morweena Eradorn Ogglejay-Wyvern. So she has to be your dark witch."

"I don't believe it. Any witch that can fry fish and chips like Meow has to be a good witch," argued Bingo, forgetting it was really Mumford who did all the frying.

Before Trumper had time to utter the word Dragonsbutts!, the front door of the Dragonbutt Arms flew open and in walked Angus Hogswood. And without pausing, he marched over to his usual place by the bar and bellowed, "A pint of Dragonstone Fire, please landlord."

Once Angus had downed his first pint of the day, he remarked, "Boys, it's been nearly a week since the three of us had lunch together at the piggery. I've been meaning to tell you that I popped into Oh My Cod! the other day to take a peek at that Mumford. You know he does look just like the old fellow who used to live at Wyvern Manor. Although the funny thing is that he really hasn't aged a day since chasing after me and my compatriots all those years ago."

While Angus took a quaff from his second pint of Dragonstone Fire that Boosey Dooley had just pulled for him, the front door of the Dragonbutt Arms opened once again. This time it was not one of the landlord's regulars, who stood before them, instead, it was Detective

Huntress of Dragonbutt police. Without uttering a word, the detective unhurriedly raised one arm and then let off an air horn that she was holding in her hand. Anyone within earshot, which included almost everyone on Dragonbutt High Street, jumped up in surprise. All that is, except Angus Hogswood who was standing motionless at the bar with his pint glass in one hand.

"Detective Huntress, I thought for a heartbeat you were one of those mooners," thundered the voice of Boosey Dooley, as he pulled himself a pint of Dragonstone Fire to calm his nerves. "Now, what can I get for you, will it be a pint of Butts Batch or Dragonstone Fire? And don't forget that if you buy at least two drinks, you get a free pie today."

"No, thank you, Boosey, I'm here on official Dragonbutt police business," answered the detective, who had a stern look on her face as she made eye contact with Angus Hogswood. "I have some questions for Angus regarding the mooning that took place outside of the Hogswood Piggery last Sunday."

The boys were not surprised in the least that Detective Huntress had learnt of the mooning they had tried in vain to keep secret. Regrettably, after Chugher Harris and Chomper Baverstock Junior had told Bertie Bovington and Flitcher Jenkins, it was only a matter of time before word spread around the village. As the cat was now out of the bag, Trumper knew that it was no good crying over spilt milk, so he listened intently to what she had to say.

"Angus, where were you last Sunday evening between the hours of six and seven?" inquired Detective Huntress, while looking directly at the big man with her inquisitive dark brown eyes. "And if you would be so kind, who were you with?"

"Now let me think for a minute, detective. Oh yes, I was at the Dragonbutt Arms for a liquid lunch, and I did not return to the piggery until four in the afternoon," disclosed Angus, who was still firmly holding onto his pint. "And I can assure you that I was there for the rest of the afternoon and evening. You can ask Typsy Braithwaite and Chomper Baverstock Senior. They were with me from around five until we had just about polished off a barrel of Typsy's Butts Batch, which wasn't until after ten as I recall."

"I have already spoken to both of them, and indeed, they confirmed that the three of you were at the Hogswood Piggery from around five until late in the evening. So that means three infamous mooners were in the immediate vicinity of a mooning. And that's not all, none of you has a convincing alibi as to your whereabouts during each of the other incidents," replied the detective, as she placed the air horn on the bar next to Angus. "Does this look familiar to you by any chance?"

"As a matter of fact it does, I have some air horns just like that one at the piggery. Back when I was mooning, I bought a bunch of them on the cheap, but that was when I thought we would be at it for years. Once it all came to an end, thanks to an overzealous Dragonbutt police detective, I came up with the idea of replacing the old butt sticks with air horns. They were perfect for shooing the Hogswood pigs along Pigswill Alley, and we've been using them at the piggery ever since," admitted Angus, who had now finished his second pint of Dragonstone Fire and was eying Boosey Dooley's pie menu.

"Then presumedly it won't come as a revelation to you that this air horn was found in the possession of Chomper Baverstock Senior," asserted Detective Huntress, thinking Angus was being strangely forthcoming for a person suspected of being one of the three notorious mooners.

"Not at all, Chomper Senior always keeps a couple of air horns handy for the days when he joins me in shooing the pigs," disclosed Angus, who was now signalling to the landlord that he was ready to make his pie selection.

"Well I find this all rather unconvincing, so I will need you to accompany me to Dragonbutt Police Station. And there you will be joining your accomplices, Typsy Braithwaite and Chomper Baverstock Senior," stated the detective, using her official police business tone of voice. This left little room for doubt in the boys' minds that Detective Huntress was not asking Angus Hogswood, but telling him.

"But what about my free pie?" protested Angus, while remembering the time twenty-five years ago when the same thing happened. Although in those days, he was young enough to get off with a warning.

"There's no need to worry about your pie, Angus. I'll tell Flanna it's going to be a takeaway, and I will have it delivered to Dragonbutt Police Station within the hour," reassured Boosey Dooley, who was not at all happy to be losing his best customer on a busy Friday night. "I assume it's going to be your usual, the freshly caught rabbit?"

The landlord was right because Angus Hogswood did choose the rabbit pie, which happened to be his favourite and also Flanna Dooley's most popular pièce de résistance. And as always it contained rabbit from Baverstock's the Butcher's and a rich sauce made with Dragonstone Fire and a large spoonful of Oh My God! chilli sauce. Before leaving, the big man accepted a dram of Dragonsbreath and then after saying farewell to his friends, the detective led him out of his home away from home, the Dragonbutt Arms.

"I don't believe a word of it," bellowed Boosey Dooley, as he helped himself to another pint of Dragonstone Fire. "If Dragonbutt police find an iota of real evidence that Angus has been mooning again, then I will take the pledge and become a teetotaler."

Trumper just smiled as he was quite sure it would never come to that. Even though Boosey Dooley could undoubtedly have benefitted from a bit of teetotaling, the older boy was now convinced of Angus's innocence. When Detective Huntress had sounded the air horn on entering the Dragonbutt Arms, he knew it was identical to the one the mooners had used at the Hogswood Piggery. And when the detective placed Chomper Baverstock Senior's air horn on the bar, he finally recalled who had been holding one just like it, and that person was definitely not Angus, or for that matter either of his friends.

Knowing that the only way to clear the good names of Angus Hogswood, Typsy Braithwaite and Chomper Baverstock Senior was to catch the real mooners in the act, Trumper was all too aware he would need to come up with a carefully crafted plan. This, of course, was going to have to wait as the boys' most pressing matter was to prevent the Grand Witch's apprentice bringing Eradorn Wyvern's spirit back from the past. Fortunately, Trumper already knew how this could be done, but it meant that when he and Bingo returned to Wyvern Manor, somehow they had to gain access to the house.

Once they had eaten the last of their pies, and Bingo had hurriedly finished his fourth bottle of Braithwaite's, it was already a quarter past five and therefore time to head home. After thanking Barry, the two boys said goodbye to the young reporter and Boosey Dooley before picking up their school backpacks and then leaving by the front door. By now it was quite dark so without delay they briskly walked down Dragonbutt High Street and then turned into Bristletooth Lane. It was at that moment Trumper noticed Bingo was unusually quiet and walking somewhat oddly, and then just as if he wanted to have a race, the younger boy unexpectedly upped his pace.

"Hey, Bingo, slow down," shouted Trumper, who after eating one of Flanna Dooley's filling pies was not in the mood to run all the way to Counting House Lane.

"I'm bursting for a pee," yelled back Bingo, as he entered Pigswill Alley through the gap between the two old willow trees.

"Dragonsbutts! How come you didn't go before we left the Dragonbutt Arms?" beseeched Trumper, who really should not have been surprised considering the younger boy had drunk four bottles of Braithwaite's in less than an hour. "Why don't you find a discrete place by one of the willow trees and I'll shine my torch so that you can see where you're going."

"Will do, Trumper, but I didn't want to go earlier. You know how it is, it just creeps up on you," hollered Bingo, as he stood with his back to the older boy a good twenty yards further up Pigswill Alley.

It was at that point Trumper detected a noise some distance away, and as it grew louder, he could tell it was coming from the direction of Dragonbutt Vicarage. Turning around, he saw a light which was getting brighter by the second, and then he heard the sound of someone's heavy breathing. Shining his torch at the bright light, all the older boy could make out was a shiny new bicycle painted in Royal Mail red bearing down on him. And then just before it was about to hit him, he jumped out of the path of the reckless rider to avoid being run over.

"Bingo, you'll have to pee higher than that if you ever want to become head boy," howled Mad Maddox, after leaving an angry Trumper in his wake and then tearing past the startled younger boy before continuing up Pigswill Alley on his sister's bicycle.

Alas for Mad Maddox, he did not get far before something quite hideous leapt from a willow tree branch and knocked him off the bicycle with a resounding crash. In the darkness, the attacker stood over the unconscious boy, seemingly unaware that two other boys were close by. Then Trumper shone his torch to reveal a monster that liked to eat naughty children, especially mischievous young boys. This was the monster whose body looked quite like a bear, yet was smaller and had short spindly legs and a face that resembled a rather ugly goblin with a long pointy nose.

"Bugaboo!" screamed Bingo, which was without a shadow of a doubt an unwise thing to do because the monster took one look at the defenceless young boy before licking its lips and running towards him.

As he had no weapon to defend himself, Bingo believed he was surely a goner that day. Then quite unexpectedly, Baxter sprang out of the darkness and positioned himself right in the path of the charging bugaboo. Uncharacteristically snarling, astonishingly, the monster was stopped dead in its tracks before hastily retreating to the spot where Mad Maddox was lying. After tossing the Butterworth boy over its bearlike shoulders, the Bugaboo then sped off on its short spindly legs back the way it had come.

"Thanks, Baxter," rejoiced Bingo, as he gave the funny-looking dog a pat on the head. "That was a close one."

After Trumper had reached the place where Bingo and Baxter were standing, he shone his torch along Pigswill Alley to ensure the bugaboo was no longer around. Thankfully, there was no sign of the frightful monster, but as he suspected, Mad Maddox was nowhere to be seen as well. The only things that remained from the attack were Mad Tolly Butterworth's now scratched and muddied bicycle and her old faded red Royal Mail postal bag.

Watching Baxter sniff the bag, which was still sitting in the basket of the bicycle, Bingo realised he could smell something all too familiar. On closer inspection, the young boy was delighted to discover that when Mad Maddox was attacked, he had been riding home with four portions of freshly fried fish and chips from Oh My Cod!.

"Dragonsbutts! What a find. Trumper, we're going to be feasting on fish and chips tonight," beamed Bingo, who after seeing the contents of the Royal Mail bag, in his excitement, had all but forgotten about Mad Maddox and the bugaboo attack.

"Bingo, Mad Maddox has been kidnapped by a bugaboo, so this is not the time to be thinking of your tummy. If we are going to save him then we have to head up to Wyvern Manor this very evening," snapped Trumper, knowing the monster would almost certainly have taken the Butterworth boy to its enclosure in the cryptid menagerie. "But before we go, we'll need your weapons, and we are going to have to enlist the help of Old Mrs Dingle too."

Thirteen

Return to Wyvern Manor

***

While Trumper pushed Mad Tolly Butterworth's bicycle down the narrow path that led to Dragonbutt pond, Bingo held on to the prized bag full of fish and chips he so much wanted to eat. However, before the boys had gotten barely halfway down the dark path, they saw Old Mrs Dingle coming towards them. She too was holding a torch in her hand and was frantically calling out to Baxter, who eagerly scampered over to the old lady on hearing his name.

Once the two boys had reached the spot where Old Mrs Dingle was hugging her beloved dog, Bingo launched into his version of the story about how Mad Maddox had been attacked and carried off by the bugaboo. And although he included the bit where Baxter had intervened and scared off the terrible monster, the young boy stressed that it was really a godsend for the bugaboo. Because, Bingo explained, if Baxter had arrived only a second or two later, he would have been forced into kicking some monster butt.

Old Mrs Dingle listened intently to the young boy while periodically nodding her head and then told Trumper and Bingo that it was fortuitous she and Baxter happened to be close by. The old lady disclosed that after Baxter had finished his daily bowl of blend number thirteen, she had taken him out for a brisk walk. But as soon as they had reached Dragonbutt pond and she had let him off his lead, without warning the funny-looking dog bolted towards Pigswill Alley. Fearing he had reverted back to his wicked little vampire ways, the old lady followed Baxter, and to her relief, it wasn't long before she found him in the company of the boys.

"There was no need to fret, Old Mrs Dingle. Baxter never turned into a vampire, but he did save Bingo from the bugaboo and probably me too," confirmed Trumper, whose recollection of the incident was somewhat different than the younger boy's. "Interestingly, he didn't seem to fear the monster at all, though the bugaboo appeared to be scared of Baxter. Maybe it has something to do with the vampire spirit that still lives inside him."

"Dragonsbutts! Of course, it does, and don't forget that Baxter was no ordinary vampire; he was a butt biting little vampire. So I think the bugaboo was afraid of having its butt bitten and that's why it beat a hasty retreat," added Bingo, who couldn't resist the smell of fried food any longer and was now munching on a handful of chips.

Trumper just frowned at Bingo and then went on to tell the old lady that bugaboos never eat their prey straight away. Instead, they prefer to devour them in the comfort of their lair, which is why the monster had kidnapped Mad Maddox and was at that very moment on its way back to Wyvern Manor. And if they were going to stop the Butterworth boy becoming the bugaboo's next dinner, the boys would need Old Mrs Dingle to take them there.

Fortunately for Mad Maddox, the old lady agreed, and so all four of them hurried themselves along to Counting House Lane. As they walked, Old Mrs Dingle informed the boys their aunty had called to say she was working late that evening, and so both she and their uncle would not arrive home before nine. With this stroke of luck, Trumper knew they would be able to go to Wyvern Manor unhindered and hopefully be home before their foster parents were any the wiser.

Upon their arrival, the boys told Old Mrs Dingle they would return in ten minutes, and then the two of them headed over to the little old house. Meanwhile, the old lady and Baxter entered their home to ready Old Mr Dingle's motorcycle and sidecar for the short but potentially perilous journey ahead. While Trumper propped the bicycle up against the wall at the back of the house, Bingo ran down the long garden path to MAOS headquarters, and then seconds later, the older boy followed.

By the time Trumper had caught up with Bingo, he had already unlocked the padlock using the key that hung from a chain around his neck and was now opening the door. Knowing that time was not on their side, the younger boy quickly switched on the light and then pulled open the large chest of drawers that held his weapons. Not surprisingly, it was the deadly Monster Obliterator he grabbed first, followed by the not so lethal punisher.

"I'll take the punisher, and you can have Little MO," barked Trumper, who also knew time was most definitely of the essence. And this meant they could not afford to stand around arguing over Bingo's weapons. "Leave your backpack and the Royal Mail bag here, and let's be on our way."

Even though the Monster Obliterator was designed for two hands, Bingo had intended to use both weapons himself; the punisher to zap any monster he came across, and Little MO to finish them off. After reluctantly handing the punisher to Trumper, he plonked his Dr Who backpack onto the brown leather sofa and then before the older boy could object, he opened the door and darted out of MAOS headquarters. Clutching his two-headed battleaxe in both hands and the bag containing the four portions of fish and chips swinging from one shoulder, Bingo ran up the long garden path and did not stop until he reached Old Mrs Dingle's house.

A few minutes later, Trumper found him sitting in the sidecar gleefully devouring one of the portions of fish and chips. And perched on the motorcycle was Old Mrs Dingle dressed in her witch's hat and robe, and just like the younger boy, she was tucking into fish and chips as well. The only one who did not appear to have his own portion of fish and chips was Baxter. Despite this oversight on Bingo's part, he sat behind the handlebars of the motorcycle wolfing down a handful of chips the old lady had given him.

"Here you go, Trumper, I saved these for you," giggled Bingo, as he handed the older boy a portion of fish and chips. Bingo kept the remaining portion for himself as wielding Little MO always used up an awful lot of energy. Therefore it was only fair he got to eat two portions of fish and chips to everyone else's one. "I thought that we should have our dinner on the go because if we don't, we'll only get hungry later. Besides, who knows how long it will take for us to rescue Mad Maddox, and that, of course, is assuming the bugaboo hasn't already eaten him."

"Alright, Bingo," nodded Trumper, who concluded the younger boy was probably right after all. So without squabbling, he accepted the fish and chips and climbed into the sidecar behind Bingo. "Old Mrs Dingle, I thought you only wore your witch's hat and robe at DWI gatherings?"

"That's perfectly true, but it's not every day I get to battle monsters. And so I wanted to make a bit of an effort and dress up a little," beamed Old Mrs Dingle, as she ate the last of her chips and gave the remaining piece of fish to Baxter. "Now, boys, pull on your helmets and fasten your goggles and then we'll be on our way."

Just like the first time that Trumper and Bingo had ridden with Old

Mrs Dingle, she started the motorcycle's engine with a couple of good kicks on the starter lever and then off they went. With a loud roar from its engine, the motorcycle and sidecar tore out of Counting House Lane with the boys and Baxter hanging on for dear life. However, unlike the previous Sunday when the old lady had taken them on a jaunt along Dragonbutt High Street, she made a hard right turn and sped up Hunnickle Drive.

As the two boys hastily ate their fish and chips, Old Mrs Dingle turned onto Upper Dragonbutt High Street and opened up the motorcycle's throttle to its maximum. In no time at all, they were speeding past the Hogswood Piggery and then the old lady made an almost impossible handbrake turn into Witches Brew Lane. She would have doubtlessly kept on riding this way until the four of them reached their destination if it had not been for the closed wooden gates at the entrance to Wyvern Manor. Frustratingly, this forced her to bring the motorcycle and sidecar to a screeching and tyre burning halt within inches of the impenetrable gates.

"Dragonsbutts! I forgot the gates would be closed. And Elvira never likes to open them to visitors at night," fretted Old Mrs Dingle, who had just turned off the motorcycle engine and was looking down at Trumper and Bingo. "Boys, this is the only way into Wyvern Manor, so I guess we are going to have to come back tomorrow."

"That will be too late. Just as sure as my name is Trumper Gallant, the bugaboo will have eaten Mad Maddox by then," insisted Trumper, as he climbed out of the sidecar and took off his helmet and goggles. "Old Mrs Dingle, you're forgetting what I told you earlier. There is another entrance to Wyvern Manor, so you wait here, and Bingo and I will have the gates open in five minutes."

Holding his torch in one hand and the punisher in the other, Trumper took the lead, and Bingo followed with Little MO and what was left of his second portion of fish and chips stuffed into his coat pocket.

Knowing that the bugaboo must have used the not-so-secret entrance to escape and would undoubtedly return the same way, the older boy shone his torch into the passageway before cautiously entering.

With no bugaboo in sight, the two boys warily advanced and soon after they emerged on the other side of the wall. After vigilantly checking for the monster in either direction and confirming it was nowhere to be seen, they ran to the main entrance. It took another minute or two of searching before Trumper found the switch to open the wooden gates so that Old Mrs Dingle and Baxter could ride in. And this allowed Bingo just enough time to finish the rest of his fish and chips.

While the old lady revved the powerful engine of the motorcycle once again, Trumper and Bingo hopped back into the sidecar. Then without giving the boys enough time to pull on their helmets and goggles, Old Mrs Dingle set off at a heart-pounding rate of speed. Oblivious to what may lie ahead; she tore down the gravel path in her husband's pride and joy with only a solitary headlight to illuminate their way.

"Black cat!" screamed Trumper, who had caught sight of its green eyes glinting off the motorcycle headlight beam directly in front of them.

"What did you say, dear?" called out Old Mrs Dingle, whose hearing was no better than her sadly deteriorating eyesight as she rode over the evil black cat that Bingo had zapped with the punisher on two previous occasions.

"It's a dead black cat now," declared Bingo, who had to shout rather loudly to make himself heard over the roar of the motorcycle's engine.

Without slowing down to recover the deceased and now very flat black cat, Old Mrs Dingle continued along the gravel path and around to the back of the house before coming to an abrupt stop beside the menagerie. As she turned the motorcycle's engine off, the boys and Baxter were relieved they had finally arrived but were somewhat surprised the four of them had made it there in one piece. And then knowing they had no time to idle around, Trumper and Bingo ran over to the blue door that as far as they were aware was the only way in and out.

"Oh dear, it seems to be locked," exclaimed Old Mrs Dingle, while shaking her head as she and Baxter joined the boys. "How on earth are we going to get in?"

"That's not going to be a problem. Stand back, everyone," ordered Bingo, as he lifted Little MO above his head and brought it down on the lock of the blue door with all the strength he could summon.

With a tumultuous sound of shattering metal and splintering willow, the wooden door immediately flew open and into the dark weapons room the four of them strode. Then Trumper shone his torch to allow Bingo to light the gas lantern that was hanging by the now broken blue door.

"Should we help ourselves to some more weapons while we're here?" asked Bingo, who at that moment was tugging on one of the metal chains which had a large iron ball at one end. Although after finding it a little too heavy, even for him, he moved on to the oversized boomerangs. "You never know, they may come in handy."

"I don't think so, Bingo; we have all the weapons we require. What's more, you need two hands to swing Little MO, and I have a torch and the punisher, so both of us have our hands full," replied Trumper, as he walked over to the bright red door on the far side of the weapons room and proceeded to slide its large iron bolt to one side.

"Wait!" yelled Bingo, while rushing to the door with Little MO elevated to the height of his broad shoulders. "We don't know what's on the other side; maybe the bugaboo is there and is waiting to pounce on whoever steps out first."

"Good point, Bingo," acknowledged Trumper, thinking it was definitely better to be safe than sorry when hunting dangerous monsters. "Do you still have your fish and chip wrapper with you?"

Luckily the greasy and noticeably smelly fish and chip wrapper was still in the younger boy's coat pocket, and so without delay, he handed it to Trumper. With Bingo standing beside him and Old Mrs Dingle and Baxter to their rear, the older boy slowly opened the door and shone his torch to see if there was anything unpleasant waiting for them on the other side. After beholding absolutely nothing, he threw the fish and chip wrapper on the ground about six feet in front of him. Then hearing a flutter followed by a squawk, something ran towards them. At which point the startled boys fell backwards just as the old lady stepped forward and holding Emilia Baggot's stun gun in her left hand, she zapped the ill-fated creature leaving it out for the count on the ground.

Once the boys had lifted themselves up from the cold hard floor of the weapons room, they saw Old Mrs Dingle spin the stun gun on her trigger finger and then blow on it before stuffing the gun into one of her pockets. Though Trumper and Bingo could hardly believe their eyes, the two boys knew they should focus their attention on the stunned and by now stupefied creature lying on the ground. So after the older boy had brushed the dirt from his clothes, he shone his torch into the darkness.

"Good shot, Old Mrs Dingle, but it's not the bugaboo you zapped or any other kind of dangerous monster for that matter. It's just a doodo," announced Bingo, after seeing the poor creature outstretched on the ground, looking as dead as its distant cousin the dodo. "Where did you learn to shoot like that?"

"I used to be a crack shot during my younger days and was the Dragonbutt Small Arms Society women's gunslinging champion for three years in a row. My reign as champion ended quite prematurely though after Bucktooth Tom Blewitt shot Three-Toed Tylor Heckett in the foot. He wasn't called Three-Toed back then of course, but after that, all guns were banned in the village. Naturally, some of the residents were disappointed, but if you ask me it made Dragonbutt a much safer place to live," imparted Old Mrs Dingle, as she squinted her eyes to see the doodo. "You know I was going to give the stun gun back to Emilia Baggot; however, old habits die hard, and so I decided to hold on to it for a few days."

With that little mystery solved, the older boy stepped out of the weapons room and into the menagerie followed by Bingo, Old Mrs Dingle and finally Baxter. Shining his torch as they peered at the motionless doodo, the younger boy gave the creature a good firm prod with Little MO. To their anguish, the doodo squawked once more and leapt into the air before landing on Trumper's head and pulling off his DPS woolly hat. If that was not bad enough, doodos began to appear from all directions until there must have been a dozen of them. Maddeningly, they tugged at the boys clothing and even managed to topple the witch's hat from the old lady's head. Before she had a chance to draw her stun gun though, Baxter came to their rescue with a furious growl. Then to their relief, the funny-looking dog scattered the screeching doodos to all four corners of the menagerie until not one doodo was anywhere to be seen.

"Dragonsbutts! I thought that doodos were supposed to be harmless," fumed Bingo, while picking Trumper's DPS woolly hat off the ground and handing it to him.

"Compared to the monsters in the cryptid menagerie, they are," assured Trumper, who like the others was grateful the funny-looking dog was with them. "We are going to have to be careful because if the bugaboo and the doodos have managed to get out of their enclosures, then other creatures may have too."

Unwilling to take a chance with the safety of his companions, Trumper made sure the punisher was on its maximum setting before the four of them set off for the cryptid menagerie. Knowing their journey would be fraught with danger, the older boy led the way while the others remained only a few steps behind. Unfortunately though, during their tussle with the doodos, neither of the boys had remembered to do the most important thing, which was to close and bolt the bright red door.

Although the menagerie had plenty of lamp posts dotted throughout the facility, and a floodlight pointed at each of the enclosures, none of them were currently on. This was because even though Trumper had seen the master switch in the weapons room, he knew that it would take the element of surprise if they were to rescue Mad Maddox from the bugaboo. For that reason, the older boy shone his trusty torch to light their way and reminded the others not to loiter as he decisively marched onwards.

Just as they reached the main compound with its door ominously wide open, Trumper spotted a doodo in the distance and then Bingo pointed to another. Then before anyone could utter a word, Baxter raced past them like the wind and chased the doodos into the darkness. Unwilling to call out his name for fear of alerting the bugaboo, the others impatiently waited there for several minutes, but to their dismay, the funny-looking dog failed to return. As they knew Mad Maddox's situation required their immediate attention, the three of them had no choice other than to continue on their way. And so they bravely trudged on while watchfully eyeing the chillingly empty enclosures.

"Did you hear that noise?" uttered Bingo, who had turned around to listen to the sound he had just heard while firmly gripping the wooden handle of his Monster Obliterator.

"I heard something as we were leaving the weapons room. Though I thought it was just my imagination playing tricks on me," answered Trumper, as he shone his torch in the direction that Bingo was now gazing. And that's when they saw the dreadful creature which had been following them. It was the monster who had the head, claws and wings of a chicken, but the body and tail of a terribly scaly and hideous-looking lizard.

"Chizard!" shouted Bingo, on seeing the horrific monster once again.

As the chizard rushed towards them with its long forked tongue and set of razor-sharp gleaming white teeth plainly visible, Trumper gripped the punisher and Bingo readied Little MO. Meanwhile, Old Mrs Dingle drew her stun gun and waited for the monster to come within range so that she could zap the foul creature to kingdom come. Though, as luck would have it, with no more than twenty feet separating them, the crocogator emerged from the darkness to confront the charging chizard. At that point, in no more than a blink of an eye, its powerful jaws snapped up the hapless creature before devouring it whole. And then after imparting a rather loud belch, the crocogator placidly toddled off into the darkness, but not before giving Trumper and the others an ever so sly wink.

"Dragonsbutts! That was a stroke of luck for the crocogator to be passing by at that very moment," muttered Bingo, who was really a little disappointed because he had been looking forward to lopping that particular monster's head off with Little MO. "Anyhow, I guess we won't be seeing any more of the chizard again."

"That's true, Bingo. And thank goodness we now have one less monster to worry about," remarked Trumper, as the three of them lowered their weapons. "However, we can't rely on the crocogator to save us the next time we get into trouble. So both of you should keep your eyes peeled as we have to be prepared for any eventuality."

After their disquieting encounter with the chizard and its subsequent demise at the hands of the crocogator, the boys and Old Mrs Dingle cautiously continued on their way. Uneventfully, they passed by a dozen or more enclosures that looked empty and then they saw a few that contained some of the menagerie's peculiar inhabitants. As the three of them reached the end of the main compound, troublingly, they had still not seen any sign of Baxter. And while they knew a terrible danger faced them, they valiantly pushed on to the spine-chilling cryptid menagerie.

"There it is. And look, the drawbridge is down, and the door is wide open. Let's enter and see if Mad Maddox is inside, but watch out for the bugaboo and the shug monkeys," whispered Trumper, with his right index finger pressed against his mouth, signalling they all needed to be very quiet. "Weapons to the ready, both of you, and follow me."

They had not taken more than a few steps though before Trumper raised his hand in the air and the three of them came to a halt. In the distance, somewhere in the cryptid menagerie, they could hear laughing, and then a boy's voice called out, "Is that all you've got!" While this was not what any of them had expected to hear from a victim of a brutal bugaboo attack who was soon to be eaten, it was Mad Maddox. And just like the rest of the Butterworths, they all knew he was as mad as one of those hatter's that used to be commonplace in Dragonbutt so many years ago.

As Bugaboos were extraordinarily finicky went it came to their food, they always spent an hour or two terrorising their young victims to ensure they were at their most succulent before eating them. And this is why the bugaboo had brought Mad Maddox back to the cryptid menagerie instead of devouring him on Pigswill Alley like almost every other kind of monster would have done. Although infuriatingly for the bugaboo, try as it might, the Butterworth boy simply laughed at every one of the monster's vain attempts to scare him.

Unable to frighten Mad Maddox, the bugaboo worked itself up into a terrible frenzy, and after jumping up and down several times, it ran around its enclosure in an awful rage. Regrettably for Trumper and the others, this is when the monster noticed the glare of the torchlight and the moment the plan to rescue Mad Maddox, unfortunately, lost the element of surprise.

Being bestowed with exceptional eyesight, and that was especially true in the dark, the bugaboo immediately spotted the three intruders, and opportunely, two of them looked like well-fed young boys. A split second later, the monster had all but forgotten about Mad Maddox and was rushing to claim his newly arrived and much-improved dinner. At the same time, a barking dog could be heard, and then moments later, Baxter was seen emerging from the darkness and running towards the advancing bugaboo.

Upon seeing the funny-looking dog again, the bugaboo abruptly turned around and sped back to its enclosure. Undeterred, Baxter followed and relentlessly chased the monster around not just its own enclosure but the whole of the barred compound that formed the cryptid menagerie. During the furore, Trumper knew that this may be their only opportunity to rescue Mad Maddox, so he and the others ran towards the drawbridge that forded the moat.

The first to cross the drawbridge was Bingo, just as the bugaboo concluded the only way to escape from this contemptuous dog was to run as far from the cryptid menagerie as possible. And the monster's plan might just have worked, if it had not bumped into the young boy and heard the forbidding words coming out of his mouth, "Say hello to Little MO!"

Once the bugaboo had taken a good hard look at the two-headed battleaxe raised above Bingo's head, it decided goodbye was preferable to hello and foolishly took three steps backwards leaving it teetering on the edge of the moat. Then just as the young boy stepped forward to dispatch his first monster, Old Mrs Dingle arrived and as quick as a flash, the old lady drew her stun gun. Without taking the time to aim, she zapped the bugaboo right between its eyes, and after a brief but hair-raising yelp, the monster fell over the safety rail and into the flesh-eating piranha filled moat.

"Dragonsbutts! I was going to finish off the bugaboo with Little

MO," complained Bingo, while watching the piranhas eat the once formidable monster, bones and all. "What's the point in me traipsing around half the night with a deadly Monster Obliterator, if when we do come across a monster, I never get the chance to use it?"

"Oh, I'm so sorry you feel that way, dear, I was only trying to protect you," apologised Old Mrs Dingle, as she returned the stun gun to her pocket. "I have to say though, if these monsters want to mess with a witch of the DWI, then this is the sort of thing they should expect."

Trumper agreed with the old lady that she had done the right thing before all three of them entered the cryptid menagerie and guardedly sauntered over to the bugaboo enclosure. With his tail wagging, Baxter led them to a large tree that Mad Maddox had climbed to get away from the bugaboo. And then after seeing the Butterworth boy sitting high off the ground on a sturdy branch of the tree, the older boy called out to him that it was now safe to come down.

"I'm quite happy where I am," retorted Mad Maddox, who had his arms folded and was stubbornly refusing to move.

While Trumper called to him a second time, without saying a word, Bingo placed Little MO on the ground and then silently slipped his hand into Old Mrs Dingle's pocket. After pulling out the stun gun, he adjusted the power to its minimum setting and nonchalantly zapped Mad Maddox. Consequently, to the merriment of the boys, the Butterworth boy came crashing to the ground with an uncharacteristic high pitched squeal.

"If you don't behave yourself, there's plenty more where that came from," warned Bingo, as he attempted to spin the stun gun on his trigger finger, just like Old Mrs Dingle had done. However, being that it was his first try, the gun slipped from his hand and fell awkwardly to the ground.

Even though Trumper forced Bingo to return the stun gun to the old lady, after glancing at the boys' weapons, the Butterworth boy got the message loud and clear. In the torchlight, the others could now clearly see that Mad Maddox was covered in mud from head to toe, so he explained to them how he came to be so dirty. Interestingly, his story not only included being unceremoniously hauled to Wyvern Manor but also how the monster had dragged him into the cryptid menagerie through a recently dug and exceedingly muddy tunnel.

They discovered the tunnel started in the shug monkey enclosure and went right under the wall of the menagerie, which is how the bugaboo managed to get out. The fact of the matter was that shug monkeys, being only part monkey and the other part dog, were exceptionally good at digging holes. If Meow had been aware of this, then she would have instructed Mumford to place the bars of the cryptid menagerie deeper in the ground. And so because this was not the case, the shug monkeys found that if you dig a hole for long enough, and not just down but also sideways, it can become the perfect escape tunnel.

As soon as the shug monkeys had finished digging their tunnel that afternoon, a bevy of them made their escape under the wall. Meanwhile, the others had broken the chain on the door of their compound and had gone to see what mischief they could get up to in the rest of the menagerie. Disastrously for the shug monkeys though, after the largest and strongest of them had leapt over the moat and lowered the drawbridge for the others to follow, they chose to break into the main compound. Then not being the cleverest of creatures, they unwisely entered the crocogator enclosure. And as one might expect, one by one, each and every shug monkey was swiftly gobbled up by the hungry crocogator.

"Trumper, the bugaboo and the chizard have both been eaten, but where are the shug monkeys?" appealed Bingo, who was pointing to the empty shug monkey enclosure. The one that just the week before had been full of the rowdy creatures.

"We haven't seen a single shug monkey since we entered the

menagerie so they must have been eaten by some other creature, just like the chizard and the bugaboo, or used the tunnel to escape. Come on everyone, if any of the shug monkeys are now on the other side of the menagerie wall then we need to hunt them down before they can do any real harm," asserted Trumper, as he marched out of the cryptid menagerie with Old Mrs Dingle and Baxter. And they were followed by Mad Maddox and Bingo, who was spurring the Butterworth boy along with the occasional prod from Little MO.

Fourteen

Mumford to the Rescue

Though all the dangerous monsters residing in the cryptid menagerie had either been eaten or were somewhere on the other side of the wall, it did not mean their return journey was entirely uneventful. In fact, with so many strange creatures on the loose, and not all of them were by any means totally harmless, Trumper knew they were bound to bump into at least a few of them. And so for that very reason, the older boy told his companions to be on their guard as he led the way with his torch shining brightly.

As they strode back to the weapons room, Baxter happily chased off several more doodos, but even he sensibly hid with the others when they came across a war party of angry looking Cornish devils. Soon after, Trumper finally got the chance to use the punisher he was holding when two wolpertingers sprang out of the darkness and startled him. Thankfully though, after zapping each of them using the punisher's lowest setting, they ran back to their enclosure, yelping and in no mood to experience anything like that ever again.

Upon hearing the cries of the sidehill gougers, Trumper and the others entered the main compound and walked over to their enclosure. And that's when they discovered, in a desperate attempt to flee from the marauding shug monkeys, the odd-looking creatures had foolishly tried to run around their hill in an anti-clockwise direction. Needless to say, as their legs were quite a bit longer on the left side of their body than their right, they had both tumbled down the hillside onto the ground below. Being unable to stand on flat ground it took the combined strength of Trumper, Bingo and Mad Maddox to return the sidehill gougers to the hill. But of course, this time they made sure both of them were pointing in a clockwise direction.

While the three boys were helping the noticeably appreciative sidehill gougers, Old Mrs Dingle looked on. And then with her gun hand beginning to twitch, she swiftly drew her stun gun and aimed it into the darkness. Worried that it might be a stray shug monkey or some other less dangerous but still harmful creature, Trumper pointed his torch at the patch of ground the old lady was eyeballing. To his relief, it turned out to be no more than three timid and quite inoffensive Lilliputian sasquatches hiding behind a small clump of bushes.

"I'm hungry," whined Mad Maddox, as he exited the sidehill gouger enclosure with the others. "Do you know what happened to the fish and chips I was carrying? There were four portions in my bag when that monster attacked me on Pigswill Alley."

"Dragonsbutts! How would we know," smirked Bingo, because two portions of the Butterworth boy's fish and chips were now residing in his tummy. "You can have these chips that I found in my pocket. They're cold and a bit soggy, but you are welcome to them."

"I'm not eating your leftovers, and I have had enough of all this nonsense," grumbled Mad Maddox, as he defiantly stomped off in the wrong direction.

"Hey, young man. If you know what's good for you, then you'll be as silent as a lamb and stay close to us," snapped Old Mrs Dingle, who had drawn her stun gun once again and was pointing it at Mad Maddox. "It's going to be some time before we can all return to Dragonbutt. So if you don't want Trumper to zap you every step of the way, then I suggest you do as you're told. Now, anyone for a spolly?"

Because he had no desire to be zapped a second time that evening, Mad Maddox simply shrugged his shoulders and grunted before turning around to join the others. Then after the old lady had handed each of the boys a spolly and they were all sucking on the tooth unfriendly treat, yet again, the five of them were on their way.

Seeing that the bright red door of the weapons room was only a hundred feet in front of them, they upped their pace and then out of the blue, something unexpected happened. Disconcertingly, it was no longer dark as the lights on each of the lamp posts that were found throughout the menagerie had suddenly been turned on. As Trumper and the others had received quite a start, it took a few moments before those that had them could ready their weapons. But once they had, each one of them was prepared to confront whoever or whatever had switched on the lights.

They did not have to wait more than a few seconds though before a familiar figure was seen stepping through the open doorway. With her long raven coloured hair that was neatly tied back in three thick braids and her unusually large and rather cat-like looking green eyes, it would have been impossible to confuse Meow for anyone else. As she hurriedly walked towards them with an uncharacteristic scowl on her face and a punisher in one of her hands, a second person who was equally recognisable exited the weapons room only to follow her with a slow thud-thud-thud. And he was carrying what could only have been described as an extremely flat and profoundly dead black cat, which the boys surmised, meant they were in a whole heap of trouble.

Meow was definitely not a happy witch after receiving a call from her aunty regarding the menagerie and what the Grand Witch termed, 'outright pandemonium'. Knowing that the inhabitants, especially the cryptid kind, were often a little boisterous in the evening, she continued to take the orders for her exceedingly popular fish and chips. However, after a second call an hour or so later in which the line ominously went dead, she was forced to shut Oh My Cod! and return to Wyvern Manor to find out what was going on.

With Mumford by her side, Meow sped back to Wyvern Manor in her MG Roadster and then immediately upon entering the grounds, she tore down the gravel path as fast as her car would go. Before the two of them arrived at the house though, to her alarm, they came across her beloved but now very flat and quite dead black cat. While this alone would have been reason enough to lose her ordinarily amiable temper, it was seeing the smashed blue door of the weapons room that finally made her fume.

Forgetting to enter the house to check on her aunty's well-being, Meow and Mumford marched straight into the weapons room. Then seeing the bright red door was unbolted and wide open, she picked up a punisher and stepped through the doorway into the menagerie. On the other side, what she beheld was certainly a surprise; a DWI witch, three young boys and a funny-looking dog that looked very much like a sheep. Although the Grand Witch's apprentice recognised the five of them, she could not understand what Old Mrs Dingle was doing with a stun gun in her hand, why Trumper Gallant was pointing a punisher in her direction, and what on earth was Bingo Malloy up to with a deadly two-headed battleaxe. And then there was the crazy Butterworth boy who had purchased four portions of fish and chips from her only a few hours earlier. What he was doing in the menagerie was anyone's guess.

"Hello, Meow, fancy meeting you here," greeted Bingo, with a forced smile on his face that looked altogether too insincere.

"I'm here because my aunty informed me of a disturbance in the menagerie. But w-w-what are you doing here?" stammered Meow, as she folded her arms and winced at the five of them standing in front of her. "May I remind you that all guests to the menagerie must be accompanied by Mumford or a member of the W-W-Wyvern family. You are not supposed to enter w-w-without so much as a by-your-leave by smashing down the door. And not only that, you forgot to bolt the bright red door!"

The thankless task of explaining to Meow what had brought them all to Wyvern Manor was left to Trumper. He told her about how the bugaboo had escaped and attacked Mad Maddox before carrying him back to the cryptid menagerie to be eaten. This meant that he and Bingo, with the help of Old Mrs Dingle and Baxter, had to rescue him by breaking into the weapons room. At that point, Bingo interrupted to say they had encountered not just the bugaboo but the chizard as well. However, seeing Meow recoil after hearing the names of her precious creatures that had only recently been brought back from the dead, he wisely chose to omit the part of the story where they had both been eaten.

"Um, and are any of you responsible for this?" demanded Meow, as she angrily pointed to the very flat dead black cat that Mumford was holding.

"It looks like roadkill to me," shrugged Bingo, while shaking his head from side to side. Then Trumper and Old Mrs Dingle joined in, and even Baxter shook his sheep-like head too.

"His name is Trevor, and if I find the guilty person or persons, they are going to rue the day they ran over a W-W-Wyvern black cat," hissed Meow, who was looking like she was about to explode.

"Trevor!" giggled Bingo, rather unwisely. "What kind of name is that for a witch's evil black cat? It doesn't sound scary at all."

"It's the name given to him by my mother! Now, I can't hang around here any longer, so it's time for all of you to leave W-W-Wyvern Manor," insisted Meow, as she pointed to the bright red door of the weapons room. "And that means right now unless you feel the need for Mumford to escort you out. Oh yes, and one more thing, you three boys are now barred from Oh My Cod! until further notice. So that means no more fish and chips for any of you."

Trevor was not just any old black cat and contrary to what the boys had thought, he was not the Grand Witch's black cat either. In fact, Trevor was Meow's black cat, and he had been with her since early childhood. Knowing what she must do, the Grand Witch's apprentice instructed Mumford to place Trevor in the vault with all the other dead creatures from long ago. And then not wanting to waste any more time blathering with the five standing before her, she told him to meet her at the cryptid menagerie.

Regretting his unfortunate comment about Trevor, Bingo was feeling quite wretched that he and Trumper were no longer welcome at Oh My Cod!. As he walked with the others, his feelings towards Meow were at long last beginning to change, and so he started to mutter to himself, "Maybe she is a dark witch after all."

Once the five of them were inside the weapons room, and Old Mrs Dingle had taken it upon herself to bolt the bright red door, Trumper walked over to the wall that contained rack after rack of weapons. By the light of the gas lantern which was still burning bright, he quickly located a dozen of the benign looking weapons he had been searching for. And then to Bingo's bewilderment, he handed three of them to the person whose hands were both free, and that was Mad Maddox.

"Butt sticks!" exclaimed Bingo, whose personal preference was to wield the most deadly type of weapon at hand. "Is that what you expect us to use on the shug monkeys?"

"No, of course not, they might have worked when Fannie Entwhistle was around, but I doubt they will be a match for Meow's reincarnated shug monkeys. We're going to need these butt sticks to capture the mooners," answered Trumper, who was the only one in the room that knew the true identity of Dragonbutt's three mooners. "Let's not dawdle because we still have to track down these escaped shug monkeys, and right now we have no idea where they are."

Fortunately, the five of them did not have far to go before they discovered where the last remaining bevy of shug monkeys had gone. After stepping out of the weapons room, they heard a commotion inside the house that sounded like a wild party was taking place with flashing lights and a whole lot of loud music. As Elvira Wyvern was hardly the type to be throwing such a raucous knees-up, Trumper was confident that all the shug monkeys were in the house. And because Meow had not mentioned anything of this, the party must have just started.

"Mad Maddox, you guard the motorcycle and sidecar while we go into the house to deal with these shug monkeys," announced Trumper, as he walked towards the tradesmen's entrance at the side of the house. "Everyone else, you need to follow me."

"I'm not staying here by myself," protested Mad Maddox, while placing two butt sticks in the sidecar and then obstinately resting the other on his shoulder before taking three long strides towards the house.

"Oh no, you don't," interjected Old Mrs Dingle, who in the time it took to say those four short words had drawn her stun gun and zapped the headstrong Mad Maddox. "Young man, it's never a wise thing to tangle with a witch of the DWI."

The moment Mad Maddox ceased squirming on the ground, Trumper ordered him to go and sit in the sidecar and remain there until they returned. Wary of the stun gun which was still pointing in his direction, the Butterworth boy did as he was told but not before asking what he should do if a shug monkey happened to come around. Bingo responded by telling him that in his experience, it is always best to look monsters directly in the eye and then with a butt stick, give them a good hard whack where it hurts the most. Failing that, he mockingly added, you should scream as loud as you can and then run like the clappers in the opposite direction.

After the laughing died down and Mad Maddox was seated in the sidecar with two butt sticks on his lap and the other held firmly in his hands, the others marched right up to the black door of the tradesmen's entrance. Then with their weapons drawn, Trumper resolutely stepped forward and turned the old tarnished door handle so that the four of them could enter.

"Dragonsbutts! It's bolted from the other side," uttered Trumper, while giving the door a good hard kick with his wellington boot.

"Stand back, Trumper," called out Bingo, who already had Little MO raised above his head to smash through the sturdy door.

Trumper did not have to be asked twice as he hurriedly stepped aside so that Bingo could take aim at the door. Although before the younger boy had the opportunity to swing his powerful two-headed battleaxe, the sound of a bolt sliding to one side was heard. And then, to everyone's surprise, the door unexpectedly swung open.

"Shug monkey!" yelled Bingo, upon seeing one of the roguish monsters in the doorway of the tradesmen's entrance. What's more, it was standing on its hind legs holding what appeared to be a half-eaten cat in one paw and clutching a pint of Butts Batch in the other.

Just as Trumper and Old Mrs Dingle fell backwards onto poor Baxter, the startled shug monkey dropped what remained of the cat. Desperately trying not to spill any of the precious Butts Batch, it looked them over to decide whether they were worthy of becoming a shug monkey's dinner. Then before Bingo could take a swing to dispatch the awful monster, the shug monkey saw the razor-sharp blade of Little MO and dropped the pint of Butts Batch before collapsing with a loud thud on the floor.

Once Trumper had recovered his senses, he lifted himself off the ground and stepped forward to examine the Butts Batch soaked monster sprawled out in front of them. After confirming the shug monkey was irrefutably stone dead, Bingo placed his Monster Obliterator on the ground and then raised his arms in frustration. For no other reason than he had been unable to dispatch even a single monster that evening, and this he claimed was simply not on. Unbeknown to the boys though, while shug monkeys were undeniably quite terrifying, their hearts were rather weak and so nasty shocks like this one could abruptly cause them to cease beating. And that was why this shug monkey, without any warning whatsoever, had just then dropped dead.

As Bingo was eager to dispatch a shug monkey all by himself, he decided not to wait for the others and instead charged down the hallway with Little MO held tightly in both hands. By the time they had caught up with him, he was standing outside of the waiting room where the boys had first met Elvira Wyvern and slumped on the floor beside him was another dead shug monkey. Trumper could clearly see that it had not been dispatched by any two-headed battleaxe. As a matter of fact, just like the first one they had come across, the cause of death had been a sudden and quite massive heart attack.

While Bingo was obviously disappointed that a second shug monkey had been dispatched without him ever having to swing Little MO, Trumper contemplated what they should do next. It could not have been more than two shakes of a shug monkey's tail though before their attention was drawn to the cries of a lady's voice coming from inside the waiting room. Strangely, the key was on their side of the door, and so without any hesitation, Old Mrs Dingle stepped forward and unlocked it. And then immediately after drawing her stun gun, just like she had seen on the television, the old lady gave the door a good hard kick before it flew wide open.

"Old Mrs Dingle, thank goodness! I knew that one of my witches would come to save the day," called out Elvira Wyvern, who had been locked in the waiting room by the shug monkeys and was to be eaten once all the Butts Batch had run dry. "And I see those boys from the village are with you and they are dirtying my lovely clean floor with their muddy wellington boots."

Seeing the Grand Witch's angry grimace, the boys decided it would be wise to slip out of their wellingtons and listen to what she had to say. But first, Old Mrs Dingle removed the key from the door and locked it again, but this time from the inside. Then Elvira Wyvern disclosed that earlier in the evening, she had been disturbed by a series of loud knocks on the door of the tradesmen's entrance and lots of rowdy behaviour going off outside. Upon opening the door, she was horrified to see a bevy of shug monkeys covered in mud from head to tail. And then to her dismay, they rushed into the house and quite rudely locked her up in the waiting room.

"You know I told Meow that cryptid menagerie of hers was a bad idea and nothing good would come of it, but she's a remarkably powerful witch and can be so convincing when she wants to be. I just hope those awful creatures haven't harmed any of my darling cats," lamented Elvira, who was none too pleased the shug monkeys had invaded her home. "If only Mumford was here, he would have seen them off."

"There's no need for you to worry, Lady Wyvern. Monsters are our specialty, and we have already dispatched two of the shug monkeys, a chizard and a bugaboo," reassured Trumper, although he intentionally omitted the fact that at least one of her cats had already been eaten. "By the way, why is Mumford so important? He doesn't even carry a weapon so he'd be no good at dispatching shug monkeys, or for that matter, any other type of monster."

At long last Elvira Wyvern revealed the truth about Meow's giant of a manservant who never appeared to age. And moreover, the reason the boys had seen him standing behind Eradorn Wyvern in the portrait that hung on the banqueting hall wall. She started by saying that Mumford was not really one of the living; instead, he was very much one of the walking dead. Seven hundred or so years ago, to safeguard future generations of Wyvern witches, the first Grand Witch had created him by stitching together dozens of human body parts that had been acquired by some rather dubious means. Then with an elaborate dark magic spell, she miraculously brought the hulking colossus to life.

Since his inception, Mumford's responsibilities had included protecting not only every witch of the House of Wyvern but also the upkeep of the menagerie and the strange creatures that lived there. As he was not actually alive, the creatures, whether dangerous or otherwise, had absolutely no interest in harming the burly fellow. And this is why he never felt the need to carry a weapon and the reason the monsters in the cryptid menagerie had no desire to eat him.

"But if Mumford was created to watch over the Wyvern witches, then why didn't he accompany Meow and her mother when they left Dragonbutt? At that time, they were the only true Wyverns living at Wyvern Manor," asked Trumper, who was pleased the Grand Witch was now in the right frame of mind to enlighten them.

"The truth of the matter is that spells, even the dark kind, have their limitations. And the spell Eradorn cast to bring Mumford to life only works in Dragonbutt and its surrounding district. So if Mumford ever tries to leave, he will simply cease to exist," explained Elvira, in a tone that implied she had grown quite fond of Meow's manservant over the years.

"Well that's a fascinating history lesson, Lady Wyvern, but we're not at Dragonbutt Primary School now. This is a monster hunt, and I've yet to bag a single one of them so far," declared Bingo, who was itching to resume their search for the four remaining shug monkeys. "Trumper, let's be on our way, and the next shug monkey we come across is going to be dispatched by Little MO."

"Bingo's right, but Old Mrs Dingle, you and Baxter should stay here to protect Lady Wyvern. If the other shug monkeys are still in the house then Bingo and I will find them," stated Trumper, in the most authoritative voice he could summon. "And make sure you lock the door behind us and don't open it again unless you hear one of our voices."

Once Trumper and Bingo had left the safety of the waiting room, Old Mrs Dingle did indeed lock the door, though not before sending Baxter out to look for Mumford as she suspected the boys might just need a little help. So the funny-looking dog scurried off as fast as his legs would carry him, past the two recently departed shug monkeys and then on to the tunnel that went under the wall of the menagerie.

Because the two boys had removed their muddy wellington boots in the waiting room, they were now silently inching their way along the hallway wearing only a pair of warm winter socks on their feet. As they moved onwards, the music from the shug monkeys' party grew louder, and then upon reaching the Wyvern library, Trumper signalled that they should go in. In the dark as to what the older boy was up to, Bingo watched as Trumper scoured the dusty book-filled shelves. Then seeing the book he had been looking for was sitting on the highest shelf in the room, Trumper climbed the ladder while Bingo placed Little MO by the doorway so that he could give him a helping hand.

Not wanting a shug monkey to corner them in the library, Trumper quickly retrieved the ancient book and then handed it to Bingo. At once, he read the title out aloud, The Dragonbutt Witch's Guide to Witchcraft and Spells from beginner to the more advanced. Though he knew it was one of the books used by the DWI witches to cast their spells, the younger boy was still at a loss as to why Trumper wanted it.

"This is the last of Eradorn Wyvern's books on witchcraft and spell making. And more importantly, it's the one that's all about dark magic," whispered Trumper, while placing the nefarious book in his coat pocket. "Without it, the Wyvern witches can never again cast their dark spells, and Meow will not be able to bring the spirit of the first Grand Witch back from the past. Anyhow, we don't have time to discuss this now as we need to locate the shug monkeys."

Bingo couldn't agree more, and so he turned around to pick up Little MO, but to his horror, it was no longer resting by the door where he had left it. After a frantic search of the room, the boys quickly came to the conclusion that the deadly two-headed battleaxe must now be in the paws of a contemptible shug monkey. Then believing things could not get any worse, the music that the shug monkeys had been playing so loudly, abruptly ended, leaving an eerie silence throughout the enormous house.

Alas, Trumper and Bingo were right to assume Little MO had been swiped by a shug monkey. In fact, the bevy of shug monkeys had all been partying in the banqueting hall with a couple of barrels of Butts Batch and half a dozen of Elvira Wyvern's cats to snack on. After polishing off the last of the cats, one of the shug monkeys had wandered off in search of their two missing companions when it came across Bingo's Monster Obliterator. On hearing the voices of the two boys, and being that shug monkeys were not the bravest of creatures, it picked up the two-headed battleaxe in its paws and hurried back to the banqueting hall to warn the others.

Now that they were armed with just a torch and a solitary punisher to battle four pernicious shug monkeys, including one that was undoubtedly wielding Little MO, the boys knew the odds were no longer in their favour, and so they chose to make a hasty retreat. Before dashing back to the waiting room, Trumper peered into the hallway, but to his dismay, he saw the terrifying monsters heading their way. Then yelling at Bingo to run, they both hightailed it out of the Wyvern library to escape the advancing shug monkeys. Fearing they were not going to be able to outrun their four-legged pursuers, Trumper called to Bingo and said they should take refuge in the drawing room. And so the two boys charged through the open doorway and into the room where they had snacked on hot chocolate and lemon drizzle cake only a week earlier.

"That's not going to hold them for long," spluttered Trumper, a little out of breath as he slammed the door shut and turned the key in its lock. "Bingo, can you see another way out of here?"

Unfortunately for Trumper and Bingo, there was only one way out of the drawing room, and that was the same way they had just entered, through the now locked door. As they listened to the shug monkeys clattering in the hallway, in desperation, the boys pushed the coffee table up against the door followed by the sofa and most of the chairs. Then chillingly, they heard a loud crack and the splintering of wood, which could only have been caused by a deathly blow from Little MO. Not surprisingly, at that moment, each boy had the same thought, that their time in Dragonbutt might just be coming to a premature and rather gruesome end.

Little did they know that help was on its way until the boys caught the sound of a barking dog and then the slow thud-thud-thud of Meow's manservant. Realising that they were saved and their monster fighting days were not yet over, Trumper and Bingo dragged the furniture away from the doorway and unlocked the door before taking a peek. What they saw was a scene of pure mayhem with Baxter biting the butts of the shug monkeys as he chased them up and down the hallway. And then there was Mumford, who was standing by the doorway and brandishing Little MO, to the consternation of every shug monkey present.

Trumper and Bingo watched as each time a shug monkey came a tad too close to the razor-sharp blade of Little MO, the monster's monkey-like face grimaced, and then in an instant, it keeled over. As the shock of coming face to face with Bingo's two-headed battleaxe

213

was altogether too much for the fragile shug monkey heart, in no time at all, there was only one of the damnable creatures left standing. Then after managing to slip away from Baxter, the last shug monkey bolted down the hallway in a desperate attempt to get out of harm's way. Though regrettably for the monstrous reincarnation, it did not get far before running across the Dragonbutt Small Arms Society women's gunslinging champion for three years in a row.

"Dragonsbutts! It's just not fair, you could have left one shug monkey for me to dispatch," griped Bingo, as he watched the old lady spin the stun gun on her trigger finger after zapping the shug monkey right between its crimson coloured eyes. "Anyhow, all the monsters are now gone, and more importantly, my tummy is rumbling, which means we should return home. So Old Mrs Dingle, I vote we hurry back to Counting House Lane for some of your hot chocolate and homemade scones, and if it's not too much trouble, we should stop for a kebab on the way."

Fifteen

One Last Moon

⚫⚫⚫

On Saturday morning, Bingo rose at eight after a dream-filled sleep in which he had fought dozens of shug monkeys, bugaboos and chizards, and dispatched each of them with the aid of Little MO. Without waking Trumper, who was still sound asleep, he checked under his bed to ensure the two-headed battleaxe was where he had left it the night before along with the punisher and three butt sticks. Then happy their weapons were where they should be, with a smile on his face he toddled off to his aunty and uncle's bedroom.

"Bingo, what would you like to eat for breakfast this morning?" asked Aunty J, while yawning as she climbed out of bed and pulled on her warm dressing gown and slippers.

"A big breakfast is what I want," answered Bingo, whose tummy was already rumbling even though he had eaten a pie, two portions of fish and chips, an enormous donor kebab from the Dragonbutt Kebab House and four of Old Mrs Dingle's scones only the night before.

"I agree wholeheartedly with that," chuckled Uncle P, who was still lying in bed clinging to his warm winter duvet. "We're going to need a full Dragonbutt breakfast."

"Great, count me in," whooped Bingo, knowing that a full Dragonbutt breakfast was another of his favourites. "I'll go and get Trumper, and then we'll meet you in the kitchen in a few minutes."

The full Dragonbutt breakfast had everything the typical English fry-up ordinarily contained and then some. However, what was most important was for each of its numerous ingredients to be fried in lots of full-fat lard, and for those Dragonbutt born, this could only ever come from the Hogswood Piggery. While variations in this celebrated Dragonbutt dish could be found in almost every home in the village, Uncle P always preferred the way his mother used to make it. And so inevitably, Aunty J learnt to prepare their Entwhistle family Dragonbutt breakfast the same way too.

Plenty of juicy Hogswood pork sausages and oodles of thick-cut smoky bacon were always a requisite along with two large eggs cooked any way you like. Then lots of freshly picked mushrooms, a large slice of black pudding and a ripe Italian tomato needed to be fried to perfection. Unfailingly, this was topped with baked beans by the bucketful and at least two slices of yummy fried bread. Though what made this lavish breakfast unique to Dragonbutt was the inclusion of a bowl of hog maw. This was prepared by simmering the chopped outer lining of a Hogswood pig's stomach in Butts Batch and then frying the delicious dish in even more of the fatty lard.

Despite the fact the two boys had to wait longer than usual for their first meal of the day, the full Dragonbutt breakfast prepared by their aunty and uncle was well worth it. With a steaming mug of hot chocolate for the both of them, they ravenously ate their way through every morsel on the visibly overflowing plates. Not stopping there, Trumper and Bingo devoured the tasty hog maw in no time at all, and to Aunty J's delight, they even licked their bowls clean.

"You two must have been hungry. Didn't Old Mrs Dingle give you enough to eat last night?" inquired Aunty J, who had barely eaten half of the food on her plate by the time the boys had finished all of theirs.

"Don't worry, Aunty J, we had plenty of food. In fact, Barry Beasley took us to the Dragonbutt Arms for a free pie and then thanks to Mad Maddox we ate fish and chips. And later in the evening, Old Mrs Dingle bought us each a kebab," responded Bingo, who failed to mention anything about their adventure that night. "I think that Trumper and I are just going through one of those growth spurts you are always talking about."

"I suppose so. And speaking of Old Mrs Dingle, these days I'm not sure the old lady is all there because when we arrived home last night, she was sitting at the kitchen table dressed as a witch. I would have understood if it had been Halloween, but we are only in the middle of January," asserted Aunty J, while shaking her head. "Oh yes, and did you hear the news that Detective Huntress has caught those mooners at long last?"

"Well we don't know that for sure, and Barry is not at all convinced she has apprehended the right mooners. He said that in his opinion, the evidence against Angus, Typsy and Chomper Senior is entirely circumstantial," interrupted Uncle P, as he finished his bowl of hog maw. "Of course, that didn't stop Detective Huntress locking them all up in the cells at Dragonbutt Police Station."

"Dragonsbutts! Bingo and I were with Barry in the Dragonbutt Arms when Detective Huntress took Angus away for questioning. But we were not aware he has now been arrested along with Typsy Braithwaite and Chomper Baverstock Senior," gasped Trumper, who knew they had to catch the real culprits and soon, so that Angus and his friends could be exonerated and ultimately freed.

"Even though Detective Huntress is not Dragonbutt born, I think she has got that old Dragonbutt saying rattling around inside her head, 'Once a mooner, always a mooner',' muttered Uncle P, while looking a little downcast. "You know Saturday night at the Dragonbutt Arms is simply not going to be the same without Angus Hogswood."

Once the boys had finished their hot chocolate and thanked Aunty J and Uncle P for the full Dragonbutt breakfast they had just eaten, Trumper led Bingo upstairs. Then after brushing their teeth and changing into some clean outdoor clothing, he confided in the younger boy that today was the day the Dragonbutt mooners would at long last meet their match. Although to Bingo's surprise, the older boy went on to add they would require the help of Bertie Bovington and Flitcher Jenkins. But first, the two boys would need to head over to MAOS headquarters.

Not wanting to leave their weapons where Aunty J may find them, Bingo concealed them all in a large laundry bag and followed Trumper downstairs. Then wearing their winter coats, DPS woolly hats and warm woollen gloves, they pulled on their wellington boots and exited the house by the back door before running down the long garden path. As the younger boy was carrying quite a load, Trumper was the first to arrive at MAOS headquarters and had already unlocked the door by the time Bingo caught up with him. On entering, the older boy switched on the light while reaching into his coat pocket to retrieve the book on dark magic spells he had taken from the Wyvern library. And then after placing the book on one of the shelves which held the Entwhistle journals, he instructed Bingo to return Little MO and the punisher to the large chest of drawers.

"But, Trumper, we're going to need Little MO and the punisher when we catch up with the mooners," pleaded Bingo, who was reluctant to leave his Monster Obliterator behind.

"Bingo, the mooners aren't monsters. That's why I appropriated these three butt sticks from the weapons room," expounded Trumper, as he picked up one of the butt sticks and swung it in the air. "Now what I need you to do is call Bertie and Flitcher and tell them to meet us at MAOS headquarters by four this afternoon. While you are doing that, I'll go over to the Bovingtons' house to talk with Bunty, and I will return shortly."

Though it was rather uncharacteristic for Trumper to want to speak with the very person he usually tried his best to avoid, Bingo just nodded his head after accepting the older boy's phone. As Bertie was still doing everything he could to avoid bumping into his sister, he had spent the night at the Jenkins house and was planning on staying there for the rest of the day. Consequently, Bingo told him to turn on his speaker before revealing what had transpired at Wyvern Manor the previous evening. After receiving heaps of praise from his school friends regarding MAOS's daring exploits, he finally got around to telling them that if they wanted to help catch the mooners, then the two of them should come to MAOS headquarters at four.

As Trumper banged on the front door of Eleven Counting House Lane with the cast-iron knocker in the shape of a horizontal letter B, he wisely looked up towards Bunty Bovington's bedroom window. Fortunately for him, after the mishap involving Bentley DuPont, she had learnt her lesson and instead merely stomped down the stairs to see who was at the door before flying into one of her infamous rages.

"Oh, it's you, Trumper, please come in," beamed Bunty, happy but a little surprised that Trumper was standing at her front door. And for once Bingo Malloy was not tagging along. "That degenerate brother of mine and his imbecilic friend are not here, and my parents are at the store, so we have the whole house for ourselves."

"No, thank you, Bunty, I just called to say that I do sympathise with you. Bertie and Flitcher were so childish pulling a prank like that on you and poor Bentley. Especially considering you are the head girl and he is now the head boy of Dragonbutt Primary School," proclaimed

Trumper, who was thinking that with a performance like this he could become a first-rate actor one day. "Something really needs to be done about those two. I even overheard them boasting to Bingo that they have never been mooned and Bertie said that because he is too clever for the mooners, they never will."

"That sounds just like Bertie," snapped Bunty, while thinking of all the ways she could make her brother and Flitcher suffer for what they had put her through over the years. "As you know, I don't really like Bentley, although I would love for him to get his revenge. Unfortunately, Bertie is quite sneaky, and no one seems to know where he and Flitcher are most of the time."

"Bingo told me that Bertie and Flitcher will be working at Bovington's Sweets and Chocolates this afternoon, and they'll finish at six on the dot," pointed out Trumper, knowing that to convincingly tell a lie you always had to keep a straight face. "Maybe you could let Bentley know."

"That's strange; my parents didn't mention anything about Bertie and Flitcher working at the store today. But thanks, Trumper, I will definitely call Bentley this morning," assured Bunty, with a wicked-looking smile slowly creeping across her face.

"Perfect, Bunty, and remember to tell him they will be leaving Bovington's Sweets and Chocolates at six," repeated Trumper, who was trying his best not to smile. "Oh yes, and make sure you let him know that Bertie thinks he is too clever to ever get mooned."

"Of course, but step into the house, Trumper, and I'll make some hot chocolate for you. And I'm sure we still have plenty of my mother's chocolate cake in the kitchen," appealed Bunty, as she stepped forward to grab Trumper's hand.

"Oh, is that the time. Perhaps another day, Bunty, right now I need to return home because Bingo is waiting for me. Goodbye, and don't forget to call Bentley," yelled Trumper, who was already running back to MAOS headquarters. Although on his arrival, to his irritation, he had to knock three times on the bolted white door before hearing the younger boy's voice.

"Who is it, friend or foe?" called out Bingo, from the other side of the door.

"It's me, Trumper," stated Trumper, rather loudly.

"How do I know you're not a mooner?" teased Bingo, as he giggled to himself.

"Bingo, just unbolt the door. Then I'll tell you who I think the mooners really are and how we're going to catch them," demanded Trumper, who was not even a little bit impressed by the younger boy's tomfoolery.

Upon entering MAOS headquarters, Trumper could see that Aunty J had paid a visit while he had been away because resting on the brown leather sofa was a tray containing a flask of hot chocolate, two large mugs and a plate of her freshly baked fairy cakes. These happened to be one of the boys' favourites and were topped with luscious buttercream icing and hundreds and thousands, which is why Bingo had already eaten two of the colourful treats and was about to help himself to a third. Not wanting the steaming hot chocolate to go cold and knowing Bingo would undoubtedly eat all the fairy cakes if he did not dig in right away, Trumper revealed the identity of the three mooners while they tucked into their mid-morning snack.

"Dragonsbutts! Are you sure that they're the real mooners?" queried Bingo, while greedily taking a bite out of his fourth fairy cake.

"All the evidence points to them, so I'm quite confident those three are the mooners who have been causing all the trouble in Dragonbutt of late," confirmed Trumper, who was nodding his head as he took a bite out of another fairy cake. "Angus, Typsy and Chomper Senior are innocent, and with Bertie and Flitcher's assistance, we are going to prove it."

For the remainder of the morning, Trumper explained how he planned to catch the mooners and then the two boys practised swinging the butt sticks. Once again, as luck would have it, Uncle P was working in his office at the Dragonbutt Smoker, and as usual, he intended to wile away his Saturday evening at the Dragonbutt Arms. Aunty J too would not be home before eight as she had taken the bus to Chelmsford and was spending the day shopping with Azalia Blenkinsop. This meant the boys would be eating their lunch and dinner at Old Mrs Dingle's house and thankfully could come and go as they pleased.

At lunch, after having their fill of the old lady's steak and kidney pudding made with Baverstock's famous beef suet, the boys were over the moon when she gave each of them a giant Knickerbocker glory topped with fresh whipped cream. Then at three in the afternoon, Old Mrs Dingle served them a veritable banquet consisting of hot chocolate, homemade scones, chocolate cake and a platter of crustless egg and cress sandwiches. By a quarter to four, their tummies were undeniably full, and so they walked back to MAOS headquarters to wait for Bertie and Flitcher. Within a matter of minutes, they heard the sound of two familiar voices, and then someone energetically knocked on the door.

"So this is MAOS headquarters," remarked Bertie, as he and Flitcher both entered through the now open door. "Not bad, not bad at all."

"Did you bring any Choco Bombs?" pleaded Bingo, whose tummy obviously wasn't rumbling just yet, but later that afternoon he knew it would be.

"Of course, my coat pocket is full of them," winked Bertie, while gazing at the shelves overflowing with Entwhistle journals. "So what's this about mooners? I heard that Detective Huntress had detained all three of them and they were now safely behind bars at Dragonbutt Police Station."

With Bingo and his two friends sitting on the brown leather sofa,

Trumper paced up and down and then once again he disclosed the names of the three individuals responsible for the recent spate of moonings in the village. He then went on to say that in two short hours, the four of them would end the mooners reign of terror and how Bunty Bovington unwittingly played a key part in his plan.

"I like your style, Trumper," sniggered Bertie, who was always trying to get one-up on his older sister. And he believed if Trumper was right about the mooners true identity, then this was going to be a whole lot of fun. "Needless to say, you can count on Flitcher and me."

"Dragonsbutts! Does this mean that Bertie and I are now members of MAOS?" implored Flitcher, with a look of excitement etched into his face. "It feels just like the old days when we were members of Bingo's gang."

"Flitcher, we'll make you and Bertie probationary members for now," interjected Trumper, thinking he and Bingo shouldn't let just anyone join MAOS. Instead, he believed prospective members must first prove they are made of the right stuff.

"Do we get to wear a uniform?" added Flitcher, who was picturing himself in a brand new stylish white jacket with the red MAOS logo emblazoned on its back.

"No, you'll get something that's much better, a butt stick," chimed in Bingo, as he leapt from the sofa and picked up one of the butt sticks leaning against the wall. Then Bertie and Flitcher did the same resulting in the three of them whacking each other repeatedly until Trumper was forced to intervene.

"As you can see, there are three butt sticks and four of us. That's because one person will have to take a photo of the mooners' faces while the others do all the whacking," confided Trumper, who was looking at the other three boys hoping one of them would volunteer. "Now, which one of you wants to take the photo?"

All at once, Bingo and his friends took a step backwards while holding onto the butt sticks as tightly as they could. Seeing that it would be nigh on impossible to get any of them to give up the opportunity of whacking a mooner with the aptly named butt stick, Trumper resigned himself to the fact that he would be the one taking the photo. This was probably for the best anyway, as it was essential to not only capture each of their faces but also the mooners had to be in the process of pulling off a full moon. And at the end of the day, the only person he could possibly trust to do this without messing it up was himself.

Thrilled that they were getting the opportunity to not only expose Dragonbutt's latest menace but also do some well-deserved whacking, Bingo, Bertie and Flitcher followed Trumper out of MAOS headquarters carrying their butt sticks high in the air. Then electing to take the shortest route possible, Trumper switched on his torch and opened the always unlocked wooden gate leading to the muddy footpath at the back of the little old house.

The four boys hurriedly marched onwards, and in no time at all, they were walking over the footbridge to Dragonbutt pond and then along the narrow path that led to Pigswill Alley. With the exception of Trumper, the boys spent their time giggling and whacking each other with the butt sticks until they stepped through the gap between the two old willow trees into Bristletooth Lane. Once Dragonbutt Victory Hall was behind them, they turned onto Dragonbutt High Street and stomped past Oh My Cod!. And although it was supposed to be open and full of customers at this time, every inch of the village's popular fish and chip shop appeared closed.

"Dragonsbutts! What are you young beggars up to?" boomed the voice of Boosey Dooley, who was standing in the doorway of the Dragonbutt Arms with a pint of Dragonstone Fire in his drinking hand. "They wouldn't be butt sticks you're carrying by any chance?"

"No, they're tennis racquets. Do you want to join us?" shouted Bingo, from the other side of Dragonbutt High Street. Then he burst out laughing, and because it was so funny, the others joined in the laughter too.

"Oh, I'm afraid my sporting days are long gone," chortled Boosey Dooley, as he slapped his ponderous belly with the hand that was not holding the pint of Dragonstone Fire. "It's a bit dark for tennis, but enjoy yourselves anyway."

After waving their butt sticks at the Dragonbutt Arms landlord, the four boys arrived at Bovington's Sweets and Chocolates with plenty of time to spare. Inside the store, they could see Hildy Bovington standing behind the counter and sitting at a table next to the window was Emilia Baggot, drinking a mug of hot chocolate and eating a mouthwatering éclair. Assuming Bunty had fulfilled her part of Trumper's bold plan, the mooners were expected to arrive sometime before six. So without delay, the older boy instructed the others to go to their assigned position and wait for the signal.

"By the way, what is the signal?" asked Bingo, who could not remember that important detail being mentioned when Trumper had disclosed the particulars of his plan.

"Don't worry about that. Just trust me, you'll know it when you hear it," smiled Trumper, as he turned off his torch and then stepped into the shadow of the house next to the Bovington family store.

Bingo gave the older boy the thumbs up and then with Bertie and Flitcher in tow, he crossed to the other side of Dragonbutt High Street to enter the dark and dismal looking Nowhere Alley. Although it was really a dead end that obviously led nowhere, the narrow alley was conveniently located directly opposite Bovington's Sweets and Chocolates. So if the mooners were to strike according to Trumper's plan, then this would be the ideal place from which the three butt stick wielding Dragonbutt Primary School boys could surprise them.

While Trumper noiselessly paced up and down in the darkness with his torch in one hand and phone in the other to take the all-important photo, the other three boys were shooting the breeze as they gorged themselves on Choco Bombs. Then just as Bertie offered his friends more of their favourite chocolaty treat, the sound of several bicycles could be heard in the distance. So with their hands covered in sticky Bovington's chocolate, Bingo, Bertie and Flitcher grabbed hold of their butt sticks, and in silence, they listened for the signal.

Trumper had been right as soon enough the ear-splitting clamour of an air horn caused them all to jump before Bingo courageously charged forward with Bertie to his left and Flitcher to his right. "Mooners," he cried, as they were confronted with three bare butts doing a full moon in the direction of Bovington's Sweets and Chocolates. Regrettably, for Emilia Baggot, who had been mooned more times than she cared to remember, the shock was simply too much. And so once again the oldest person in the village fainted, but this time the old lady's face came to rest on what was left of her Bovington's chocolate éclair.

Although none of their faces could be seen at this point, that all changed after Bingo whacked the butt of the tallest mooner revealing an astonished expression on his face. Then once Bertie and Flitcher had whacked the butts of the mooners on either side of him, the startled faces of the other two were now clearly visible as well. At that moment, Trumper rushed forward with his torch shining brightly. And then he took the photo that not only lay bare the butts of the three mooners, but it also captured the bewildered looks on the faces of Bentley DuPont, Chugher Harris and Chomper Baverstock Junior.

To Bingo's annoyance, in the middle of their unscripted confrontation with the mooners, the Dragonbutt Primary School head boy and his two accomplices were able to pull up their trousers and make a mad dash for their bicycles. Somewhat out of breath from all the whacking yet still brandishing their butt sticks, Bingo, Bertie and Flitcher chased after them as best they could. Though to the disappointment of all three, the mooners were able to retrieve their bicycles and ride past

Fanshaw's the Baker's before disappearing into the darkness.

"Just let them go," called out Trumper, who was the only one that had not run after the fleeing mooners. "I've got the photo, and that's all the proof we need."

"Trumper, it looks like you were right all along," exclaimed Bertie, as he stood puffing and blowing beside Bingo and Flitcher. "But how did you know the real mooners were Bentley, Chugher and Chomper Junior?"

He explained that his suspicions were aroused while eating a pie at the Dragonbutt Arms only the day before. That was when Detective Huntress let off Chomper Baverstock Senior's air horn, which happened to be the same type the mooners were known to use. It was at that moment Trumper recalled seeing an almost identical one in the hand of Chomper Junior, the day he and Chugher rode their bicycles into Wyvern Manor and nearly collided with Bingo and himself. And that's when he realised Bingo's two classmates had to be the real mooners, and of course, how they knew of the mooning which took place near the Hogswood Piggery.

"Dragonsbutts! Well that accounts for Chugher and Chomper Junior but what made you suspect Bentley was a mooner as well?" questioned Bertie, while handing each of the boys a Choco Bomb.

Trumper revealed he had always thought it rather odd that Chugher Harris nominated Bentley DuPont for the position of head boy. For no other reason than both he and Chomper Baverstock Junior, like most of the boys and girls at Dragonbutt Primary School, had previously shown only disdain for Dragonbutt's most spoilt boy. According to Trumper, this newfound comradeship, along with the fact that Bentley had bought brand new bicycles for the two of them, could mean only one thing. And that was Bentley DuPont must be the third mooner.

"Brilliant, Trumper, but you know what this means," laughed Bertie, with a devilish-looking grin across his face. "Once Dr Wimbish hears about this, and I am quite confident he will, Bentley DuPont will no longer be our head boy. So that means you're going to be the next head boy of Dragonbutt Primary School and unfortunately for you, Bunty is still the head girl."

Sixteen

Doing a Runner

"**B**oys, your pancakes will be ready in about half an hour," announced Aunty J, from the doorway of Trumper and Bingo's bedroom. "Try not to disturb your uncle because he had quite a boisterous time at the Dragonbutt Arms last night."

'Boisterous' was definitely somewhat of an understatement when describing her husband's evening which took off in a big way after the arrival of Angus Hogswood, Typsy Braithwaite and Chomper Baverstock Senior. After Trumper had sent Detective Huntress the photo showing the faces of the real mooners, the sceptical police officer was compelled to admit the three professed mooners sitting in the Dragonbutt police cells were not the mooners she had been searching for after all. Thankfully for Angus and his two friends though, their timely release meant they could spend the rest of the evening at the Dragonbutt Arms, and that is precisely what they did. Then as one would expect, on calling last orders at the end of the night, Boosey Dooley ushered all his regulars through to the backroom for one of his infamous lock-ins. And naturally, that included Uncle P.

As the boys descended the stairs for breakfast, Trumper was not at all surprised to hear an exceptionally loud rumble emanate from Bingo's tummy. Even though he had eaten five slices of The Beast and three pieces of a Bovington's chocolate cake at Old Mrs Dingle's house the night before, as usual, the younger boy was feeling rather peckish. Luckily for him, Aunty J had cooked an enormous stack of pancakes and had already made their favourite hot chocolate with a gooey marshmallow and plenty of fresh whipped cream.

"I didn't get a chance to talk with you after arriving home last night," remarked Aunty J, who had just sat down at the kitchen table with a fresh cup of English breakfast tea. "Did anything interesting happen while I was away?"

"You can say that again, last night we caught the mooners in the middle of a full moon outside of Bovington's Sweets and Chocolates. And Trumper took a photo of them for Detective Huntress," exclaimed Bingo, while placing a large knob of creamy Dragonbutt butter on top of half a dozen fluffy pancakes before pouring lashings of Botters honey over each one.

"Oh no, dear, you must be mistaken," replied Aunty J, as she slowly sipped her tea. "Don't forget I've already told you that Detective Huntress arrested the mooners on Friday evening, and they are now languishing in the cells at Dragonbutt Police Station."

"Dragonsbutts! Not those mooners. The last time they were active was before Trumper and I were born," groaned Bingo, who was too preoccupied with devouring as many pancakes as his tummy could hold to tell his aunty the full story.

Seeing Aunty J was none the wiser, Trumper explained that he had only recently discovered the true identity of the mooners. Knowing that no one would likely believe him, he and Bingo, with the help of Bertie Bovington and Flitcher Jenkins, had no other choice but to expose Bentley DuPont, Chugher Harris and Chomper Baverstock Junior as the real mooners. And because photos never lie, happily, Detective Huntress was forced to release the three grown-ups she had wrongly accused only the day before.

"So what's going to happen to these three boys?" asked Aunty J, as she helped herself to a couple of pancakes and a second cup of English breakfast tea.

"Well I would lock them up in the cells at Dragonbutt Police Station and throw away the key," barked Bingo, while placing another piece of sweet buttery pancake into his mouth. "The next time those three should see the light of day is when they are as grey-haired as Old Mrs Dingle."

"I don't think so, Bingo. You're forgetting they're only kids, just like us," stressed Trumper, who had been doing most of the talking, so he had only eaten three pancakes to Bingo's five. "All they'll get is a good telling-off from Detective Huntress and Dr Wimbish, and then they will probably have to perform some sort of community service in the village. But trust me, once my photo is on the front page of the Dragonbutt Smoker then there will be no more mooning in Dragonbutt for those three."

Though the younger boy knew Trumper was right, he simply shrugged his shoulders and drank his hot chocolate and then went on to eat another four pancakes before climbing the stairs. Twenty minutes later, they were both standing in the hallway dressed in clean clothing with Bingo holding the three butt sticks ready for another dreary January day. Then wearing their winter coats, DPS woolly hats and warm woollen gloves, the boys pulled on their wellington boots by the back door and ran down the long garden path to MAOS headquarters.

Because Bingo had his hands full, Trumper was the one who unlocked the door and therefore was the first to enter and switch on the light.

Then after the younger boy had placed the butt sticks in the large chest of drawers for safekeeping, Trumper told him that the only thing left for them to do now was to destroy Eradorn Wyvern's book on dark magic spells.

"But why do you want to do that, Trumper? No one knows we have it, and besides, the book can't cause any more harm if we keep it safely locked away in MAOS headquarters," argued Bingo, who was thinking if ever Old Mrs Dingle was to master the basics of dark magic, then one day she just might teach him how to cast a spell on Mad Maddox.

"Bingo, how long do you think it will be before Meow discovers her prized book is missing from the Wyvern library? That's if she hasn't done so already, and then it'll be only a matter of time before she realises we were the ones who took it," pointed out Trumper, as he picked up the troublesome book of dark magic. "Never again can we allow this book to fall into the hands of a Wyvern witch, and needless to say, that includes Meow."

"Alright, Trumper, whatever you say," acknowledged Bingo, who by this time was only half-listening to the older boy. "I guess Meow will have to make do with practising regular magic from now on, just like the rest of the witches in the DWI."

"I hope so. Anyhow, Barry Beasley is sure to want to know how we caught the real mooners. So I will give Barry a call after sending him the photo I took last night," responded Trumper, as he returned the book on dark magic spells to the bookshelf and picked up his phone.

Once Trumper had sent the photo with a message that simply stated, 'One Last Moon', he called the young reporter and luckily got through to him straight away. With a look of surprise on his face, he paced up and down MAOS headquarters while shaking his head. Then as Bingo looked on, the shaking turned to nodding, and after two or three minutes, Trumper finally ended the call.

"According to Barry, Meow is no longer at Wyvern Manor," divulged

Trumper, who was deep in thought and at a loss for words for once.

"Dragonsbutts! You mean to say that she's done a runner?" uttered Bingo, looking somewhat perturbed the owner of Dragonbutt's only fish and chip shop had flown the coop.

"It looks like it. Barry said there was a ruckus in the village last night because Oh My Cod! was closed and so first thing this morning he drove over to Wyvern Manor to see what was up. When he got there, Elvira Wyvern told him that Meow had already left with a suitcase of clothes and her most precious possessions. She didn't take Mumford with her and refused to say where she was going, so Barry thinks Meow must have left Dragonbutt," nodded Trumper, who was thinking what he and Bingo would do now that Dragonbutt was bereft of mooners, monsters and dark witches. "Oh, and he wants to interview both of us for his front-page article on how we caught the mooners. In return, Barry is going to treat us to Sunday lunch at the Dragonbutt Arms. He's already cleared it with Aunty J, so we're going to meet him at twelve-thirty, and Bertie and Flitcher can join as well."

Bingo was tickled pink knowing he would be eating one of Flanna Dooley's mouthwatering roasts and no doubt a bowl of her famous sticky toffee pudding. As it was only a tad past ten-fifteen, he suggested they first go to Flitcher's house to play video games and then all four of them could walk to the Dragonbutt Arms together. Trumper agreed and so after Bingo had called his friends to tell them about the exciting news, they left MAOS headquarters without delay, though not before the younger boy slipped something unseen into his coat pocket.

"Cheer up, Bingo. I thought that you would be happy to eat Sunday lunch at the Dragonbutt Arms," called out Trumper, after turning around to see the younger boy looked decidedly glum. "I know you're sad to hear Meow has gone, but Dragonbutt is going to be a much safer place to live without her."

"Dragonsbutts! It's not that. I just hope that someone is going to take over the running of Oh My Cod!," spluttered Bingo, who couldn't stop thinking about the first-rate fish and chips he had consumed over the past few weeks.

Trumper laughed out loud because even with everything that had happened over the weekend, it was just typical of Bingo to be thinking of his tummy. However, he believed the younger boy was absolutely right, they were excellent fish and chips and would be sorely missed by every resident of the village.

With all this talk of his favourite fried food, Bingo's tummy began to rumble just as they entered Flamingo Crescent. Fortunately for the boys, when they rang the doorbell of the outlandish flamingo pink coloured Jenkins' house, it was snack time. And so both of them gladly accepted a steaming mug of hot chocolate and a plate of freshly baked sticky Chelsea buns served straight from the oven.

At twelve on the dot, the four boys left Flamingo Crescent for their Sunday lunch at the Dragonbutt Arms where Barry Beasley would surely be waiting with a welcoming smile and a pint of Dragonstone Fire in his hand. Chattering incessantly about the mooners and arguing which of them had received the most whacks and from whose butt stick, they marched down Hunnickle Drive. Then just as the boys were about to turn onto the cobblestone path that bordered Dragonbutt pond, they heard the screeching of brakes as a speeding car came to an abrupt stop right next to them. To their trepidation, what they saw was an open-top denim blue MG Roadster with Trevor the very flat dead black cat lying motionless on the passenger seat. And walking in their direction from the driver's side was none other than the Grand Witch's apprentice, Meow.

"W-W-Where is my book?" screamed Meow, as she pointed at Trumper and Bingo who by now were running for all they were worth with Bertie and Flitcher towards Pigswill Alley.

As it turned out, Meow was a surprisingly good runner for someone who was a mere five feet tall, and so she easily caught up with the boys before they could enter the narrow path that connected Dragonbutt pond with Pigswill Alley. Knowing that they were never going to outrun her, the four of them came to a halt and then Flitcher, to his and Bertie's misfortune, made a rather ill-advised and clearly fateful mistake.

"You don't scare us. We're MAOS, and we were the ones who caught the mooners. It'll take more than a little witch to get the better of us," blurted Flitcher, as he winked at the others with an uncharacteristic air of confidence.

Without saying anything in response, Meow slipped her right hand into the pocket of her coat and pulled out Eradorn Wyvern's well-worn wand. Pointing it directly at Flitcher, she mumbled a few of her ancestor's magical words and in the blink of an eye poor Flitcher Jenkins was transformed into a small and somewhat weedy looking tree.

"Dragonsbutts! You crazy witch, what have you done to Flitcher?" yelled Bertie, who did not get a chance to say another word because Meow was now pointing the wand at him. And after a few more words of magic, Bertie Bovington was turned into a chubby English bulldog.

"Meow, the book you are looking for is safely hidden and you will never be able to find it, not in a hundred years. So there is no point in using your magic on Bingo and me," protested Trumper, as confidently as he could while staring at the wand now pointing at them. "Bertie and Flitcher may never amount to much, especially Flitcher; nevertheless, you need to change them back to the way they were, right now."

"There's no need for you to get in a tizzy. These spells are not permanent, and so inside of an hour, your friends are going to return to their former selves," retorted Meow, just as Bertie the bulldog cocked his leg and watered Flitcher the weedy looking tree. "Lady Eradorn's books are meant for w-w-witches eyes only, and her last book, the one in Bingo's coat pocket, can only be understood by me. So hand it over, Bingo!"

Speechless, Trumper could not decide which was more jaw-dropping. How the Grand Witch's apprentice knew the book she had been so determined to find was hiding in Bingo's coat pocket or that he had foolishly taken it from MAOS headquarters in the first place. Understanding he had made a colossal blunder, the younger boy accepted there was no choice open to him other than to hand the last of Eradorn Wyvern's books to Meow. And so without delay, apprehensively, he pulled the book from his coat pocket and warily placed it into the witch's outstretched hand.

Holding the heinous book in her left hand and the wand pointing towards the boys in her right, Meow uttered more of Eradorn's ancient words of magic. Though to her disbelief, the two boys remained just as they were. After repeating the same words a second time and then a third, she became increasingly frustrated that her spell had failed to work. Believing she must have mixed up some of the ancient words, the Grand Witch's apprentice then tried a whole myriad of different kinds of spells. Although to her bewilderment and increasing dread, not one of them had any effect on Trumper and Bingo.

"W-W-Wizards!" fumed Meow, as she gazed at the boys with a guarded expression on her face. "Who are your parents?"

"We're not wizards," huffed Bingo, who had no idea why Meow's spells had not worked on him and Trumper, but he was glad they hadn't all the same. "And we live with our Aunty J and Uncle P."

"I mean your real parents?" repeated Meow, in an increasingly agitated tone of voice. "Only a w-w-wizard is protected against W-W-Wyvern magic. So you two boys must be the offspring of insidious double-dealing w-w-wizards."

Having discovered Trumper and Bingo were no ordinary Dragonbutt boys, and because she was again in possession of Eradorn's irreplaceable book on dark magic, Meow turned and ran back to her car then started the engine before speeding away. While this latest turn of events had left the boys somewhat bemused, Trumper being Trumper at once pulled himself together. Then seeing that Bertie the bulldog was running in circles in a failed attempt to chase after his own stubby tail, the older boy told Bingo to round up his friend and to keep him away from Flitcher the weedy looking tree.

"I've got Bertie," beamed Bingo, who was a little breathless after chasing Bertie the bulldog halfway around Dragonbutt pond. "But what are we going to do with Flitcher?"

"Meow said that Bertie and Flitcher will return to normal after her spell wears off. So I guess we have to hang around here for awhile," answered Trumper, as he gave Bertie the bulldog a gentle kick when he waddled over to sniff the older boy's trouser leg. "I'll send Barry a message to let him know we have been delayed. In the meantime, I'm not sure what I should call my next journal. Do you have any ideas?"

"That's easy, it has to be 'Fearless Bingo Malloy defeats a bunch of hellacious monsters and a really bad witch'," declared Bingo, who was struggling to hold onto a rather playful Bertie the bulldog.

"Um, I don't think so, Bingo," smirked Trumper, while deep in thought. "However, I do like the bit about the witch, so how about 'The Dragonbutt Witch'."

"Don't you mean 'The Dragonbutt W-W-Witch'," chuckled Bingo, as he picked up a stick and through it for Bertie the bulldog to retrieve.

"Dragonsbutts! Bingo, that's it," laughed Trumper, who knew that even Meow would be able to pronounce this title. "I'm going to call my second journal 'The Dragonbutt Itch'."

Trumper Gallant and Bingo Malloy will return in

The Beast of Fangorn Abbey